THE REBEL AND THE FINAL BLOOD WAR

THE REBEL AND THE FINAL BLOOD WAR

NEW YORK TIMES BESTSELLING AUTHOR

K.A. LINDE

RED TOWER BOOKS™

Entangled Publishing, LLC
644 Shrewsbury Commons Ave., STE 181
Shrewsbury, PA 17361
rights@entangledpublishing.com

Cover design by LJ Anderson and Bree Archer
Edge design by Bree Archer
Interior design by Britt Marczak

Paperback ISBN 978-1-64937-974-0
Ebook ISBN 978-1-64937-534-6

Manufactured in the United States of America
First Edition April 2026

10 9 8 7 6 5 4 3 2 1

MORE FROM K.A. LINDE

BLOOD TYPE

The Monster and the Last Blood Match
The Captive and the First Blood Game

THE OAK AND HOLLY CYCLE

The Wren in the Holly Library
The Robin on the Oak Throne
The Raven at the Ash Door

ROYAL HOUSES

House of Dragons
House of Shadows
House of Curses
House of Gods
House of Embers

ASCENSION

The Affiliate
The Bound
The Consort
The Society
The Domina

To the girls who never stopped fighting—
for love, for hope, for yourself.

The Rebel and the Final Blood War is a dark supernatural romance filled with vampires, the humans they rely on for survival, and the last grasp of a greedy company that wants to win control. As such, the story includes elements that might not be suitable for all readers. Violence, death, gore, blood, gun injuries, references to torture (off page), medical experimentation, emotional and physical abuse, depictions of mental illness, and dark romance themes including control, jealousy, possessiveness, and graphic sex are depicted in the novel. Readers who may be sensitive to these elements, please take note, guard your hearts, and prepare for the final battle…

Chapter One

Beckham was dead.

A gunshot pierced the air, and another followed.

Reyna Carpenter ignored it all. None of it mattered.

Beckham was lying on the ground and hadn't moved an inch since Harrington snapped his neck and dropped him like a sack of potatoes. She'd opened her own wrist to feed him her blood. After all, they were a perfect blood match. She should be able to save him.

Instead, she had watched her soul mate die.

And there was nothing she could do.

Tears wouldn't come. A sob caught in her throat and buried itself there. She couldn't think or see or breathe or even feel. Everything was caught up in that one moment. As she stared down at the man she loved with all her heart while it ripped in two.

Harrington had moved so fast. Beyond her ability to even comprehend, and then in that second, he'd ruined everything. She thought she hated him before. Hated him for kidnapping her, stealing her blood to keep himself alive. Abusing her. For the psychological torture.

But all that was nothing compared to this.

Commotion ensued all around her, yet she couldn't drag her eyes away from Beckham to find out what was going on. Did it even matter?

An arm grabbed at her. She tried to fight the person off. She screamed. She clung to Beckham. No. She wouldn't move. They couldn't take her from him.

"Reyna!" Gabe shouted at her. "Reyna, look at me. I just shot Harrington. All the vamps are down. We have to go."

"No! No. Get off me," she screamed back at him.

"We're all going to die if we don't move now."

Reyna tried to shrug him off, but it was pointless. Gabe was a fighter, an Irish mob boss, and one of the most fearsome leaders of the rebel organization Elle. She could no more move him than bring Beckham back from the dead.

He grasped her around the middle, then hoisted her over his shoulder. She reached for Beckham. Her hand outstretched into open air. Slowly her brain pieced together everything around her. Harrington on the ground, blood pouring out of bullet holes. Roland next to him trying to staunch the blood loss. The backstabbing traitor Penelope bleeding from a gunshot wound, hysterical. People flooded out of the mayor's New Year's Eve party downtown after seeing the chaos and death and destruction.

Beckham.

She needed to be there with him. She fought against Gabe's hands, trying to get back to him. But Gabe was strong and persistent. He refused to let go as he carried her farther and farther away. Beckham was gone, and Gabe was taking her away from him.

"Put me down. Let me go back to him!"

"Reyna, fucking shit!" Gabe yelled at her.

She kicked and clawed at him to release her. As they moved, her heel fell off and onto the patio floor. She couldn't do this. Fuck! She couldn't lose him. She refused for this to be her reality.

Gabe cursed and then dropped her on the pavement, tugging her hastily into a secluded alcove. He grabbed her roughly by both shoulders.

"Snap back to reality, Reyna. There's nothing we can do right now. Harrington told the snipers not to shoot you, but people will come after us. If you want to live through the night, I need you to run!"

"But Beckham," she whispered.

"Live, Reyna," Gabe pleaded with her, his voice tight. "All you can do is live."

She hardly saw his sympathetic look as she stared over his shoulder to the patio beyond. Beckham hadn't moved. Living didn't feel possible. How could she live when he didn't? Maybe it was outrageous to even consider, but she felt as if a bomb had detonated in her mind. Shrapnel tore her apart from the inside out.

Then to her horror, she saw Roland stumble to his feet. His eyes caught hers across the divide of people. They promised blood and torment and destruction. Roland was now Harrington's only remaining second-in-command, and he had always wanted Reyna—to break Reyna. She could see then and there that he would stop at nothing to get what he wanted this time.

Beckham couldn't stop him. Harrington wouldn't stop him.

Leaving now was the only way to escape a fate worse than death.

She couldn't continue to stand here. She couldn't go back in time. Nothing she did could fix this situation.

She had come here to kill Harrington. And he'd gotten the better of her…of all of them. But if she died here, what would happen to the world?

"Reyna, please," Gabe said.

She turned clear, devastated eyes to him and nodded. Beckham's death would not be for nothing.

He released a harsh breath of relief, and she realized then that she'd scared him. That he'd thought he'd lost her. He didn't know how right he was, but she would have time to think about that later. Right now, she needed to survive.

She compartmentalized all her doubts into one space in her brain, kicked off her other shoe, and took off sprinting after Gabe.

Barefoot and freezing in nothing but a strapless dress and Beckham's suit coat, she didn't dare stop.

They made it to the end of the block and nearly ran smack dab into Meghan. Her red hair box braids were pulled into a high pony, and her silvery dress was obscured by a black jacket that went nearly to her knees.

"What took you so long?" Meghan gasped, moving into position next to them.

"I'll tell you later," Gabe said.

Reyna glanced over her shoulder. Her eyes rounded in horror. "Fuck."

"What?" Gabe asked. He followed her line of sight and cursed violently, before grabbing Meghan's hand and running again. "We need to pick it up."

Reyna measured her breathing and increased her pace. Roland followed them, and considering vampires ran at incredible speeds they were lucky he hadn't reached them yet. Maybe Beckham throwing him into the brick building actually hurt him. She'd seen Roland crumple at the hit, and it took him a long time to stand up again.

Reyna glanced back one more time to see that the crowd seemed to keep Roland off their back. Between the New Year's Eve mob and the mayhem from the gunshots, he had no clear path. And everything was so haphazard that he had to physically push people out of his way as he attempted to weave through the crowd. No one made it easy on him.

But after that glance, she couldn't keep looking. Not if she wanted to get through the crowd herself.

They ran down three blocks, weaving in and out of traffic and taking turns and corners, hoping to lose Roland and trying to get away from the mass of people to reach their getaway car.

Gabe checked once more and flashed them a victorious smile. "I don't see him."

Reyna nodded and Meghan shot them both a quick grin. But Reyna couldn't get rid of the uneasy feeling in her stomach.

"Almost there," Gabe said. "Just this corner."

They whipped around the next corner to an unmarked black van idling on the street. As they rushed toward it, the back doors flapped open.

Then Roland appeared and cut off the end of the street. No longer meandering, he launched himself toward them. He saw the van. He knew that they could get away and had every intention of stopping them.

Everything happened in slow motion. Meghan reached the van first, careening into the empty interior. Gabe was next jumping inside. Reyna was the last and the slowest, her breathing jagged. No matter that she'd spent months training for this very moment. Her time on the treadmill hadn't actually seemed to prepare her for running outside, barefoot, in unbearably cold temperatures.

She knew Roland was almost upon her. She didn't dare look over her shoulder, but she could tell it was too close for comfort.

Meghan pulled her gun out and pointed it toward them. Gabe placed his hand on the barrel.

"You'll hit her!"

Meghan shook him off, lifted it again, and aimed. Gabe reached his hand out toward Reyna, and she used her last burst of energy to throw her body toward him.

His hand locked on her wrist. But she fell short and her knee hit the metal bumper. Her shoulder was tugged so hard she swore it felt as if it dislocated as he hauled her inside. She was nearly there when she felt a hand clasp her ankle.

"Go, go, go!" Gabe yelled at Tye, who was driving the getaway car.

He moved to wrap his arms around her chest as he tried to pull her farther inside. But Roland was stronger. The van kicked into drive and suddenly they were all thrown off balance. Gabe scrambled to get his footing again, but even with them rumbling down the street and Roland having no leverage, he was still pulling her from the van.

"Let me go!" she shrieked, trying to dislodge Roland from her.

"You think this is over? That you can just walk away?" Roland spat at her.

"Fuck you," Meghan yelled.

Then Reyna heard a series of gunshots. Roland shifted fast enough to miss most of the spray, but a bullet must have hit. He grunted and gave a bit of release on her ankle. Reyna reared back and kicked him in the face. He let go, falling backward across the pavement.

Gabe tugged Reyna all the way into the van. She gasped on all fours as she stared through the open doors at Roland's furious face. Even after being shot, he still got back on his feet and raced to catch them.

But he couldn't take down a moving vehicle barreling down the street. Their eyes met in the distance, and a chill ran down her spine, as if he was saying that he would come for her. This wasn't over.

But it was over.

It was all over.

Chapter Two

The van skittered around another corner and toward safety as Meghan and Gabe pulled the doors closed. The noise from the outside disappeared, sending them all into a stony silence, their labored breathing the only sound.

Reyna didn't recognize the woman with brown skin and a bindi on her forehead who turned to the back from the passenger seat. She rummaged through a black duffle bag and handed warmer clothes to Meghan and Gabe. She moved toward Reyna, but Gabe put his hand out to stop her. His eyes shot to Reyna's and then back. He shook his head as if she were a volcano about to erupt.

The woman shrugged and passed the clothes to Gabe. He walked through the large open area in the back to where Reyna was still seated on the floor, shell-shocked. She tucked her knees to her chest, pulling Beckham's jacket tighter around her. She wouldn't relinquish this. No matter what anyone said.

"Hey," Gabe said, crouching down. "You're going to get sick if you don't change into this. You don't want it all to be for nothing."

He held out a pair of pants, thick socks, a sweater, and a jacket to match Meghan's. When she didn't respond, he put the clothes next to her and went to talk to Meghan, who appeared a minute later with a haunted look in her eyes.

She didn't try to talk to Reyna. She didn't try to tell her that things would get better. She didn't lie to her. She acted like the nurse that she was trained to be. She helped Reyna into the pants and socks. Reyna only protested when Meghan tried to remove Beckham's jacket. This was all she had left of him.

Tears filled Meghan's eyes at the sight. She slung the other jacket on top of Beckham's, rubbed Reyna's hair gently, and then stepped away. She returned a minute later to bandage her wrist and then left her alone.

The adrenaline of the escape and chase had suddenly left Reyna's body, leaving her utterly empty. Leaving her with her memories.

Beckham's broken body. Him falling to the ground. Not moving. Dead.

She felt as broken as he had looked in that moment. Broken and bleeding and empty. Just empty.

Reyna could hear everyone whispering about her. "What happened to her?" the woman asked.

Gabe shook his head. "Beckham…"

"He's gone?"

Meghan cleared her throat noisily. "Prisha," she hissed.

"Yeah," Gabe replied. "He's gone."

Tye cursed softly.

Meghan hiccupped around her own tears.

"She saw it?" Prisha murmured.

"Yeah," Gabe whispered.

"Poor thing."

But Reyna didn't feel like a poor thing.

She wasn't a wounded animal.

She was destroyed. Obliterated. Demolished.

She was as cold as ice and just as frozen. Inside and out.

She had left him behind.

And her entire heart with him.

...

Reyna lost track of how long they drove.

It could have been hours. She had no sense of where they were going. She didn't bother asking.

Her mind was a merciless place. As much as she wanted to burrow down into her numbness and forget what had just happened, she couldn't. She pressed her palms against her eyes and tried to block out the images assaulting her. But it was no use. She didn't think she'd ever go a day without seeing them.

Eventually, they pulled off the main roads. The van rumbled to a stop, and they parked inside a garage. The door shut behind them, casting them into darkness. Reyna took a measured breath to still her unease before Gabe hauled the back door open again.

"Come on," Meghan said, reaching for Reyna's hand. "Let's get you inside."

Reyna let Meghan help her out. She straightened her spine at her friend's look of pity and then left the truck. Gabe and Meghan followed her to where Prisha stood with Tye. Prisha gestured for them to move toward a back door.

The house they entered was plain, with hardly anything in it. Just some used furniture and a foldout table in the kitchen. It didn't look like a place where someone lived. Another safe house.

"There are three bedrooms," Prisha said. "Washington has already taken one. I'm happy to share my own. You can decide who gets the third. I also have a couch and an air mattress."

"Thank you for getting this set up, Prisha," Meghan said warmly. "It will only be for a night."

Prisha waved her hand. "It's all gone now, isn't it? You'll need the space."

"We don't want to compromise you," Tye said. His features were drawn. "It's enough that the bunker was destroyed. We won't be able to get inside to see the full damage until the smoke has cleared."

Reyna's heart tugged again. The bunker was destroyed. She had spent the last month living there, in Elle's headquarters on the outskirts of the city. Elle had rescued her from Harrington and brought her into the fold. Her brothers had gotten onto the security team. Brian had married his fiancé, Laura, before he had been captured on a raid. Drew and Laura had been at the bunker while she had left to kill Harrington. A lot of good that had done.

She couldn't even think about all the other people who had been in the bunker when Harrington had bombed it.

"How many are accounted for?" Prisha asked.

Tye shook his head. "We haven't heard from any other safe houses. Communications are down. We probably won't hear until tomorrow."

Which meant they wouldn't have word on Drew and Laura until tomorrow either. Reyna sighed.

Meghan put an arm around her shoulder. "Why don't we get you into the shower and clean you up? Then I think you should rest. You can have the other bedroom."

"I'm fine. I'll take the couch," Reyna said.

Meghan reached out to her, but Gabe grabbed her arm. "Let her go."

A moment later, Reyna glanced over at them and saw that Meghan collapsed into Gabe's shoulder, her own muffled tears loud enough for Reyna to hear. Gabe escorted her from the room.

Reyna pulled Beckham's jacket tighter around herself. She could see that the others grieved as well, worried about what happened to the rebellion. They all suffered greatly for what Harrington did.

One error had cost them everything. Not just Beckham but the entire rebellion.

All the people that they had known for years. She might have lost Beckham, but they lost everything. Maybe they all needed to be alone tonight.

She curled up on the empty sofa, Beckham's jacket her only blanket. It still smelled like him. What would it be like when it no longer held that smell? When his jacket was as lifeless as his body?

She choked on the sob that was stuck in her throat and the dam broke. Tears fell down her cheeks. They blurred her vision and superheated her skin. She felt like she could vomit. She couldn't breathe. She was hyperventilating. Her chest hurt. There was a hole where Beckham had been.

She'd gotten away. She'd survived. There were important things left to accomplish. But right now, all she felt was grief.

Beckham was really gone.

And she had to find a way to live with that.

• • •

Beep, beep, beep.

Reyna awoke in a burst of fear and desperation. For a second, she didn't remember where she was. It was as if she was put back into that prison cell beneath Visage, where she lived as a blood bag for that monster Harrington. She could distinctly remember lying there, an IV in her arm and the familiar sound of the heart rate monitor beeping noisily after she had been kidnapped.

Visage had appeared to the outside world as a benevolent company that saved them in the midst of the great recession. Vampires came out of the darkness with the invention of the blood type cure, which was less a cure and more a Band-Aid. Vampires drank from specific humans that matched their blood type, and it curbed their baser tendencies. It created "men" like Harrington and Roland.

Reyna had only recently found out that much of what she had thought she had known was a lie. Some vampires were already predisposed to higher cognitive function. Harrington and the three vampire lords he'd recruited—Cassandra, Roland, and Beckham—had engineered the recession for the purpose of starting Visage. To take over the world.

And they were winning.

Now only Harrington and Roland remained. Beckham had killed Cassandra. And Beckham…

Reyna opened her eyes to dispel the lingering feeling of unease. She was in a quaint little house on the outskirts of the city. She wasn't at Visage. She wasn't still kidnapped. Everything was all right.

Except, it wasn't.

Beckham was…dead.

"You're up," a voice said behind her.

Reyna shot to her feet and whirled around. She was still wrapped in Beckham's jacket. Roger Washington stood in jeans and a high-neck sweater. She had never seen him look so normal. He was the vampire doctor who had invented the blood type cure in the first place. He'd worked with Harrington for years before turning coat and helping Elle.

He had determined that she and Beckham were a perfect blood match. A once-in-a-lifetime pair whose blood matched the other's blood composition, the equivalent to a soul mate.

"I'm up," she said softly.

"I'm so thrilled that you made it out. I was asleep when you came in last night and missed everything," Washington said.

Reyna sank back into the couch. "Do you have any word on what happened with the bunker?"

Washington shook his head as he poured himself some coffee. He held the pot up to her in offering. She nodded. "Unfortunately, I know no more than you do. Sydney sent me out of the bunker to separate all of Elle's high command as a precaution, so I was already here when I got word." He crossed the living room and handed her the coffee. She took a long sip, shuddering against the bitterness. "How did last night go?"

"It was a disaster."

"I'm sorry for that, Reyna."

Sorry. He was sorry. Washington couldn't have changed the outcome, but it still rankled her.

"You don't understand. Harrington won. Penelope is a vampire." She hated the taste of Penelope's name in her mouth after she'd fucking double-crossed them. Penelope's "love" for Beckham had turned her rotten and in the end, she had doomed them all. "And Beckham…" She couldn't force the words out. Her heart felt as if it were being ripped from her chest all over again. "He's…he's dead. Harrington killed him."

"I didn't realize. Is there anything I can do?" he asked cautiously.

"No," she said, letting her anger extinguish. It wasn't his fault that Beckham was dead. The only blame belonged to Harrington.

Washington held his hand out as if he was going to try to comfort her, try to say something to make it better. But perhaps his years had shown him what could and could not be fixed. Because he let his hand drop and closed his mouth. He didn't look at her with pity like the others. Only with deep understanding. And somehow that was worse.

Why did it have to be this way? It wasn't fair. Life wasn't fair, and she had never expected it to be. Not when her parents had died when she was eight, or when her alcoholic uncle had abandoned them three years later, or even during the weary years living in the Warehouse District. It had been a tough life, but she had always had highlights. Her brothers and Beckham. Now she was alone.

"Hey, I thought I heard voices out here," Meghan said, appearing from the hallway. There were hollows under her eyes. She looked bedraggled and defeated. It was not a sight Reyna was used to seeing on her. "Everything okay?"

"Reyna was filling me in on what happened yesterday," Washington said.

Meghan winced. "Sorry. We should have done that last night."

"No need. I think I have the basics now. Would you like some coffee?"

"Please." She looked toward Reyna. "How are you doing this morning?" Meghan asked. Worry creased between her brows.

"I'm alive. So, what's the plan?" Reyna asked, forcing her shoulders back.

Meghan opened, then closed her mouth. She looked a bit like a fish out of water.

Reyna froze. "Wait, we do have a plan, right?"

"We have a plan," Gabe said. He appeared behind Meghan. His dark red hair was frazzled as if someone's hands had been in it all night. Looking between Meghan and Gabe, it wasn't too hard to guess what last night's grief had resulted in. "Tye went to switch out plates and get Prisha another vehicle. We need something secure before we can leave."

"And where are we going to go? The bunker is gone. The plan was to get back to the bunker after all of this. Safe houses were Plan B in case we needed a quick escape. What the hell now?" Reyna snapped.

"Plan C," Washington said.

Reyna arched an eyebrow.

"No one knows where all the safe houses are—that way if someone got kidnapped then they couldn't out the entire operation. I'm going to take you to a safe place outside of the city until this blows over," Washington informed her.

Reyna let the news sink in. "We can't just run away."

"We're not," Gabe said. "We need a place to regroup, and we can't stay here."

Reyna didn't like the sound of that. She'd rather figure out a way to make the bastards pay. But as she was about to say as much, Tye and Prisha came through the back door in a rush.

"They're casing the neighborhood," Prisha said.

"Time to go," Tye said.

"Shit," Gabe spat.

"Prisha, you should head out," Meghan said earnestly. "You don't want to be found."

"Will you be safe?"

"Yes," Meghan said. "Thank you again."

Prisha kissed Meghan on the cheek, nodded at the rest of them, and then disappeared into the garage.

Gabe and Tye grabbed their remaining supplies before hustling them out of the house. An SUV with heavily tinted windows was parked where the van had sat last night. They all piled inside as Tye took the helm. Reyna tucked her legs up underneath her and waited for what felt like an eternity as the garage door opened behind them. Tye slowly backed them down the drive and out onto the main streets.

Reyna didn't know what she was looking for. She expected something like the police waiting for them, but what she saw instead was a small army of black vehicles in all shapes and sizes. Reyna held her breath as they passed one of the cars and saw the little red *V* logo for Visage on the side. Her stomach flopped.

Meghan grabbed Reyna's hand. They locked eyes and Reyna saw her own fear reflected at her.

She held her breath as they drove past another Visage vehicle. A vampire got out of the front seat at that precise moment. The woman stared at their SUV as it rolled by. For a second, Reyna swore the woman had X-ray vision and was able to see through the tint to the people behind it. She narrowed her eyes at the SUV. Reyna watched the woman's hand move to the phone in her pocket.

"Please don't. Please no. Please, please, please," Reyna whispered in the backseat.

Meghan clutched her hand until it was painful. But Reyna didn't stop her, and she didn't take her eyes off the vampire who took a step toward them. Her hand tightened around the phone. She opened her mouth but didn't form words. She stared as if she just knew.

Reyna tensed. Ready to sound the alarm if need be.

Then something distracted the vampire. She glanced down at her phone, frowned, and brought it to her ear. She took one last look at the SUV before turning away as it sped past her.

Reyna released her breath. They drove the rest of the way out of the neighborhood in silence. They weren't in the clear yet. But at least they were away from the worst of it.

If only the same were true for their morale as they drove the remains of their broken rebellion from the city.

Chapter Three

They weren't pursued.

Reyna couldn't believe it.

She was sure that someone would look at their vehicle and assume it held rebels. But no, they drove out of the neighborhood and onto the open roads without a hassle. Tye listened to the police scanner and narrowly missed a roadblock or two, but once they got on the interstate, the coast was clear.

Tension hung heavy in the SUV, and it was a silent hour before Washington finally directed them off the main roads and onto a long bumpy drive. Once they moved from under a copse of trees, they came upon a large iron gate.

Reyna's eyebrows rose and she leaned forward to get a better look at it. The gate was straight out of some Victorian period piece. As if it should be a dark and stormy night with lightning announcing their entrance instead of a bitter cold but sunny New Year's Day.

Tye punched in a passcode and the gates creaked apart slowly. Very slowly.

They inched forward onto the grounds. Everyone was rubbernecking, trying to figure out where the hell Washington had brought them. They passed what must have once been lush gardens but were now overgrown and ignored. And after a couple more minutes, they got their answer.

A circular drive ended right before a three-story stone mansion.

"What is this place?" Reyna asked as they came to a halt.

"Yeah. I've never seen this in any records," Meghan said.

"It's not in any records," Washington said. "It's my home."

"Does Harrington know about it?" Reyna asked, terror suddenly lancing through her.

"Yes, but he would never in a million years suspect that I would come back here. I haven't stepped foot in it in fifteen years."

"Why?"

He glanced back at her. "Because my wife was killed here."

Then he opened the door and slid out of the SUV. They looked at one another in confusion and sorrow before following him. Reyna's feet hit the gravel drive, and she stared up at the imposing structure. Vines covered much of the entrance. The stonework, which must have once been beautiful, had deteriorated from the elements. Reyna could see at least one window that was broken, and a tree had fallen into the roof on one corner of the building. Would they have running water? Electricity? The house had clearly been built long before those things existed.

"We left for *this,*" Gabe voiced what everyone was thinking. They might have had no choice, but some run-down old mansion didn't seem like the salvation they'd been looking for.

Tye stretched his lean muscles out. "Looks like a piece of shit."

"I can hear you," Washington said. He had ambled up to the entrance and was prying the front door open.

"We know," Gabe said with a grin. "Doesn't change the appearance of this place."

"I'll have you know that I have had this home since after the turn of the nineteenth century," Washington said, turning his nose up at them. "It has come a long way since 1805."

Reyna's mouth fell open. She sometimes forgot how old vampires could be. Beckham was so young for a vampire and yet he still was sixty-seven. The thought hit her like a sucker punch to the stomach.

Past tense.

He'd been so young. He had been sixty-seven. He was no longer.

She squeezed her eyes shut and rode out the pain until it subsided. It was easier in the moments when she didn't have to think about the immediate consequences of him being gone. It was hard to wrap her brain around the fact that he wasn't about to walk up the drive with his usual stoic look and burning broody passion.

"Hey," Meghan said, placing a hand on her shoulder. "You okay?"

Reyna didn't want to think or talk about her feelings. "Let's just get inside."

She followed Washington into the cavernous interior of his turn-of-the-nineteenth-century mansion. The foyer had vaulted ceilings that reached up to an impossible height. It was dark inside and when Washington reached for the lights, only a few flickered on, casting the entire place with an eerie glow.

"Creepy," Reyna whispered.

"You can say that again," Gabe said behind her.

"I thought you were bringing us to a rebel operation," Tye said. "If you haven't been here in fifteen years, what are we going to do here?"

"I have not been here, but I have a colleague who has been maintaining the premises since I joined Elle. It will suffice for the time being. Now, follow me," Washington said.

Gabe and Meghan exchanged a look before pulling out their phones to use as flashlights. With the entrance fully illuminated, they could see the layers of dirt that said no one had stepped foot in here for years. It certainly didn't look maintained.

Washington pulled open an enormous wooden door that led from the historic foyer into a gorgeous and stately living area. The furniture was carefully preserved beneath sheets, and the windows were covered to keep the light out, presumably to save the antique artwork lining the walls. Reyna felt as if she had stepped back in time.

They toured the mansion, finding thirteen bedrooms on the second floor. The third floor was one big suite. Though the tree falling in clearly disrupted that. When Washington showed them the basement, Reyna expected a dark dungeon or prison or something equally medieval. But no, the basement was a fully finished medical lab with all the equipment he'd had back at the bunker. Plus, a store of firearms, communication devices, and pretty much everything else they would need to pick up where they'd left off.

"I've never worried much about upkeep in the main parts of the house, but the basement was completely refitted in recent years." Washington seemed more comfortable now that he was back in a lab, downstairs, and away from the memory of his dead wife, upstairs. "All of my research has been uploaded to the servers, and the lab was created as a just-in-case option."

"Wow," Gabe said, admiring the impressive gun collection, "appearances are deceiving."

"I'm glad that I pass your muster," Washington said dryly.

Gabe tipped him a two-finger salute.

"We should all pick rooms and clean up. I have a superior olfactory system and can tell you that everyone needs a shower," Washington said with a small smile. "I'll contact Genevieve to come by with food."

"You trust her?" Meghan asked.

"She has been taking care of this house longer than you have been alive. She's trustworthy."

"All right," Meghan agreed. "A shower sounds nice."

Gabe, Tye, and Meghan immediately fell into a sense of normalcy, arguing over which bedroom to take for themselves. They all seemed extravagant. Reyna didn't really care.

Washington stopped her on her way toward the stairs. "Reyna…"

"Yeah?"

"Beckham stayed here in the past. Before I abandoned the place, he had a room." Reyna's heart constricted. "I thought you'd want to stay there."

She nodded, unable to form words.

"Turn left and it's the room at the end of the hall."

"Thank you," she choked out.

"I am terribly sorry for your loss. Beckham was a good vampire. A great man. He deserved better than William Harrington," Washington said. "As long as I was friends with William, I never knew him to get his hands dirty. He must have felt very threatened by you to do something so out of character."

"Little consolation."

"Indeed. But don't ever forget the power that you have over him. He seeks to control you, but he doesn't understand you. It's his greatest weakness. I do not think he has realized that harming you was a tactical error."

Reyna raised her chin. "He will one day."

Washington let a small smile grace his cheeks. "I believe you."

With that, Reyna grabbed fresh clothes out of one of their duffle bags downstairs, climbed two flights of stairs, turned left, and faced down the door to Beckham's room. She slowly walked toward it and placed her hand on the metal doorknob. Her hand shook on the knob before she worked up the courage to turn it and push the door open. She flipped on the lights, and the room was bathed in a soft glow from the antique lamps.

Beckham's space felt homey. A four-poster bed took up the center of the room, complete with a canopy and navy duvet. An entire wall was full from top to bottom with books in every shape, color, and size. An old-fashioned writing desk sat unoccupied in a corner, still littered with papers he'd apparently left behind.

The Beckham who had lived and worked at this residence had not been the Beckham she had known. This was the ruthless vampire who had risen to the top with murder and destruction. The vampire he had been before he'd turned his back on this life and started to help Elle. Before he became hers.

She sensed it in every fiber of her being. Still, somehow, she was completely connected to Beckham in every way. He was gone, but she felt him like phantom pain in a severed limb.

Reyna swallowed back the bile rising in her throat and then for the first time since Beckham wrapped his jacket around her shoulders, she removed it from her body. She found a wardrobe against the wall still stocked with clothes. The smell of him nearly overwhelmed her. For a moment it was as if he were standing directly behind her. She could close her eyes and feel his hands on her and breathe him in.

She pushed all the clothes together, took out a hanger, and hung the jacket in the wardrobe. She hated the absence of it already. She wouldn't let it go, but she would keep moving forward. If she stopped entirely, his death would be for nothing. Beckham would want her to go on. He would want her to use his death to further their cause. He would want so much more from her. He always had.

Mourning would be a long process, but she couldn't let it cripple her. Not when there was so much left to do.

After her shower, Reyna felt much clearer and levelheaded. She dragged on new clothes, pulled her hair up in a tight ponytail, and knew what she needed to do.

An hour later, she had everyone assembled in the dining room. The room was much too big for their motley crew of five, but it was better than nothing. Tye stood on the antique table to light the candles on the chandelier, which somehow had survived all this time and not been replaced by electric.

"Do you know how old that table is you're standing on?" Washington tsked. Reyna didn't know how *else* he was supposed to light it.

"Probably not as ancient as you, old man," Tye said teasingly before jumping down and taking his seat.

"I take no offense to having three hundred or so years on you," Washington said.

Reyna stood from her seat at the head of the table. It had been purposeful to take what had been Sydney's place. None of them knew if the leader of Elle had survived the attack on the bunker.

"I called this meeting," Reyna said, "because I don't want to waste any time. Though I am thankful that we have a place to stay, there's *a lot* that needs to be done."

"Reyna," Meghan said with a sigh, "this is really not the time. You should rest. You should grieve. You need the time to recover."

Reyna held up her hand, and to her surprise Meghan stopped talking. "I understand where you're coming from, but no. I don't need downtime. I don't need to grieve. I'll sleep when I'm dead. Right now, we need to regroup and hit them back. They'll never expect us to rally."

"Because we have nothing to rally around," Meghan said.

"That's where you're wrong. We have everything to rally around. Everything. Visage is still going to unveil their plans for a feeding camp. They still have humans imprisoned beneath their building in the city. They're trying to take over the world. We can't let them get away with it."

"I agree with you," Gabe said, holding his hands up. "But we need more time."

"You said that I needed to live so that this wouldn't all be for nothing," she said, throwing his words back at him. "Let's not make it for nothing."

"I'm sorry, Reyna. But you just saw Beckham murdered. You're not ready for this," Meghan said.

"Kid gloves off, Meghan. I appreciate you breaking me out of Visage, but please don't baby me. You all lost as much as I did and you're not falling apart. I'm ready to step up. Are you?"

Meghan leaned back and pursed her lips. She didn't respond. Reyna shrugged and faced the guys.

"Well?"

"Whatcha got?" Tye asked.

Gabe winked.

Washington smiled and tilted his head toward her.

"We have a lot to do, but first, we need to figure out what happened with the bunker. Tye and Meghan, you two should figure out how bad the damage is and work with Washington to contact whoever survived."

"And you and Gabe?" Meghan snapped. "Where do you fit in all of this?"

Reyna turned and faced her friend. She loved Meghan. But something had broken in her with this. She was no longer the upbeat woman that could charm the pants off of anyone with a smile. "Gabe and I are going to get Jodie."

Meghan's eyes rounded. "Jodie left almost a week ago. We have no idea where she is. It's a waste of resources to look for her right now."

"Jodie escaped Visage with us. She's our responsibility and my closest friend. She has never been on the streets alone. Ten years inside Visage and now this? No, we have to find her. The mission is to get all of Elle back together. Jodie is part of Elle, and we *do* know where she went. I have an address. Once we have our team back together and more information, we can get back to the real matter at hand—taking down Harrington."

"It's a good plan," Washington said. "We have much to do to get Elle back on its feet. This is as good as any place to start."

"And we will get Elle back on its feet," Reyna said passionately. "Visage will not win. They will not break us. No matter how they try. We will always come back swinging."

Gabe, Tye, and Meghan looked up at her with a newfound respect. As if she had suddenly grown into the person she was always meant to be. And Reyna vowed to do whatever it took to live up to this new role. Beckham's sacrifice would not be in vain.

Chapter Four

"So, you really up for this?" Gabe asked as he pulled out an assortment of guns.

"Please stop asking that question. Between you and Meghan, I think I've been asked enough about my feelings on the matter."

"Hey, you should go easy on Meghan."

"I know," Reyna said with a sigh. She pinched the bridge of her nose. "I know what she's lost. I know what it all feels like, but I can't stand being babied. I'm not the same person I was when I joined Visage or the person Meghan met when she broke me out."

"I can see that. But Megs can't help but look out for you. It's in her nature."

Reyna shrugged. "You're right. Just trying to keep the train on the rails. I don't want us to get so lost in our feelings that we stop doing shit."

Gabe chambered a bullet in his weapon and then smiled at her. "Don't worry. I'm all for doing shit."

"You're ridiculous," she said with a laugh.

Gabe collected all the guns and loaded most into a duffle bag. He stuffed one into his waistband and attached several others to holsters on his body. Then he handed one to Reyna. "Hope you don't need this."

"Me too." She took it reluctantly, checked the safety, and then strapped it to her side. She pulled her jacket over it, and they headed out the door.

"Can you believe that Washington has had this place since 1805?" Gabe said with a shake of his head. "Fucking vampires, man. How fucking old is he?"

"Old."

When they reached the garage, Reyna's eyes doubled in size at the amazing selection of vehicles that Washington had. From flashy sports cars to SUVs to a fucking Hummer. The guy was a collector. This must've been where the groundskeeper spent most of his time. Thank God, he kept the garage outfitted with up-to-date tech. Reyna and Gabe hopped in the passenger seat of one of the more inconspicuous cars.

"Why the hell would he work as a doctor with this loot?" The car revved to life and then Gabe peeled away.

"It clearly didn't start as an Elle establishment," she said, voicing the thought she'd had all along. "Fifteen years ago, he would have been helping Harrington start Visage."

"It's a little poetic that the rebel organization that's going to take Harrington's ass down is working out of a base he started all this shit in."

"Couldn't agree more," Reyna said with a vicious smile.

They drove for over an hour in companionable conversation. Gabe was a carefree, flirtatious sort. When she'd first met him, she'd immediately pegged him as trouble. That much was still true. Except now it was one of her favorite qualities about the quick-witted Irish mobster.

As they moved through more decrepit streets, their conversation slowed until it lapsed into silence. The neighborhood was decrepit to say the least. Waste and refuse littered the street. Most of the streetlights were out and left an eerie glow on everything. Graffiti littered the buildings and only a handful of people walked around, none of them looked particularly friendly.

Her heart sank. She sure hoped Jodie had already left this place.

"I'm not sure what to do about the car," Gabe said. "I thought it would blend. I greatly underestimated how shitty this neighborhood is."

"Yeah. I think we need to find a place to stash it."

"You okay with a bit of a walk?" Gabe grimaced.

"Whatever we need to do."

It was probably a mile away from their destination before Gabe found a place to leave the car that didn't look as if it would be stripped down for parts before they returned. The weather was brisk, but it was nice to be out actually doing something. She hardly noticed the walk or the cold as anticipation fluttered through her stomach.

"Try not to get your hopes up," Gabe muttered. "This isn't the kind of place people linger if they don't have to."

Reyna ducked her head and tried not to make eye contact with anyone on the streets. She'd grown up in the Warehouse District. She'd thought she'd known hardship but that was nothing compared to what she saw now.

A few guys approached Gabe, who bucked up to twice his size at their approach.

"You got some cash?" the first guy asked.

"No."

"What, you're too good for us?" the second guy asked.

"How about your little girly, then?" The last guy took a step toward Reyna. She sidestepped closer to Gabe.

Gabe shot them a menacing glare and then pulled back the front of his jacket. The handguns he'd secured there earlier were clearly visible. "You're making a terrible mistake. Just keep walking."

One guy showed off his own gun, but his friends looked warier.

"Promise I'm faster on the draw," Gabe snarled.

"Come on, Dom."

"Yeah, Dom," Gabe spat. "Listen to your buddies."

Dom offered some choice expletives before being dragged away by his friends. Reyna only took a breath when they were a block away from them. She sure hoped that they didn't run into them again. That encounter wouldn't go as well.

"Fucking cocky bastards. Thinking only with their dicks," Gabe growled relentlessly as they walked the last few blocks. "Think they're so bad. They wouldn't survive a night on my fucking streets."

Reyna smiled at him. She liked seeing Gabe be all big bad tough guy. No wonder Meghan was into him.

"Well, here we are," Gabe said.

They stared up at the dilapidated apartment building. Most of the windows were boarded up. A group of kids played with a kickball in the street, and a few elderly men played backgammon on the stoop. It didn't seem as bad, until she spotted a drug deal happening on the corner.

"Great place," Reyna muttered.

They approached the entrance, which had an electric gate that had long been deactivated. One of the elderly men called out to them, but they both ignored him and hurried up the steps. They checked the registry for Jodie's cousin's name, June Gardner. There was no one by that name, but they'd been expecting that. They buzzed the apartment number. No one answered.

Gabe shrugged and took to the stairs. They went up five flights before finding the apartment off the landing. Gabe knocked on the front door long enough for someone to finally crack it open. It was a large woman in nothing on but a bra and underwear. Her hair was in curlers, and she wore a permanent sneer.

"What?" she spat. "I don't need nothing. Don't need you banging on my door. Fuck off."

Reyna jumped forward. "So sorry to bother you, ma'am. We were wondering if June Gardner lived here."

"Don't know no one by that name."

"Or Jodie. Tall, Black woman, curly hair?"

"Yeah, she came by. So what?"

Reyna's heart leaped. "When?"

"Don't fucking know. But I sent her on her way like I'm about to send you on yours."

"Do you know where she went?" Gabe interjected.

"Do I look like someone's fucking keeper?" the woman said and then slammed the door in their faces.

Gabe looked like he wanted to barrel through the door. She put her hand on his arm and shook her head.

"She's not going to be any more help. I think if she was this nice to us then she wouldn't have been any kinder to Jodie."

"True."

"Come on. Let's find someone more willing to give information."

They headed back downstairs and walked over to the elderly man who had tried to flag them down. He at least had wanted to talk to them.

"Hello," she said with a smile.

"Well, hello there," he said with a toothless grin. "I'm Harold."

"Nice to meet you. We are looking for our friend June. She used to live here, and we haven't heard from her in a while."

"June, June, June," the man said as if looking deep into the recesses of his mind.

"Our other friend, Jodie, came looking for her last week." Reyna gave him the same description she'd given the woman upstairs.

"Oh, I remember her," the man said. He moved a backgammon piece before turning back to them. "She came around asking the same questions as you."

"Yes, we're worried about our friend June."

"Oh, June?" another man asked, glancing up. "She worked at the pie place. I go every week. Best pie in the city. Try the cherry cobbler."

Reyna sagged with relief. A lead.

They got instructions from the men, relieved to find it was only a few blocks away, and then hurried from the horrid apartment complex. She and Gabe didn't speak as the anticipation coursed through them. After botched mission following botched mission, they needed this win. They needed to prove that they could get one person back. Because if they could get Jodie, then maybe they could save everyone else too.

This joint would have answers. She was sure of it.

The pie place was actually named Pie Place. It was a simple diner. Not exactly clean, but it had waitresses in vintage yellow dresses with white aprons over them. None of them looked too pleased to be there.

She and Gabe pulled out red-cushioned stools and sat at the bar. A woman roller-skated up to them from behind the bar, holding a pen and notepad.

"Welcome to Pie Place, where we have the best pie in the city. Can I recommend the cherry cobbler?" she said with little enthusiasm.

The backgammon guys must come all the time. They even had the spiel down.

"Cherry cobbler would be great," Gabe said. Reyna shot him a look. He shrugged. "Who turns down pie?"

Gabe waited until he had his pie in front of him before grinning wickedly at the waitress. Reyna watched with admiration and disgust as he charmed his way into conversation with this woman who clearly hated her job. She giggled and flirted, came back twice for drink refills, and ignored her other tables to talk to Gabe.

"Be right back," he said with a wink and then followed the waitress through to the kitchen.

Reyna huffed in frustration, finishing off the rest of his helping of cherry cobbler. She had to admit it was really good. Damn. She'd been hoping it was an exaggeration.

After five long minutes, Reyna was ready to head back into that kitchen herself and bust up whatever was going on. She couldn't believe that he'd basically abandoned her for some waitress.

Then Gabe appeared, looking grim.

"What?" she asked, glancing around to check her surroundings. "What's wrong?"

"You're not going to like this."

"Well, I didn't like you abandoning me out here either."

He glanced at the bar. "You ate my pie."

"You were gone forever."

Gabe sighed and threw down a twenty. "Come on. I know where Jodie went next."

"How the hell…?"

"Sometimes interrogations happen with a smile."

"You really are trouble."

"No worries, nothing too wild." He flicked her a devious grin. "But I am."

"So, where did she go?" The bell chimed overhead as they exited.

Gabe pointed across the street. "Meredith told me that girls who get fired from Pie Place 'go across the street.' Apparently, it's quite literal, because girls who get fired from a mediocre diner can't get a job anywhere else."

Reyna glanced across the street and saw a nondescript brick building with a neon sign that read Bottoms, a gentleman's club.

"Ugh," Reyna groaned. "A strip club?"

"Yeah. And they don't open for a couple more hours so we're going to have to kill time until we can get inside."

"Great."

"The stakeout. My least favorite part of a job," Gabe muttered.

They hiked back to the car to make sure it was still in one piece and then whittled away the next couple hours until Bottoms opened for business. Gabe phoned Meghan to let her know that they'd be later than anticipated.

They made their way back to Bottoms right before it opened and watched the line of regulars file in the front door. When Gabe gave her the okay, they trotted across the street and inside.

It was the first strip club Reyna had ever been in, and it was even seedier than she could have imagined. There was a small stage that jutted through the middle of the room, with shiny chrome poles spaced across it. Seats ringed the stage and tables took up dark, secluded corners. She could see a few marked doors that she assumed were for private dances. A bar ran along a whole wall and waitresses in lingerie strutted around offering drinks to patrons. A busty blonde was onstage in nothing but a G-string and black thigh-high leather boots.

"Let's get a table," Gabe said.

"Are you out of your mind? Let's talk to the manager and get out of here like we agreed."

"Change of plans."

Reyna groaned. "Why? What the hell could have changed it?"

Gabe pointed his finger at the stage. Reyna whipped around. Striding onto the stage in a ruby-red negligee and clear, mile-high heels was Jodie.

CHAPTER FIVE

"Fuck," Reyna muttered.

"Sit. Now," Gabe growled in her ear.

Gabe put a hand under her elbow and drew her into a corner.

"What the fuck?" Reyna said as she plopped down.

"I've seen people do worse to survive," Gabe reminded her.

"Yeah," Reyna whispered. She had seen people do much worse. It wasn't like Reyna was completely innocent. Being a blood escort came with its own litany of issues. And that was before she had become a permanent escort for Beckham, let alone going to a vampire sex club.

It still made her ache that Jodie hadn't trusted Reyna enough to come back. Jodie had been taken to Visage at such a young age, and she wanted her own life and to find her cousin. Reyna hoped this was one step on the way to that.

Still, Reyna had about a million questions running through her mind. All of which she wanted to jump on the stage and demand answers to immediately. If it wasn't for Gabe's hand on her arm, she would have done just that.

"If we disturb the show, we'll get kicked out. Then what will we do?" Gabe asked her.

She grit her teeth at him. "Fine."

It became clear almost at once that Jodie knew Reyna and Gabe were in attendance. Her eyes kept shifting to their table. Reyna hoped that she would march off that stage. But she didn't. She did some sexy little dance, removing her negligee and baring herself to the crowd.

Reyna sighed heavily. "How much more of this do we have to endure?"

Gabe snapped his fingers twice. A woman scurried over and started dancing just for him. He stopped her. "I want a solo room with the girl onstage, for me and my girl here."

He grinned wickedly at Reyna, who had the sense not to bite his head off.

"I can get that solo room now for me and you," the woman said with a wink.

"The one onstage," he said. "Now."

"It'll cost you."

"Now," he growled.

The woman lifted an annoyed shoulder and then disappeared. Within the next minute, another woman was taking over Jodie's spot on the stage and Jodie was being ushered offstage.

"You've done this before?" Reyna asked dryly.

A manager came to escort them to the back and take payment for what was clearly an expensive private room. Jodie was in a flimsy nightgown and had her arms crossed over her chest.

"What the hell are you two doing here?" Jodie snapped as soon as the door closed.

"What the hell are *we* doing here?" Reyna gasped.

"Ladies," Gabe said with a sigh.

"Don't," Reyna spat.

"Yeah, if she has something to say, then by all means," Jodie said, waving her hand out to the side.

Reyna took a deep breath and then let it out slowly. Getting angry at Jodie wouldn't help anything. She wasn't even mad at Jodie. She missed her. She loved her. And she wanted her back. It wasn't fair to channel all the shit that she'd gone through into her closest friend. Someone she definitely did not want to lose.

"I'm sorry you felt that you had to leave. We want you to come back," Reyna said.

Gabe shot her an appreciative look. "To what's left, that is."

"What's left?" Jodie asked. She dropped her arms to her sides and glanced between them. "What do you mean?"

"A lot has happened since you left," Reyna said. "We'll fill you in when we get you out of here."

"Wait, I'm not leaving," Jodie said. "You think I'm doing this for nothing? I have to find June."

"And are you any closer to finding June than you were before?"

"Yes," Jodie spat.

"She worked here?" Gabe asked.

Jodie nodded solemnly. "Two years ago. One of the girls said that she just stopped showing up. She'd been here for a long time. Kind of a mom of the group. But the owner says he knows more."

"Let me guess," Gabe said with a sigh. "He'll tell you if you can afford it. Since you can't afford it, you work for him until you can afford the information."

Jodie ground her teeth together. "So what?"

"It's called exploitation." His hands curled into fists. "The owner saw a pretty girl down on her luck. If he had his way, you'd never get out of here."

"What a piece of shit," Reyna muttered.

"I can take care of myself, thank you very much," Jodie said. She looked furious that Gabe was suggesting she was being taken advantage of.

"Why don't you point me in the direction of this owner, and I'll handle it," Gabe suggested.

"I'm not letting you fight my battles for me," Jodie said. "You should both leave so I don't get in trouble."

Reyna pinched the bridge of her nose. "This is a disaster." She glanced at Jodie. "I know that you want to find your cousin. I want to find June too. But what happens if Visage finds out that you're here? What happens if the owner finds out that they're looking for you?"

"The owner doesn't know shit, Reyna," Jodie shot back.

Reyna held up her hands. "Fine. Okay. I get it. This is a shitty situation."

"It's not just a shitty situation. It's my cousin is missing and she is the only family that I have left in the entire world," Jodie argued. "What would you do if it was Drew or Brian? Or Beckham?"

Reyna jerked at his name and Gabe winced.

"What? I know exactly what you would do. You'd burn the world down and between Elle and Visage. I have never made a decision of my own, so forgive me that I'm going to stay here until I find June."

Reyna's cleared her throat. Now wasn't the time to mention what had happened to Beckham. All that mattered was that Jodie was right. Her life had been controlled since nearly day one. She deserved her own independence. Reyna wished she could give it to her, but if Jodie stayed here, she would die. Everything caught up to them eventually.

"We want to find June, too, but Jodie, this isn't where you belong. You're not safe here, and we can still help you."

Jodie turned half away from her. "I wanted to do this on my own. I thought I could…"

Reyna took a step toward her and held her hand out. "Why should you have to when you have me? When you have all of us who would stand behind you when you need it?"

Jodie glanced between them with a sigh. "Y'all are really annoying. You know that, right?"

Gabe snorted. "Pretty much."

Jodie reluctantly dropped her hand into Reyna's. "We're going to find her?"

"Yes," Reyna said, tugging Jodie in for a hug. Having Jodie back felt like a win. And any win was something they needed at this point.

When they separated, Jodie agreed to lead Gabe to the owner of the strip club. They left the private room and headed down a side hallway to an office at the back of the building. No sign announced the room, as if the owner was used to unwanted attention.

Jodie held her hand up and knocked on the door. "Ricky?" Jodie said, using an uncanny, submissive voice. "It's Jodie. I got some cash for you from my performance tonight."

A series of locks released before the door cracked open. "Hurry up and get in here. I don't have a lot of time."

Jodie arched an eyebrow at Gabe and Reyna before walking into the office.

"Where's my money?" Ricky demanded.

Gabe and Reyna followed behind Jodie. Ricky's eyes widened in surprise, then he dashed to his desk.

"Wouldn't do that," Gabe said, holding his gun leveled at Ricky's chest.

Ricky stopped moving as if he were a mouse caught in a trap. "What the hell do you want? I'm running an honest business here."

Reyna shut the door and bolted it back up. Jodie crossed her arms over her chest in disgust. "Psh, honest."

"You work. You get paid," he spat. "I don't care if you're a whore or a snitch. I'm still honest."

"You're exploiting her," Gabe said roughly. "Now divulge what you know about June Gardner or else things will be less than pleasant for you."

"I can have the cops here in seconds. I have the whole place wired. They'll know you were here."

"You can't have the cops here before I shoot you," Gabe reasoned.

"You wouldn't…"

Gabe cocked the pistol. "Try me."

Ricky gulped.

Gabe pointed the gun at a chair. "Sit."

Ricky did as he was told, grumbling all the way.

"June Gardner. Everything you know," Jodie said.

"You're a real bitch," Ricky shot at her.

"You haven't seen the worst from me yet." Then she walked across the room and punched Ricky in the face. She pulled back hissing, but the crunch of Ricky's nose breaking and the blood gushing from it were all too perfect.

He bent over, holding his nose. "I don't know shit about June. She worked here for a couple months two years ago. She was in and out like all the pathetic girls who filter through the place. She didn't leave a forwarding address. She just stopped showing up. Christ."

"What?" Jodie asked in horror. The realization that she'd been working here for no reason hit her. "But you told me you knew where she was."

He shrugged. "That's the biz, baby."

"Motherfucker," Reyna spat.

Gabe shook his head. "A bullet is too good for you—but man, I would love to use one."

"We need the tapes," Jodie said.

Reyna and Jodie ruffled through his office until they found the system that recorded the interior of the strip club. The video screens were up for his viewing pleasure, including all the private rooms. Not so private.

Jodie ripped the machine from the wall and watched as the screens flickered and then the images disappeared. "There. That's better."

"For real," Reyna said, as she looked for something to destroy the machine with, but she finally shrugged and tucked it under her arm.

Gabe passed Jodie a gun while he tied Ricky to the chair with some rope. Always prepared. Once that was done, Gabe clocked him across the head with the butt of his gun. Ricky collapsed forward, unconscious.

"Good riddance," Jodie spat. She nodded her head toward the door. "There's a back way out."

"You're going to need to change," Gabe said.

"I'll meet you out there after I grab my stuff."

"I'll go with you," Reyna insisted.

"It'll be less suspicious if I go alone," Jodie said.

Reyna opened her mouth and then eventually nodded. Jodie needed to be able to make her own decisions. "Good luck."

Jodie smiled a real smile at her this time before hurrying down the long hallway. Reyna followed Gabe out the back door with the recording machine. It was about ten minutes before Jodie dashed from the doorway in street clothes with a worried look on her face.

"No one liked that I quit," she said with a grimace. "We should get going. I bet they'll all complain to Ricky soon. We do not want to be here when that happens."

They jogged away from the club, back to the car. They kept glancing over their shoulders, wondering if someone would come after them. It was a long shot, but totally possible that they would at least call the cops.

The trio jumped into the car and zoomed away from the scene of the crime. They were tired and breathing heavy but jubilant and excited. Jodie even giggled from the back.

"That was amazing. I can't believe we just did that," she said. Then she seemed to sober up. "But what am I going to do about June?"

"We'll keep looking," Reyna assured her.

"Yeah," Jodie said with a sigh. "I thought this was going to be easier."

Reyna frowned. She felt that way about most things at this point.

"Y'all said a lot had changed?" Jodie prompted.

Gabe and Reyna shared a look as if to ask who should start. Reyna chewed on her lip and faced Jodie. "We went after Harrington, but he knew we were coming. Penelope double crossed us and became a vampire. Then Harrington bombed the bunker and killed…killed Beckham."

Jodie's mouth dropped open. "What?"

"So yeah. A lot has happened," Reyna said, crossing her arms around her stomach.

"The bunker? And Beckham?" Jodie asked in utter disbelief. "Holy shit, Reyna. Are you okay?"

Reyna didn't respond to that. She didn't know if she would ever be okay, but she was moving forward. She was doing what Beckham would have wanted her to do. And so she crawled over the divide to the backseat and wrapped her arms around her best friend. They were both mourning the loss of someone they loved. They were both learning this new life. Reyna was glad that she had someone else to move forward with.

Chapter Six

They made it back to Washington's mansion an hour later. Meghan and Tye had come back hours ago, and Washington came out of the basement with the good news.

"The housekeeper arrived," he said mildly.

A woman appeared with a smile on her face and a plate of sandwiches. "You must be hungry."

"Reyna, this is Genevieve," Washington said. "She's a vampire and an excellent cook. She's been taking care of the place on and off for me and agreed to come on fulltime while we're here."

"Nice to meet you," Reyna said, tentatively taking a sandwich.

Jodie took the whole plate. "I'm famished."

"Same," Gabe admitted. "Nice to meet you, Genevieve. Welcome to the team."

"How do you know Washington?" Reyna asked and then bit in her sandwich, which was toasted turkey and cheese with some kind of sauce, and it was unbelievable.

"We go way back," she said with a shrug.

"Don't interrogate, Genevieve," Washington said, pushing up his glasses. "Just be glad someone can take care of the place."

"Thank you, Genevieve," Jodie said as she stuffed her mouth. "Now which room is mine?"

They went off together as if Jodie had never left and Genevieve had always been there. Meghan and Tye came back downstairs to inform them that they'd checked out the bunker and it was destroyed. They couldn't even get through the main entrances. They'd had to find another way in, and even then, it was clear from the heat coming off the place from the fire that nothing could survive.

No one knew what happened to the people. To Drew and Laura, who had been inside. Or Everett, who had been imprisoned for turning Reyna in to Visage and acting as a spy for Harrington. Or Sydney…their leader. The very person who had started Elle, who *was* Elle. Everyone thought Elle had died, and in some ways she had. They'd turned her into a vampire and when she'd come back, she'd no longer been Elle. She'd become Sydney. Now it was possible that she was really gone.

Jodie integrated well. Maybe even better than she had when she'd initially joined Elle. Back then, she had gotten her first real taste of what the world was like. And now she realized the good that she could do working with Elle. She still didn't like Washington. He had been one of the doctors who had experimented on her when she had been kidnapped at a young age. But he respected her space and worked hard to earn her trust, so she was coming around. And it was good to see them all work together.

"Why don't we have communication with the other safe houses?" Jodie grumbled. "It's been a week since New Year's. Shouldn't someone be able to reach us?"

Tye sighed. "I wish I knew. Meghan and I have checked a lot of the safe houses. Some of them look like people were in them, but now they're empty. They look abandoned."

"Where could everyone have gone?" Jodie inquired. "Are there places other than the bunker?"

"Yes," Washington said. He frowned. "But for safety reasons, we weren't supposed to know where they all were. So much of the information that Elle had—what do you say?—went down with the ship?"

"If we had Tony, we might've been able to access it," Meghan said. Tony was Elle's resident techie, but he had been at the bunker on the day of the explosion.

"You think it might be on a server somewhere?" Reyna asked. "Or in the Cloud?"

She was still wrestling with these terms. After years without internet or phones, she was picking up all these new things as quickly as she could.

"The main servers were in the bunker," Washington said.

"There had to be backups though, right?" Gabe suggested.

"But we don't know where those are either," Tye pointed out, crossing his arms and sitting back.

"We need a fucking break," Jodie snapped. "Where haven't we looked? What can I do? Do we not have phones or something? Technology should help."

"We've called all the numbers we have. A lot of the phones were burners so they couldn't be tracked. We really didn't plan to be this disconnected from one another," Tye said with a grimace.

Reyna leaned back in her chair and kicked her feet up on the antique dining room table. She ignored Washington's pointed stare at her audacity. Getting Jodie back had been a win. Not only was she Reyna's closest friend and a link to the Visage prison experiments, but Jodie had special blood too.

Reyna's blood was the very rare Rh null negative with so few matches in the entire world. And unfortunately, one of those was William Harrington. But Jodie's had the potential to unlock a possible blood antidote—which would make it so that vampires could drink anyone's blood, not just their blood type match, and have the same benefits.

Yet, despite having Jodie back, they were still a pathetic crew of six now.

Six people to take on all of Visage.

A week ago, when she'd stepped out of the shower, she had felt so certain that they could do this. Now she was wondering what the hell she'd been thinking. It was still possible to stop Harrington, but was it hubris to believe that six people could succeed where an army had failed?

She shook her head. There was a link that she was missing. But she didn't know what it was.

"What do you think, Rey?" Jodie asked. The nickname that her brothers used hit her like a punch to the gut.

"We need to think about this more. We're missing something." Reyna stood from her chair. "It's almost dinner. Why don't we all come back after that and plan our next moves? We can go from there."

Reyna trudged from the room. Sitting around and talking in circles wasn't helping her. She wanted to walk the grounds to clear her head, but what she really missed was her camera.

Beckham had given her a camera when she had first lived with him. He'd said it would give her perspective. And it sure as hell had. She could use a piece of that perspective right about now.

She walked up the steps and to the landing where Beckham's bedroom was, but the familiar smell alone made it difficult to even be in there. She hadn't been sleeping much to begin with. Nightmares haunted her every time she closed her eyes. They made her want to scream like a teakettle to escape. But no, she was trapped in a cage of her own making—a musky smell, fierce handwriting, black suits, an inexplicable presence.

Beckham was the other side of her coin. And now she was one-dimensional.

She went to the bookshelf and gently ran her hand along the leather bindings. She'd already surveyed them, but she couldn't get enough of it. They smelled like fresh parchment and long days tucked away in alcoves devouring the material. She kept hoping one of the books would reveal a trapdoor. It would swing open and show all of

Beckham's secrets. An easy way to fix everything. A deus ex machina.

But no.

There was just her.

She had to make it happen.

Reyna sat at the desk and pulled Beckham's papers toward her. As she sat amongst his materials, she felt so connected to him. So close to him. A powerful emotion ripped through her. It started in her heart and expanded outward, encasing her entire body. This was Beckham.

Her Becks.

She coughed as tears came to her eyes. Why did the connection have to be so strong even when he was gone? She didn't want to lose it either though. Feeling him like this was a grasp at the real thing. It prolonged the inevitable. One day she would wake up and realize that there was no more connection. That he was really and truly gone even from her.

A severed connection.

It struck her and she had to force herself from the chair before she collapsed into sadness.

This wasn't helping. This wasn't helping anything.

Reyna rushed from the room, desperate to be free of his ghost.

But as she raced down the stairs and outside into the brisk cold, the feeling only intensified. She wasn't running from him. She was getting closer.

She clutched her chest. The sensation was so real. She'd felt it before but never this strong, not even when he'd been alive.

As if she could reach out and touch him, even though it was impossible.

She ran her hands back through her dark hair and lifted her eyes skyward. She missed him something fierce. She was strong. She was ready to take on the world. But she wasn't ready to move past him. Her heart ached for him. It was actually beating fiercely in her chest.

She shook her head in confusion and started walking. Why was she having this reaction? A tear slipped down her cheek as she kept going down the gravel road. She was nearly to the gate when she picked up to a run. She didn't even know what she was doing, but she couldn't stop.

When she rounded the last corner, the gate was hanging wide open. Fear pricked at her. They surely had not left that open. None of them would be so careless. And yet the only way into Washington's mansion was open for anyone to come in.

She stilled her feet as she approached. Her heart was still pattering away, and the feeling only intensified the closer she got to the gate. What was happening? Why was she walking right toward danger?

And then a figure appeared at her right. A vampire woman with ruby-red hair and two wicked-looking blades. Another vampire was beside her—a short, Black woman with a shaved head. The next two men she recognized on the spot—Beckham's driver, Gerard, and Reyna's bodyguard. Both also vampires.

Her stomach twisted at the sight of them. "What…what are you doing here?"

She felt him before she saw him. Reyna whirled around. Her heart was in her throat. The sense of rightness overwhelmed her.

"They're with me, Little One," Beckham said.

Chapter Seven

Reyna's hand flew to her chest.

Beckham.

Beckham.

Beckham.

Her mind raced ahead of her. Her heart ceased palpitating. She simply froze.

This made no sense.

It was impossible.

Beyond impossible.

People didn't come back to life. Well, not more than once. Once a vampire was dead, they were dead. There was no second life as another vampire.

Yet, there he was.

Her heart contracted painfully.

There.

He.

Was.

Her perfect Beckham. Tall, brooding, with midnight eyes that whispered threats and echoed passion. A figure so imposing that others shrank back at the sheer size of him, the promise of death on the razor-edged planes of his face, and the confidence that oozed out of every pore. And that was before they even learned of his reputation. A person didn't need to know it to recognize the threat before them.

And yet, he wasn't a threat to her. He never had been. He never would be.

"How?" she finally gasped out.

"It's a long story," Beckham said.

Reyna shook her head. She wanted to run to him, to put her arms around him, to believe what she was seeing. But how could she?

She had watched him die. Seen his body slump to the ground and die before her very eyes. It wasn't secondhand knowledge that she could refute. She had been there. She cut open her own arm to try to save him, and it hadn't worked. How could he possibly be here right now?

"No. It's…it's not possible," she stammered out.

"It appears that it is."

"Tell me…tell me something only I would know," she said. "You could be an imposter."

That was practically impossible. No one could pretend to be Beckham. She could feel down to her very being that it was him. She had sensed him upstairs in his bedroom and run the length of the driveway to reach him. It had to be him. And yet she needed to be sure.

His dark eyes clouded with frustration at having to prove himself. But he never let the words slip from his mouth. He just considered what to tell her.

"White roses are for new beginnings," he told her, taking a step forward. "I used to focus solely on my phone because your presence was such a distraction." Another step forward. "I can sense your blood." They were practically touching now. "I can sense it right now.

You. All of you. The smell of you. The taste of you. The way your body vibrates at my nearness." He dipped down and brought his lips close to her mouth. "I am who I say I am, Little One. I am yours."

The dam broke.

Reyna threw her arms around his shoulders and crushed her body against his chest. He tucked her in close, burying his face into her dark hair.

"You're back. You're really back," she gasped as her tears soaked through his shirt.

"Shh." He stroked her affectionately.

"I don't understand. I don't…"

She pulled away to look up at him. They were facing down the impossible. Vampires didn't return from the dead, yet Beckham was here. He shouldn't be standing before her, but he was.

Their eyes locked and she lost sight of everything else. The pain disintegrated. The cold was gone. She didn't even notice their breath fogging between them. Or the people he had brought with him. Or the trees. Or the gravel. Or the gate.

Nothing.

It was just her and Beckham once more.

"How are you alive?" she whispered. "I saw you die. I watched it happen."

His brow furrowed at that. "Let's get you out of the cold and I will explain everything."

He gestured for her to walk. Her boots crunched against the gravel and the cold bit back into her consciousness. It was subfreezing temperatures, and she didn't even have a coat on. What had she been thinking?

Well, of course she hadn't been thinking.

The four people with Beckham formed up around them as they moved forward. They all looked lethal and kept assessing their surroundings for threats. She wondered what their stories were and how they had ended up with Beckham.

She had a lot of questions.

"I can't believe you're really here." She touched the sleeve of his jacket. He was solid and firm. Real.

"I'm as surprised as you are," he admitted.

"It isn't every day that your boyfriend comes back from the dead."

He arched an eyebrow. "Has it happened to you before?"

She laughed. It was the first time she had laughed in over a week. It made her feel lighter. As if she walked on clouds. She glanced up at Beckham. "No. Just you."

He wrapped an arm across her shoulders, and they continued the rest of the way to Washington's mansion. Gabe and Meghan were arguing out front. Reyna suspected it had something to do with her sprinting out of the house at top speed. But when they saw her coming back with Beckham and a retinue, both of their jaws dropped.

"Oh my God," Meghan said.

"Is that…" Gabe let the question trail off.

"Yes," Meghan breathed.

"How?"

The million-dollar question.

"Meghan. Gabe," Beckham said with a head nod.

"Is this some kind of joke?" Gabe asked.

"It would not be a very funny one."

"It's really him," Reyna told them.

"I'll explain inside," Beckham said. He faced the four who were following him. "Philippé, do a perimeter sweep. Katarina, check the defenses. Return to me when you're finished. Gerard, Zoya, you're on me."

Then he strode into the mansion as if he owned the place, with Reyna at his side. The entire exchange left Reyna even more confused. More questions sprung up. She ached to ask them all, but at the same time she felt at peace. She demanded a miracle. And she received one.

The entourage assembled in the dining room. Gabe rushed to get Tye and Jodie, while Meghan found Washington speaking to a young woman in the kitchen. Their looks of shock at him appearing out of nowhere perfectly mirrored Reyna's.

"Roger," Beckham said, extending his hand to Washington.

"Beckham," Washington replied with awe.

"And the lovely Genevieve," Beckham said. His attention turned to the vampire woman Washington had brought from the kitchen. She was only about five feet tall and looked not a day over twenty. She wore her straw-blonde hair parted down the middle and in a braided bun at the base of her neck.

"Mr. Anderson," she said demurely. "It's a pleasure to have you back in residence."

"You know each other?" Reyna asked in confusion.

"Yes," Beckham answered.

"Genevieve has been a close associate of ours for a long time," Washington said.

"Indeed," Beckham agreed. "I'm certain everyone here wants to know how I am not dead."

The room went silent except for the scraping of chairs as everyone sat.

"William tried to kill me, but he managed to fracture my neck that day. Essential ligaments and veins were still attached, and he rendered me unconscious. I healed because I fed before going to the New Year's Eve party and was informed when I awoke that Reyna had given me her own blood as well."

That made sense in its own way. Vampires were difficult to kill on a good day. Guns only slowed them down. Sunlight when they were feeding the wrong blood type could also incapacitate them but did little when they were drinking from the blood cure. Decapitation was the easiest way, but severing the spinal cord was known to work as well. Starvation was the hardest and most gruesome.

Reyna had been sure that Harrington snapping Beckham's neck had done the trick. It had been horrifying to witness and just as bad to live through.

"Reyna is your blood match. It would make perfect sense that her blood would help you heal," Washington said.

Beckham's head whipped toward Reyna. He clearly already knew that term, but she had never had the chance to tell him that fateful night. "Is this true?"

She nodded, her heart expanding at the intensity in his gaze.

"I'm gathering a blood match is something special?" Jodie asked from the other side of the table.

"A perfect pairing of the blood composition. Beyond blood type itself but down to its very foundation. A one-to-one match," Washington explained.

The room fell silent again as they stared at Beckham and Reyna. As they saw how unique they were to be in one place. To have discovered each other.

"Well, that explains much," Beckham concluded.

"It could explain everything," Washington said.

Beckham nodded. "I remember nothing after William attacked me until I woke up in a morgue. I was in a metal container, on the docket to be incinerated that afternoon. I escaped the confines of the metal tube and found a blubbering Penelope. She had been watching over me. Mourning, I suppose, in her own way."

Reyna cursed.

"I was weakened, but I managed to use my last bit of energy to overpower her and discover what had happened. After the chaos of New Year's, Harrington had my and Cassandra's bodies taken to a morgue to be incinerated. Penelope insisted on going with me. In fact, I likely would have already been incinerated before I woke up if not for Penelope's presence. I should have killed her then. I had the advantage." He shook his head. "But the damage had been severe—I don't know anyone who would have been able to come back from it. Once I got the information I needed, I gathered what strength I could, knocked Penelope out, and fled the facility."

"Did she tell you anything else?" Tye asked greedily, starved for more intel. "Any information about what Harrington is planning?"

Beckham turned his attention to Tye, who shrank back a little at the full force of Beckham's terrifying visage. "No. She's not important enough to have that information. Just what happened after they believed I was dead."

"Damn," Tye grumbled.

"I managed to get to a safe house where I could get in contact with Gerard." He gestured to the man Reyna had only ever known as Beckham's driver. "We have known each other for a very long time. He helped me out of the vulnerable position I was in."

Reyna cringed at that. She didn't want to know what it must have been like for him to be so weakened. Or what he had to do to feel better.

"We stayed in a safe house until I was back to full strength." Something in Beckham's expression said that he still wasn't at capacity. That he was pushing himself beyond his limitations a mere week after his "death." But he would never acknowledge it here. "Then I came to help."

At that moment the flaming-haired Katarina and Reyna's former bodyguard, Philippé, entered the hall. Everyone's eyes raked over the newcomers.

"This is my inner circle." Beckham gestured to the menacing group.

The Black woman, Zoya, spoke up first, a wry expression on her face. "It was time to get the band back together."

Katarina snorted and twirled one of her twin blades in her hand. "I'll take the drums, please."

"Is that because you like to wail on things?" Philippé asked with a straight face.

"She likes to use both hands, if you know what I mean," Gerard added.

Beckham coughed and all four members of his inner circle straightened. They went from camaraderie to deadly calm in a split second.

"The band," Beckham said, amused by his company. "Gerard is my second. Philippé is my muscle. Katarina is…"

She beamed before he even said her particular skill. Her flaming red hair stark against her alabaster skin. Her blades whirled in her hands.

"A show-off," Beckham finished.

Katarina laughed unabashedly. "That I am. I'm also the best weapon's master and trained assassin you'll ever have."

"Zoya," Beckham continued as if Katarina hadn't tooted her own horn, "is my strategist. They'll be helpful moving forward."

"Are you assembling your army again?" Washington asked quietly.

"I am doing what I must."

"A-army?" Meghan asked. "What army?"

"Elle has failed," Beckham said evenly. "It's clear that a covert rebellion with minimal resources doesn't have the capabilities to stop Visage. They are too strong. I know because I helped Harrington build the company. As much as I wanted to believe in Sydney's vision, the vision is dead. I am a vampire lord. I once had an army so deadly that I conquered this city in five years. We will do it again, starting today."

Reyna finally stood from her seat and with a brave, quiet voice said, "No."

All eyes turned to her. Beckham faced her as well and she could see the questions whirling in his dark orbs. But his face showed none of it. He waited patiently for her to explain herself. He put the ball in her court. She intended to keep it there.

"What do you mean?" Tye finally asked. "We don't have a plan. We don't have an army. We have five humans and a single vampire scientist. We're a ragtag team of survivors. We can't even find the rest of Elle after the bombing. It makes perfect sense to use what we have. And if Beckham is willing to build an army of vampires for our cause, how the hell can we say no to that?"

"I'm not saying no to an army. We desperately need more people," Reyna agreed. "But Elle is not dead."

"The bunker was destroyed. We're scattered," Meghan reminded her. "We're not much of Elle."

"Elle isn't a place. It's an idea. It's the idea of equality between humans and vampires. That we can work and live and thrive better together than against each other. As long as that idea exists, then Elle isn't dead. It is within me. It's within all of you."

Washington beamed at her. "I'm still Elle."

Jodie stood up. "I'm Elle."

Gabe grinned and shot her a two-finger salute. "I'm Elle."

"I'm Elle," Meghan said with a tender smile. "Always have been."

"Me too," Tye said.

Beckham's eyes were appraising, as if seeing a different creature than the one he had left back on that patio on New Year's Eve. As if she had molted her skin and come out as someone else entirely.

"I guess I didn't understand my own philosophy on the subject. I am Elle," he conceded to her, acknowledging her as the leader she had somehow developed into. "But it seems that you are now the heart of it."

Chapter Eight

Reyna stood on a precipice. Her life irrevocably changed. Altered and rearranged. No longer was she on the sidelines of her life. She was in charge.

"We all know that the main goal is to take out Harrington and hamstring Visage. With Harrington out of the helm, we can go a long way toward reducing Visage to their actual purpose rather than stretching their influence as they have been doing the last decade. No more prisoners and medical experimentation under their headquarters. No more taking advantage of the poor. No more Blood Census or identity bracelets. Absolutely no feeding camps," Reyna said. "Balance. Equality. That's what we want."

Everyone nodded. As if they were all getting back on the same wavelength after so much loss.

"Our first priority remains making contact with the safe houses and regrouping with the rest of Elle." Reyna turned to Beckham. "You have someone good with tech?"

Beckham's grin was a feral thing that sent chills down her spine. He gave her a look that said he wasn't used to being ordered around. There were few he allowed it from. Very very few.

"Zoya," he finally said.

She stepped forward. When she smiled, it was more like a grimace, her fangs revealed in all their glory. Reyna was glad to have never met her before she started working for the good guys.

"At your service," Zoya said with a wicked gleam in her eye.

Reyna paused for a second before speaking. She didn't know how she felt about ordering around Beckham's army. But she'd deal with that later. "Zoya, work with Tye, Gabe, and Meghan to reach the rest of our group. Once we're back to capacity, then we can begin to form a plan as to how to stop Harrington."

A well-thought-out and thorough plan. Not like the one she'd ad hocked together out of anger from Brian's capture. One that would cripple William Harrington for good.

Zoya moved to speak with Meghan, Gabe, and Tye while Beckham addressed the rest of his inner circle. Katarina laughed at something he said and then dragged Philippé out of the room. Gerard melted into the background and stood like a statue. It was hard to believe this sinister vampire had been her driver. What had he been doing acting as chauffeur when he was Beckham's second-in-command?

"Inspiring speech," Genevieve said, appearing at Reyna's side.

Washington was standing next to her. "It truly was."

"Reminded me of the old days with Elisa," Genevieve said with a dreamy expression on her face. It was as equally hard to believe this meek and demure woman was a vampire.

"Who is Elisa?" Reyna asked.

"Was." Washington's lips turned down. "My wife."

Then he walked away.

Genevieve patted her arm. "I shouldn't have brought her up. She and Washington were together many years before she passed on. She was a fearsome leader of the vampires. Had a vision for Visage much like yours. It was Harrington who manipulated it."

Reyna sighed and stared off after Washington. "And he killed her for it?"

Genevieve nodded. "Unfortunately."

"Sounds like a horrible loss."

"It was. It truly was. Well, I must be getting back, but if you need anything at all, let me know. I will be around."

"Thank you, Genevieve."

Reyna sensed Beckham's presence at her back before she felt the brush of his fingers against her sleeve.

"Elisa was before my time with Visage as well," he said. "They say she was a visionary."

She faced him. Her heart melted at the sight of him.

After hearing everything he had to say and getting the rebellion back on track, she suddenly felt exhausted. Beckham didn't need her to say anything. He wrapped his arm around her shoulders and escorted her upstairs to his room.

He swept a blank glance around. "You're staying here?"

"Washington told me it was yours." She nearly choked on the words. "It was all I had of you other than the memories."

He tilted her chin up. "You've changed."

"I thought you were dead."

"I told you that if the world didn't break you, I would. And here you are." He looked suddenly pissed. As if he was going to start raging about the room, even though he was the most in control person she had ever met.

"I was broken," she admitted hollowly. "But then…then you put me back together."

He shot her an incredulous look.

"If I crumpled, then your death would be for nothing. You wanted better than that for me. You always protected me, but you also kindled the fire within me. Letting it go out would dishonor your memory."

"And in the meantime, you became the leader of Elle?" he asked, pushing his hands into his pockets. His voice was dry with sarcasm.

"That would certainly keep you safe."

"Truthfully, I didn't much care about my own safety." Reyna ran a hand back through her hair. "I'd lost both of my brothers and my sister-in-law. Jodie was missing. Elle was blown up. And the person I cared the most about—my blood match, my *soul* mate, was dead."

"Soul mate," he said slowly. Reyna had never seen fear in those onyx eyes, but suddenly it was there.

"Yes. Washington said that a blood match is similar to a soul mate. A one-of-a-kind match."

He seemed incredulous. "I'd have to have a soul for that, Little One."

Reyna took a step back. "Becks, of course you have a soul."

"No. That much I'm certain of."

"You are determined to see the worst in yourself."

"I see the reality," he told her.

"Why am I surprised that even when you come back from the dead you argue with me?" Reyna shook her head. "How did you find me?"

"I sensed you."

"Out here?" she asked. "We're an hour from the city."

"You came into the city. When I woke up and got to the safe house, I thought you must be dead because I tried to sense you and felt nothing. If Gerard hadn't come to help me, I would be dead right now. But then I felt your presence. I knew precisely where you were."

"I went to get Jodie back. I can't believe you could sense me then. I didn't feel anything. Definitely nothing like when you showed up here."

"Maybe it was because I had your blood in my system. Either way, I nearly went mad trying to get to you, but Gerard wouldn't let me."

"Why?" she whispered. "Did he not want you to see me?"

"No. It wasn't that. I was too weak to leave," he admitted with distaste. "I used all my energy in getting information out of Penelope and then fleeing. I'd never been so drained in my life. As if my body had used every last bit of energy to knit me back together and I was left with nothing."

She could see the toll that had taken on him. After thinking she was dead, he couldn't even go to her when he'd realized she was alive. She would have gone mad too. Especially considering his physical prowess was integral to who he was losing that had to have been debilitating.

"It took a week of near-constant feeding to begin recovering. I'm still not where I was." He growled that last bit. A condemnation of himself.

She gently touched his hand. "You found me. I'm here. We're both alive and safe." Her hand moved to his jaw, and he met her gaze. "Let me help you get healthy."

His eyes narrowed. "No."

"Becks," she said softly. "I am your blood match. My blood helped save your life. We need you at full capacity. Let me help."

He took a step back.

"When are you going to trust me?" she asked in frustration.

The look he shot her said everything she needed to know. He trusted her but he wasn't going to put her at risk. He'd done that time and again. Even when he'd seen that he could control himself drinking from her. Now more than ever she wanted them to surrender to this.

She'd left that patio with his death on her conscience and his bloody jacket on her shoulders. She never wanted to waste another moment.

Reyna took his hand in hers and pulled him toward the bed. She didn't say anything. Words were useless between them anyway. They could speak with stolen glances and quirked lips and heated skin and gentle touches. Their bodies could speak for them. Express all the things that they couldn't bring themselves to say. All the fears that had clouded their minds for too long.

No more.

She wouldn't live in fear.

She would only live in the moment.

She had her Becks back. It was a miracle, and she was going to treat it like one.

She slipped her hands under his jacket and pushed it off his shoulders. He didn't move to stop her. Just quirked an eyebrow in her direction, which she returned with a smirk of her own. Then moved to the buttons on his black shirt. She started at the top, slowly unbuttoning it until his chest was bare before her. Her nails grazed the solid chest and muscular abdomen. He was as formidable as a brick wall and every inch promised certain death. But not for her.

His shirt followed his jacket onto the floor and her hands skimmed over his shoulders, across the bulging biceps, over his forearms, to his hands. Those beautiful hands with long fingers and broad palms. Hands that had caressed her cheeks and grasped her ass firmly and commanded her body.

Reyna stripped out of her shirt and placed those amazing hands on her waist. She shivered at his touch, which was a shade cooler than her superheated body. His fingers flexed into her skin. They were possessive. Claiming her flesh as his own, running those fingers up her ribs and around to her back. He flicked the clasp of her bra. Her breasts fell forward and the bra hit the floor. His hands skimmed around to the front of her body, covering her breasts. The pads of his thumbs flicking against her erect nipples.

A moan escaped her lips. Her back arched into him as she closed her eyes. Desire shot straight to her core. He pinched a nipple roughly and she squirmed under the attention. Her body pulsing as desire soaked her panties.

"I can smell you," he said, brushing a fang against the shell of her ear.

She shivered in anticipation and reached for his belt buckle.

"I can sense everything about you." He dipped his hand inside her jeans. "But the smell of you is purely primal."

She yanked his belt loose and tugged down his zipper.

"Oh and you're so wet," he groaned like a prayer.

She shuddered under his touch as he slicked a finger through her wetness and dragged it back up to her clit. He stroked slow methodical circles around her most sensitive area, and she lost all cognitive thought as he toyed with her.

"Oh fuck," she gasped.

In that moment, she didn't care how he had come back. Just that he was here. And she needed him more furiously than she had ever needed anyone or anything.

Her body responded like a struck match. Every touch fanned the flames until she was ready to combust. And still, he didn't stop. His fingers dominated her clit. His touch clouded her senses. Everything coalesced into the one thought: *Beckham is alive.*

He was alive and here and touching her. He wanted her and needed her. Her life still moved forward and wasn't completely derailed. And he was here to see her come out on top despite the hell she'd had to endure. His death had only made her want to fight back. To make people pay for what had been taken from her. And she wasn't going to stop until they did pay.

Because he may be here, but they'd done everything they could to take him from her.

"Stop thinking," Beckham said, as if he'd read her mind. "Come for me, Little One."

She moaned on a breath and released all the tension in her body. Her brow smoothed, her jaw relaxed, her body sagged—and then it hit her like a freight train. The orgasm ripped through her as unexpectedly as Beckham's presence here.

She crumpled forward into him. He kissed her hair softly and then lifted her into his arms. She put hers around his neck as he placed her on the bed, then crawled in after her. Her jeans melted away and he shucked off his own pants.

Reyna stripped back the comforter with a coy smile and sank onto the dark blue silk sheets. Her hair fanned out around her head while he towered over her, alluring and terrifying. An unlikely match—and yet somehow perfect in every way.

"I have waited a lifetime for you," Beckham said.

"I thought I'd have to live mine without you."

He stroked a finger across her cheek before slanting his mouth on hers. It was a kiss of claiming. A kiss filled with loss and heartbreak and renewal and hope. It was everything she could ever want in a kiss, and more. It meant he was here. He was really here. Above everything else, he was here and he was hers.

She wanted to take her time getting reacquainted with his body, but one kiss was her undoing. She clawed at the remaining clothes that separated them. He grinned against her mouth before obligingly removing his boxers.

When he got to her black underwear, he didn't seem quite as in control as he'd been with his own. He hastily ripped the material in two and tossed them onto the floor. She laughed at the abruptness and then immediately groaned as his mouth replaced his hands.

Just when she thought she was going to come all over again, his mouth moved to her inner thigh. He inhaled sharply right at the apex and leisurely ran his tongue along the main artery.

"Oh God, Becks, please," she groaned. Sure, he needed to heal, but she'd be lying if she said she didn't want him to sink his fangs into her. To claim her in every way that he could.

"Reyna..."

She thrust her pelvis up and rolled her hips achingly. She wanted him so bad. She wasn't above begging.

Then she felt the prick. She gasped at the first feeling of pain, which was instantly smothered by pleasure as he sank his fangs in her artery and began to drink. Endorphins flooded her system. The vamp venom heightened everything in her body, especially the intense pleasure. If she got too much, it could disorient her and even knock her out. But she trusted that he was going to take only enough to make him feel better and to make her see stars.

Fight or flight kicked in, amping up the adrenaline in her body and sending her into a frenzy. It was what sent her running from Beckham the first night that he drank from her. It was what made humans fear vampires. But the adrenaline could make you want more too. It was a rush. Hot and primal and exotic. It sent heat straight to her core, warming her up and making her body practically vibrate with need.

Then as quickly as he'd gone in, he came up, breathing heavily with blood on his lips and looking as if he was ready to orgasm. His pupils blasted out and his sharp features heightened.

"You," he groaned.

"Me?" she asked breathily.

He moved up her body and she reached in between them, taking his cock in her hand. His eyes closed for a split second at the touch. She stroked him idly as the rest of the venom flooded her system, giving her the best high of her fucking life.

"Taste like Heaven."

"My blood or my pussy?" she joked.

He arched an eyebrow. "Both."

Then he kissed her, filling her mouth with the taste of her body. He grabbed both of her hands and pushed them over her head before thrusting forward into her body. His mouth muffled her cry of desire as he moved in and out of her in the most delicious way.

Beckham Anderson had stolen her heart, he owned her body, and as they came together, their souls touched.

Chapter Nine

Kisses trailed down her naked back.

Reyna hummed happily in response. "I like that."

"Mmm," Beckham murmured against her bare skin the next morning. A finger glided up her spine, touching every vertebra until she shivered uncontrollably.

She sighed. "I could stay in this bed all day."

His mouth returned to her skin, tasting every inch of her. "If only you didn't have to save the world."

She humphed. "A girl can't have a day off?"

"Sure. Let me take care of it."

"Yeah, no," she said, turning her head to look at him. He was grinning as if he'd known that she would never relinquish the power she claimed since New Year's.

"Do you know many people have openly disagreed with me?" Beckham asked casually.

"And lived?"

He arched an eyebrow, which only made her giggle.

"I'm going to guess not many."

"Before Visage, when we became more civilized very, very few."

He'd stumbled over the word *civilized* as if it didn't quite fit them. Beckham had been one of the most dangerous vampires. For his cleverness and sheer brutality.

"Well, you're not going to hurt me," she sassed him.

That rare unabashed laugh burst out of him. "Watch it, Little One."

"Or what?" she teased. She flipped over, shooting him a sultry look.

"Or I'll have to tie you to this bed until you remember who is in charge here," he said with a dangerous glint in his eye.

Unfortunately, it only turned her on more.

"I think you like that I took charge," she told him defiantly. "I think you like that I'm as strong as you. I'm not a porcelain doll."

He dragged his tongue along his teeth. Then he moved so fast she could barely register it before he pressed her backward in the bed. "I am not emasculated by your leadership," he told her. "But you are still fragile, and I will always protect you with everything that I am."

"As long as it doesn't interfere with me saving the world, then that kind of turns me on."

His black eyes danced. "Kind of?"

A knock sounded on the door. Beckham groaned and leaned his head into the crook of her neck.

"What?" he snapped.

"Got a lead, boss," Katarina's musical voice rang from the other side of the door.

"Noted."

They dressed hastily, and he opened the door for Reyna.

"So this inner circle business. We can trust them?" she asked.

"With my life."

"I didn't know Gerard and Philippé were that important when you had them acting as my driver and bodyguard."

"I only sent the best with you. They understood your significance. Plus, it was an easy way to have them close at all times."

"And Gerard only became your second after Bronwyn?" Reyna asked.

It was Beckham's turn to freeze. He clenched his fists. "I wouldn't mention that name in present company."

Reyna frowned. She had the unfortunate experience of meeting his sister, Bronwyn, who she had known as B, when she had been a prisoner in Visage. His sister had been Beckham's second-in-command and supposedly she had been killed. But really, Harrington had kidnapped her in an effort to get Beckham to work for him.

Beckham continued forward without answering her question. She decided not to press it. He'd only found out that Bronwyn was alive a week ago. The wound had to be too fresh to touch.

Together they marched into the sitting area, where his inner circle sprawled.

Next to Tye, Zoya tinkered with some technical equipment. Katarina had her dual blades out and whirled them back and forth in her hands. Philippé stood like a statue, facing the entrance, his arms crossed over his chest. Gerard lounged in a chair, holding a small book open, seemingly oblivious to everything else going on around him.

"What do you have?" Beckham asked as soon as he entered the room.

Zoya jumped to her feet. "Found a few possible locations of other Elle safe houses. I looked into the phone numbers for the burner phones distributed and did a backward check…"

Beckham held up his hand. "I trust you. You have locations?"

"Three," she said with a curt nod. "Working on the others with Tye."

Tye grinned at her like a lovesick puppy.

"Good," Beckham said.

Reyna buzzed with excitement. "Three locations? We should get teams together and go check them out."

"I've already got Meghan and Gabe packing for the city," Tye told her with a grin.

Reyna broke into a smile. "When do we leave?"

Beckham shook his head. "You're staying here."

"Like hell I am."

"Reyna..."

"No. I'm not sitting on the sidelines anymore." She turned away from him as if that was the end of the discussion. From the look in his eyes, it was clear he didn't agree. "Let's get moving. We're wasting daylight."

Reyna grabbed a jacket and went in search of Meghan and Gabe, to help where she could. On the way outside, she ran into Jodie.

"Hey, I was looking for you," Jodie said.

"What's up? We're heading out to check on a lead on the safe houses. You want to come along?"

"That's great, but I think I'm going to stay here and maybe work with Washington."

"Seriously?" Reyna asked, her eyes bugging in confusion.

"What Washington did was wrong, and he acknowledges that. I won't forget what he did to me, but after everything I've seen, I can... forgive him. With time. Everyone's doing their part. I thought it was time I did mine."

"You're sure?"

"Better than doing nothing."

Reyna took Jodie's hand in hers. "You're under no obligation to forgive him. You know that, right? Nor do you have to do this, to work with him."

Jodie swallowed hard as she nodded. "I know."

"I'm serious. You are doing enough just by being here and working with the rebellion."

Jodie bit her lip. "I want to take down Harrington every bit as much as you do. He's the one who did this. He's the one who locked us both up. So yeah, if I can find a way to fuck him over, then that's what I want to do."

"Commendable," Beckham said, appearing behind them.

"Thanks," Jodie said with a smile.

Reyna was worried for her, but at the end of the day, it was her choice. That was the point of bringing her back. To support her through her new independence. If this was what she wanted, then that's what Reyna wanted for her.

"I love you," Reyna told her, drawing her in for a hug.

"I love you, too," Jodie whispered. As she pulled back, she added, "Good luck today." Then she trudged down the stairs into the basement below. Reyna was proud of her.

...

"Just because it's called a safe house doesn't mean it's actually safe," Beckham said as he observed her checking a loaded gun.

"We can't send your band of merry men into safe houses. The people of Elle don't know them. All it will do is spook them. We have to go ourselves," Reyna reminded him. "And you already know that."

Beckham took the gun from her hand and rechecked the magazine. Then he slid it in the holster on her thigh. "Doesn't mean I like it."

Reyna held her hand out. "We're doing this as a team."

He slowly put his hand in hers and tugged her in close. "I don't want to lose you again."

"I know," she choked out.

Just because she survived didn't mean that she felt like a survivor.

"You don't have to put yourself in a dangerous situation."

"And when you became a lord, when you took over the entire city, you let others lead the charge, right? You sat back and directed. Stayed out of danger."

Beckham's eyes smoldered.

"That's what I thought."

Reyna pulled back from Beckham to put her jacket on.

"I believe in you," he said softly. "And I will be at your back through this," he promised with a kiss.

Her insides fluttered at the words. He looked like he wanted to argue with her again and demand her safety. It was a huge shift for him to let her walk into the fire even with backup.

At that moment, Tye and Meghan marched into the garage. Reyna could see that they were excited and nervous. Probably about who they might find and who they wouldn't.

"We're ready," Tye said, jingling the keys to a van.

"You have the radio link?" Beckham asked gruffly.

"All set to go." Tye patted his inner pocket. "Phone too just in case. I know all the codes and signals. We won't be out of contact."

"Good," Reyna said.

"Wish I was going," Gabe said. He sulked with his arms crossed over his chest, leaning back against the doorframe.

"Next time," Reyna said with a smile.

She'd asked Gabe to stay behind and keep an eye on the place. He gave them a two-finger salute as she followed Beckham into an SUV. She settled into the passenger seat, and he revved the engine.

"Wishing it was your motorcycle?"

"Always."

Reyna's heart fluttered as she remembered her one glorious ride on the back of his bike. So much had happened since then. She hoped that after all of this she'd get one more ride.

They peeled out of Washington's place and onto the open road, toward the city. The route was all but deserted, as the promise of icy temperatures kept many inside. Reyna took Beckham's hand in her gloved one. She was nervous about what they would find, but optimistic. Her stomach was full of butterflies thwacking away at her insides, but she tried to relax the rest of the ride.

Another hour later they reached the city limits. Beckham pulled into a nice neighborhood with car-lined avenues and people all bundled up walking unhurriedly down the sidewalks.

"There's a safe house here?" Reyna asked in surprise.

"They're all over. Sydney wanted an extensive list for any circumstance. I don't think she really considered this one though," he admitted as he expertly parallel parked the SUV.

"Talented."

"You can't parallel park?"

She snorted. "I can't drive."

Beckham frowned. He clearly didn't like that news. "I could teach you."

"Really?"

"I escaped death once. I can probably do it a second time."

Reyna shook her head. "He has jokes."

"Are you ready for this?"

"Right," she muttered. Her eyes met his once more and she nodded. She was ready. Whatever may be.

They exited the SUV and regrouped on the sidewalk. No one paid them any attention as they ducked their heads against the wind and hurried down the street. Reyna could see her breath. She shivered. This was probably the worst day to do this. But none of them had been prepared to wait until after the snowstorm hit.

Beckham gestured for them to take the stairs to an inconspicuous brownstone. They pulled open the front door and entered an apartment building lobby.

Reyna moved to the list and scanned it for apartment 4B. Her finger hovered over the button. "Should I buzz up?"

Beckham nodded before he bent down to look at the door.

She took a deep breath and then pressed the button. It buzzed noisily, echoing off of the walls. Then everything was silent.

"No one home?" Reyna said to Beckham.

His leaned to the middle of the door, messing with the lock. "Try one more time."

She laid on the buzzer, hoping that would do the trick. "Hello, anyone home?"

But once she removed her finger, nothing happened, again. Either no one was there or everyone ignored her. It wasn't out of the realm of possibility. She probably wouldn't trust someone buzzing if she was in hiding.

"And now," Beckham said, as the door popped open. He held it wide for her with a cocky grin.

"Oh, nice."

Beckham grinned at her. Then they were both climbing the endless staircase. One story, two, three, four. Beckham wasn't even breathing heavily. Reyna didn't care how much she ran on a treadmill. Stairs were an entirely different ballgame. And she hated them.

"Okay," she said, trying to regulate her breathing. "Apartment 4B." She started down the hallway. "G, F, E, D, C, and B."

She stood before a nondescript doorframe with 4B in gold letters on the front. The peephole was covered. But light came from a crack under the door.

Reyna nodded her head toward the light and arched an eyebrow as if to say, *Someone's home.* Beckham steadied himself, preparing himself for a fight. The only thing Reyna wanted to prepare for was seeing her brother.

She took a deep breath and then knocked on the door. "Hello, anyone there?"

Again, silence.

"I don't like this," she whispered.

"Me either." He moved between her and the door. "Stand back."

"Becks."

His hand went to the doorknob—ready to break the lock and burst inside. As if anything could be more suspicious. But as he wiggled the handle, the handle moved freely. Their eyes met with mirror images of concern.

It wasn't supposed to be open. No one from Elle would be careless enough to leave it unlocked.

Beckham moved forward into the room, and before Reyna could follow, a sharp hiss escaped Beckham. "Reyna, don't."

But she forced herself to follow him. She wouldn't abandon Beckham. No matter how he wanted to protect her.

She stepped inside. Her hand flew to her mouth. A strangled gasp escaped her lips. Her stomach rose to her throat, and she gagged.

"No," she moaned.

A dozen bodies were scattered around the room. Blank eyes, mouths twisted into the beginning of a scream, blood everywhere. Discarded. It was the only way to describe the bodies, no, people. Whoever had done this hadn't cared about the mass murder. They'd drained their blood or broken their necks and simply discarded them like used tissues. Trash.

Her stomach rolled again at the imagery. Of all the dead Elle members. All of the people she hadn't been able to save.

"Breathe."

"Oh my God. Drew," she gasped. "What if it's Drew? Or Laura?"

"I didn't see them, but I will check for you." Beckham blocked her view, but even he wasn't big enough to cover it all. Or to scrub it from her memory. "Keep breathing, Little One. In through your nose and out through your mouth."

"How could someone do this?"

Beckham didn't respond. He rubbed her back as she retreated into herself at the sight of the carnage. Her stomach twisted and no amount of careful breathing could change it. She turned away from Beckham and vomited up everything in her stomach. She coughed until tears rolled down her cheeks. Her eyes stung, her heart ached, and she was burning up. She threw up again and again until she had nothing left.

This was the world she lived in.

Vampires massacred a dozen innocent people for shits and giggles.

Or worse, just to send a message.

"We should get you out of here. Why don't you wait in the hallway? Let me know if anyone approaches. I'll check for your brother and comb through to see if anything was left behind."

"Becks," she whispered. Her red-rimmed eyes stared up at him in horror. Such senseless murder.

"I know. We'll stop him."

Reyna nodded and then teetered out of the room. She felt like a coward for leaving him in there alone, for not being able to face it. But the day that she was okay with what was in that room was the day she lost her humanity.

She leaned her back against the wall in the hallway and waited. A minute later a crackle sounded in the empty hall. Reyna nearly jumped out of her skin before grabbing for the two-way radio in her jacket pocket. She fumbled it out with shaky hands and pressed the button.

"Reyna, here. What's up?"

"Reyna!" Meghan's muffled voice shouted into the speaker. "Reyna, is that you?"

"Yes, Meghan. What's going on? Everything okay?"

"No. You need to get here now! Ooph!"

Reyna's eyes widened as she stared down at the speaker, willing it to say more. But the line was filled with static.

"Meghan? Are you okay? Tell me what happened." No response. "Meghan? Tye? Anyone? Answer me."

Panic set in.

Beckham appeared in the hallway, yanking the door closed behind him. "We need to leave. Now."

"Meghan and Tye are in trouble."

"I heard." He gestured for her to move.

"What about the bodies?" Reyna whispered nervously. "Drew? Laura?"

Beckham shook his head. "They weren't there."

Static cut through whatever else he had been about to say. Then one word from Meghan broke through the line.

"Everett…"

Chapter Ten

Reyna ran for the stairs.

Everett was alive. He was at one of the safe houses with Meghan and Tye. What a disaster. A massacre and the spy returned from the dead.

When she had last seen Everett, he had been comfortably housed in one of Elle's more secure rooms with an around-the-clock guard. He'd turned her in to Harrington the day that she'd been kidnapped. When she'd escaped, he'd admitted that he was a spy for Visage and had been researching Beckham for over a year to keep track of him for the enemy. He had delivered pertinent information about the reconnaissance mission her brother Brian had been on though. Information that could have stopped Brian from being captured and MIA. Everett had claimed he'd done all of this because they had his brother, Edmond, as collateral. She understood that, but it didn't make it okay. And it made his next move unpredictable.

Beckham didn't try to slow her down as she took the stairs two and three at a time, barreled out of the door, and into the open. The cold hit her like a two-by-four. They hadn't been upstairs that long and somehow the temperature had already taken a nosedive.

"Harrington left a note," Beckham said once they were in the SUV and far enough away from the safe house.

Reyna steeled herself for it.

"It said, 'I'm watching.' It was written in blood near one of the bodies. I think he had the building monitored."

"Fuck."

Beckham nodded as he glanced hastily at the rearview mirror. "I don't want to get away only to bring him onto our doorstep."

Reyna craned around to look through the back window, but she didn't see anything that seemed out of the ordinary. "Do you think Harrington would suspect where we're staying?"

"Honestly?" Beckham asked. "No. I couldn't even believe it as I was following your trail. I never thought Washington would step foot in that house again. Let alone bring other people. He kicked us all out and didn't even let us take a single thing with us that wasn't already on our person. That's why my room is still full of papers. There's no reason for Harrington to suspect Washington's mansion."

Still, Beckham meandered them through the city for a full twenty minutes before angling toward the other safe house. Better safe than sorry.

"I don't know if I should be more uneasy because no one has followed us or if someone had. At least with the latter we would know," Beckham said. "But we've wasted enough time. We need to get to the others."

Beckham continued to check the rearview mirror often all the way across town. The tension was thick. It only madc Rcyna morc nervous when he finally pulled over and killed the engine.

"Stay close to me," Beckham told her.

She nodded. No argument there.

Reyna jumped out of the passenger seat and fingered the guns strapped to her thighs and ones hidden in holsters against her ribs just like Gabe. Her new security blanket.

As they approached the house, Beckham nodded his head toward an alleyway. They found a back set of stairs around the corner and Beckham moved forward first, keeping himself in front of her.

He paused on the threshold, preparing himself for what was to come. Putting away the Beckham who made jokes about teaching her to drive, pulling out the animal. She could feel the shift and the stillness that resonated. She loved both feelings. How easily he could become the person he needed to be. She tuned in to his calm, and it seemed to radiate through her. She took a deep breath and tethered herself to it.

Beckham snuck a quick look back at her in surprise. As if he'd read what had just happened. She flashed him a grin. She was composed again. Composed and ready.

He could see it. Feel it. Sense it.

Beckham burst through the door without warning and barged into the house. They entered a scant kitchen where two girls who couldn't be older than fifteen had their heads buried in the refrigerator. They took one look at Beckham, screamed, and then ran for the living room.

Reyna would have laughed if their fear wasn't so genuine. Beckham was imposing and these girls had been ousted from their house. Perhaps a little more tact would have been better utilized.

When they entered the living room, Meghan had both girls by the arms. "What do you think you're doing down here? We told you to stay in your room until we have this all sorted."

"We were hungry," the blond girl complained.

"We sent someone out for provisions. Now go back to your rooms and stay there until we get you," Meghan commanded. Then her eyes swept over to Reyna and Beckham. They warred between relief and frustration. "Thanks for scaring the girls."

Reyna frowned. "You seem all right. Why didn't you respond to our calls?"

Tye was seated in the corner. "Radio isn't working. Sorry. The safe houses sometimes mess with them."

"Drew and Laura?" she asked, looking at Meghan.

She shook her head once. Reyna sagged. Still no Drew and Laura. She didn't even want to think about the possibilities. One more house at least.

"Where is he?"

Tye nodded his head toward what appeared to be a closet under the stairs. "We restrained him and kept him out of the way until you got here. We didn't want him to get any ideas."

"Do you know how he weaseled his way in?"

Meghan and Tye shook their heads.

"Let's find out, shall we?" Beckham asked, wrenching open the closet door.

Everett sat on the floor of the dark closet like a trussed-up turkey. His hands and legs were tied. A gag was in his mouth, and he had a black eye. He arched his eyebrows when he saw Beckham standing in the doorway. If he could have spoken, some smart-ass remark would have flown from his mouth. Beckham hauled him up with one hand and dumped him like a sack of potatoes into a chair. Then yanked the gag from his mouth.

"Give me one reason why I shouldn't kill you," Beckham said in his most threatening tone.

"Hello to you too," Everett drawled lazily.

Beckham punched him in the face. Everett's head snapped to the side and a sick crunch sounded. Beckham had broken Everett's nose. Blood spurted out and down over his lips.

Everett coughed twice. "Always thought I'd look better with a bump in my nose. A little more devil-may-care."

"Let's try this again," Beckham spat.

"Oh, I do love second chances."

"Everett," Reyna snapped. "Just talk to us. Why are you here?

How did you get out? Why the hell should we trust you?"

"Never trust a spy," he said with a lopsided grin in her direction.

"This is how he went on with us too," Tye grumbled.

"If he doesn't speak, then we don't need him," Reyna said callously. She wanted to believe that Everett had changed. That everything they'd been through mattered. But he was dangerous and a liability.

"I couldn't agree more," Beckham said.

Everett laughed. It was more pain than anything.

Reyna could sense that Beckham was about to break his neck any second for the audacity of it all. His patience wore thin when it came to people who had hurt her.

She rushed forward and batted Beckham aside. His surprise was evident. She liked keeping him on his toes.

Reyna slid one of her guns out of its holster and leveled it at Everett's head. "We've been here once before. You all bloodied up after a beat down you deserved and me questioning you. But unlike last time, we don't actually need anything from you right now. You had something we wanted—information. You don't have that this time. I'd wager the only reason you're here is to save your own skin and hide out as long as you can. Because you're not just on our shit list, you're on Visage's too. Must feel great to be hunted by everyone. And now we're here and you're cornered, and you think your bullshit posturing will save you. I'm here to tell you that it won't." Everett's expression shifted from laughter to a hint of fear. "So again, why shouldn't we kill you?"

"We're on the same side," Everett ground out. "You know that Visage has my brother, Edmond. I've been gone too long. He's probably already dead. You think I want to work for Visage? That I ever did? I'm not pro-Visage."

"But you still haven't told us how you're in the safe house. Or even what you're doing here."

"An announcement went out in the bunker. A woman on the speaker issued an evacuation. My guards disappeared. I followed a crowd of people and made it here with them. I was on a low enough level to get to the vehicles. Look, I'm not into joining your lot, because it seems like a good way to die. But the way I see it, I have resources, you have resources, we can work together."

"No," Beckham said.

"I know a place we can take these people," Everett went on. "I have some friends. They're not too keen on the whole vamp equality thing, but they have a facility big enough. They're kind of hoarders too, so food isn't an issue. Unless you have a better plan."

Silence followed his statement. They didn't really have a plan for the people in the safe houses. Washington's home couldn't house enough people, and it didn't have the resources. And after Harrington's blood note, they couldn't leave the people here.

"Why should we trust you?" Beckham demanded.

"Don't," Everett said with a shrug. "But you already know my reasons for offering to help."

"So are you going to turn on us at a moment's notice? Will these friends of yours keep our secret too? There are too many unknowns."

"We need as many allies as we can get," Reyna said.

"They're not allies."

"Send someone in that you trust to scope the place out before dismissing it. I know that you have people in the city." She'd overheard him send Philippé and Katarina in after them for backup.

"Fine," Beckham said, then disappeared into the kitchen, his phone to his ear.

"Don't fuck this up," Reyna told Everett.

"Do you think this is a good idea?" Tye asked.

"Do we have a choice?" Meghan asked.

"When you put it that way..." Tye shook his head.

It was only a couple minutes before Philippé and Katarina appeared at the safe house. With both Beckham and Philippé in one tiny living room, everything felt cramped. Reyna couldn't imagine having *more* people here. The two of them alone was imposing. And while Katarina may be small, she strutted into the room all cool grace and wicked smiles. Her blades secured to her back. Her hips swaying exaggeratedly.

"This the runt we have to babysit?" Katarina asked, checking Everett out. "Oh, look, you already got him ready for me. I love my men all tied up." She nipped at him suggestively.

"My friends are not going to like having two vamps tailing me," Everett said. "They're not exactly a vampire friendly kind of people."

"Tough shit," Katarina said. "We're what you've got."

"I'd listen to her," Philippé said.

"And what are you going to do?" Everett asked.

"Enough talking." Philippé hoisted Everett casually over his shoulder and hauled him out of the room. Reyna snickered.

"We have to go check on another safe house. Our first one didn't exactly go as planned," Reyna told Meghan and Tye. She explained the situation they'd found themselves in. They both paled.

"Go," Meghan said, drawing her into a hug. "Be careful."

Reyna nodded and then followed Beckham outside and into their SUV.

"You knew I had my circle with me," he observed.

"Yep."

He drew her mouth to his. Her head went light and fuzzy at the intensity of the kiss.

"What was that for?" she whispered when he pulled back.

He arched an eyebrow and put the car in gear. Her body hummed to the tune of the engine. This thing with Beckham was pure magic.

The safe house was about ten minutes away. Same kind of neighborhood, with medium-sized houses and relatively nice streets. This was her last chance to find Drew today.

Her stomach was sick with worry and anticipation. Drew could be anywhere. She knew that. And at the same time, he *had* to be here. He had to be.

Beckham put a steadying hand on her back as if he could sense her growing anxiety and they both shuffled forward. They made it to the back door when a voice called out from inside.

"Oh my God, who left the door open? It's freezing in here," a soft female voice said.

Reyna's heart stuttered to life and then she was dashing through the door. "Laura!"

"Reyna!" Laura gasped. Reyna threw her arms around her pregnant sister-in-law as tears flowed freely down her face.

"What's all the commotion—?" someone said.

Reyna nearly collapsed at the sound. "Drew?"

And there he was. Her brother. Soft brown hair and eyes nearly identical to her own. The boyish features and flannel shirt.

"Rey?" He scooped her up and swung her around in his arms. "You're alive! God, it's so good to see you. We were so worried."

Reyna held on to her brother for dear life. This was home. This had always been her home.

Beckham followed in behind her, closing the door. Laura gave him a quick hug of welcome. Beckham looked startled by the affection.

"Are there others who made it?" Drew asked.

"Yes. So far we've gotten in touch with another safe house with about twenty people. We lost another house. How many do you have here?"

"Fifteen."

"So few," she whispered. Then something dawned on her, and she pulled back to look at Drew. "Gregory?"

Drew shook his head once. His boyfriend was gone. Just like that.

"I'm so sorry."

"It's okay," he lied. "So, what's the new game plan? What are we doing to get Brian back? Is that what Penelope is announcing today? She's in on it, right?"

Beckham and Reyna glanced at each other. Uh-oh.

"Penelope is announcing something?" Reyna asked carefully.

"Yeah, at City Hall before the storm hits." Drew glanced between them. "That's why you finally came to get us, isn't it?"

Reyna shook her head in dismay. "Penelope doubled crossed us."

"Fuck," Drew spat. He rarely cursed. It had always been Brian with the hot temper.

Laura pressed a hand to her stomach, stricken. "What are we going to do?"

Beckham crossed his arms over his chest. "Trip to City Hall?"

CHAPTER ELEVEN

Reyna couldn't get warm.

No matter how many layers she had on or the hand warmers in her gloves. Her bones ached. Her skin had gone past the point of numb to a painful stinging. Her nose was bright red, and she kept having to sniffle. The rooftop overlooking City Hall downtown was a bad location right before a blizzard.

Beckham had spent the last hour securing their position. He didn't want to take any chances. She sure as hell didn't either. Being here was a huge risk. They were exposed and a lot of people wanted them—dead or alive.

Her gaze traveled to the waiting crowd in front of City Hall. The streets were filled for as far as she could see. People came to hear the big news the beautiful mayor, Penelope Sky, would deliver. No one cared that she had been turned into a vampire or that she was most assuredly a puppet.

The last time an announcement was made at City Hall—when

the old mayor, Penelope's father, began the Blood Census, issued mandatory identification bracelets, and initiated a curfew—Reyna had been swept up in a riot and nearly knocked unconscious by the crowd.

"This feels awfully familiar," Reyna muttered. "Except for the cold."

Beckham's eyes turned to the crowd, and he frowned. "I'm glad we're not down there this time."

"Yeah. No angry mobs for me."

The crowd suddenly quieted down as figures walked onto the stage. She was lucky that Drew's safe house had a pair of binoculars; he'd given them to her before she'd left. It had been hard getting him to stay behind but convincing him to watch Laura did the trick. Her stomach had already settled knowing he was alive.

Reyna brought the binoculars up to her eyes and watched Penelope walk onto the stage erected in front of City Hall. Roland followed behind her and took a seat to her right. A few people she didn't know or recognize filed in. To her surprise, Harrington was absent.

"Where is he?" she muttered.

Reyna looked and looked and looked. But it was useless. If he was going to be there, then he would be front and center next to Penelope. He wasn't the type to stand in the shadows and let someone else take the credit. Which begged the question—where was Harrington if not here?

Someone introduced the mayor to the crowd, which cheered at her introduction. Reyna returned her binoculars to Penelope's long, lithe body. She was dressed in a sensible black pantsuit. Her dark hair was glossy and expertly curled. There were no longer any traces of the fire that had ravaged her body. She must have healed just from feeding. There was no trace of her humanity left, just smooth skin and perfectly puckered pink lips and shining blue eyes. Reyna had always thought she was the most beautiful human she had ever seen in her life. As a vampire, she was dazzling.

If only she wasn't a two-faced snake who had attempted to claim Beckham, and when she had lost, had done anything necessary to try to fix it. Even becoming a vampire and blowing up their entire operation on New Year's Eve, all because Beckham didn't want her. Whatever pity Reyna had felt for her had evaporated. The gunshot to Penny's heart that night had been less than she deserved.

"Thank you. Thank you," Penelope said into a microphone, holding up a gloved hand. "Thank you all so much for coming out today in the midst of this cataclysmic weather. First, I would like to remind everyone to prepare adequately for the storm. It's not like anything we've seen in a long time. Probably since before I was born."

She let out her little tinkling laugh that endeared everyone to her. Then she suddenly sobered.

"Now to address the other occurrences around the city. I'm not immune to the death and destruction happening. As you know, there was a spree of murders on New Year's Eve, and I was targeted. Luckily, I was spared from certain death again. I can't say the same for Cassandra Dressla, a top official in Visage, and a close, personal friend."

Reyna rolled her eyes. Yeah, right.

"Couple that tragedy with the blood disease sweeping the city, we are in dire times. Humans are unknowingly being affected and passing it on to vampires through their blood. Then the disease rampages the vampire's system and turns them into starving monsters. These rogue vampires try to kill everything in their wake. We have identified this as Cogitare Anemia."

Reyna drew in a sharp breath. Washington had told her about this before everything had gone south. They both suspected that Visage had been the one to unleash this deadly disease onto the population. If treated quickly, the vampire could survive, but the longer they went, the worse they got. And from Penelope's speech it sounded like things were getting a lot worse, fast.

"Because of the domestic terrorist groups and this blood disease, we have come up with a solution."

Beckham tensed next to her.

"With the full support of the government, the city is going to work with Visage to secure human safety housing. Anyone who believes that they may be infected or would like to be moved to safer housing during this, you are welcome. The housing is completely free. The only thing we ask is that you help us fix this problem in our city. Together we can eradicate this illness and bring peace back on the streets."

A cheer rose up from the crowd.

Her stomach had sunk all the way to the floor. Free housing. Trying to cure a disease that Visage had unleashed. This sounded way too fishy to her.

"The city is providing our bus service to take people from specific locations to these designated areas. All costs will be covered. For more information regarding the new housing, stay tuned for a Visage representative."

Penelope flashed a brilliant smile. But for a second, Reyna thought she saw something else in it. Fear. Distaste. It was only there for a second before it disappeared.

"Thank you all so much!" Penelope waved her hand and the crowd cheered even louder for her. They loved her. She quickly departed, anxious to get off that stage. A woman who had delivered a death sentence with a candy bar.

The Visage representative moved to the microphone and droned on about protocol, effectively losing the crowd. Reyna moved her binoculars to where Roland stood and approached Penny. She visibly flinched away from him. Oh, yeah, she was not enjoying her new role in this.

"We should go," Beckham said.

"You don't think we should go down there? Find out more information?"

Beckham sliced his head to the side once.

She nodded and followed behind him. It was likely that what Penelope had said was all she actually knew. Beckham had been

Elle's insider for so long. They all felt a little lost without him feeding them information about Harrington.

Reyna sensed that he felt a little out of sorts without it too. Though he'd never say so. He'd continue to go on and put on his big bad mask for the world. And she'd let him. They both needed it.

They took the endless stairs down to the main floor. Round and round they went until her legs ached.

When they finally made it to the ground again, the wind whipped her hair in her face, and she cursed. Beckham tucked the loose strand into her beanie. She looked up at him and smiled. Beckham gently took her hand in his and then hauled her through the crowd that dispersed down the street.

They veered toward the getaway car. It had been damn near impossible to find a place to stash their SUV on the way in. She wouldn't mind the walk if it weren't so bitterly cold. The wind chill was some obscene negative number. Like even the weather disagreed with Visage's new plan to take over.

Halfway to the SUV, snow began to fall. Big, beautiful snowflakes so white and picturesque. A soft flurry that cascaded from the clouds and over the dark city streets.

Reyna couldn't help it. Despite everything going on, the snow still amazed her. She hated the cold, but the snow was different. It was too beautiful to hate when it first fell and blanketed their world in a winter wonderland. Before it turned to black ice or gross tramped-through slush on the sidewalks.

She stopped in her tracks, pulling Beckham to a stop beside her. Then she opened her mouth like a little kid and tasted the snowflakes on the tip of her tongue.

Beckham watched her in utter fascination. She might as well have sprung a second head for all her behavior made sense to him.

In the midst of the dire, the world produced beauty.

She intended to revel in it.

"You are a mystery," Beckham said. His eyes followed her as she skipped a circle around him with her arms wide and her head tilted back.

"The world is a mystery, and I live in it."

"So human."

She twirled toward him and planted a kiss on his lips. "You were human once."

"Might as well have been a lifetime ago."

She shrugged and stole another kiss. "We have a lot ahead of us. You can enjoy the snow for a full second. I won't tell anyone."

And for that full second, he did. He dropped all his guards. Looked at her like his glorious snow queen and tasted the snow on his tongue.

She giggled and then traded her snowflake for his. As their kiss heated the space, the snowflake melted between them. She sighed against him forgetting the world in this moment of security.

And when she pulled away, a wind picked up, the snow all around them spiraling savagely toward them. She looked up as if she could find the source of the sudden current and just saw a blur barreling toward them. She got out a gasp before Beckham said, "Get back."

He barely touched her when he tried to move her backward, but it was as if he'd forgotten his own strength. She tumbled back a foot and landed in a heap in the freshly falling snow. She groaned as she righted herself. That hurt like hell. Her tailbone was definitely going to be bruised. At least she'd had a lot of extra clothes on to pad the fall. She wondered what the hell had freaked Beckham out enough to react like that.

Then she saw it.

Roland.

Her heart stuttered and she scrambled backward as Roland collided with Beckham at full force. They skidded into the brick building, the force of their collision shaking the entire block. Whatever had accumulated on the rooftops fell to the ground.

Roland had his hand around Beckham's throat and was holding him in place. There was fire in Beckham's eyes. He'd seen it coming. And had spent a crucial second making sure she was out of harm's way. Reyna scrambled farther backward and tensed.

Her hand drifted into her pocket, and she reached for the phone that she'd taken with her. She pressed down the number three. Beckham had told her to call it if she was ever in trouble. This probably qualified.

"You traitor," Roland snarled at him. "Did you think I wouldn't know you were here? That I couldn't spot you on that rooftop? You and that *bitch*!"

"Watch what you say about her," Beckham said, low and dangerous. He wasn't even frazzled. In fact, although Roland was holding Beckham down, he was also the one who looked out of control.

"And you defend her. After all of this. You gave up everything for one fragile human."

"Are we going to fight or do you want to keep running your mouth?"

Roland snarled in his face. "I should kill you right now."

Beckham knocked Roland's hand away from his throat. "But you can't."

"You're not my hit."

"Still following daddy's orders, I see."

Roland straightened. His face was a mask of fury. Gone was the civilized and dignified Frenchman who had tried to seduce her. In his place was a monster. Beckham had pushed him to the edge. He was trying to get a rise out of him. He wanted the fight.

"You are a disgrace to your kind. Humans are food. She is food," Roland said, pointing at Reyna. "A sweet delicacy, sure, but nothing more. When did you forget that? The moment she spread her legs for you?"

Beckham's fangs flashed dangerously. "Tell me why you are here or let's get this over with. I tire of you."

"How could you throw your lot in with theirs?"

For the first time, Reyna realized that Roland might actually be offended. If it was possible for someone so vile to be hurt, this would be what it looked like. Despite their differences, Roland had believed that Beckham was on his side. They'd spent years working together. Their word was their honor. Roland felt betrayed.

"You have arrived alone with orders not to kill me on sight," Beckham said, ignoring his question. "You either want something or you have a death wish. Which is it?"

"A truce," Roland said. Beckham arched an eyebrow. "An alliance, then."

"And what would give you the idea that I would want to ally myself with you?"

"Think about it." Roland straightened. This was the part he must have prepared himself for. The rehearsed address. "You and I spent years circling each other. Harrington brought us together with a vision of a better future. That future is now. Let's grasp it. Together."

"Speak clearly."

"Depose Harrington. Take back what we had and rule as we once did. Not just lords but kings."

Reyna's head swiveled in terror between the two vampires. She could imagine the world Roland foresaw. Vampire lords once ruled with ultimate power. As far from equality between vampires and humans as possible. Reyna could never condone a world in which Roland ruled. Harrington may be horrible, calculating, and sadistic, but Roland was crude, base, and cruel.

Beckham released a laugh. Both she and Roland snapped their heads to look at him. It was such an unusual sound. She heard it so rarely. She doubted Roland ever had.

"No," Beckham said plainly.

"Harrington is holed up. You will never get to him without me."

"No."

"You don't know what you're refusing."

Beckham laughed again. "Oh, I do. And the answer is still no."

Then he grabbed Roland by the front of his jacket and threw him into the brick wall as he had done on New Year's Eve. Reyna shuddered at the impact.

"Coward," he spat over Roland's crumpled body, and then held his hand out for Reyna. "Shall we?"

"You're not going to kill him?" she asked in surprise.

"He wasn't here to kill me. I do have some honor."

Her eyes were wide as she stared at the deadly man she had fallen in love with. There was no fear in her when she looked at him. She would do whatever it took to stop the trajectory Visage was on. She couldn't fault Beckham for who and what he was for wanting to do the same. And she loved that by stopping just short of killing Roland, it proved what she had always said—Beckham wasn't a monster.

She placed her hand in his.

Chapter Twelve

Beckham and Reyna were off of Roland's radar by the time Philippé and Katarina sprinted toward them.

"We received your distress call," Katarina got out. She was actually breathing a little heavy. "Why do you not seem in distress?"

Beckham's eyes moved to Reyna. She shrugged one shoulder. They *had* been in distress when she'd made the call.

"I had it covered."

Reyna rolled her eyes. "Well, when Roland had you against the brick wall by the throat, I wasn't so sure."

"Roland was here?" Katarina gasped. "And you were alone."

"I can handle Roland."

"Right. What did he want?"

"We'll discuss it later."

Katarina fell into step beside them and Philippé took the rear. "So is he still smoking hot?"

Reyna's head whipped to the side. "He's disgusting."

"Well, yeah. I was kind of into that for a while."

"Katarina has interesting sexual tastes," Beckham said with a smirk.

"What can I say? I like the kink."

Reyna laughed. "I'm going to assume that you don't know this from personal experience."

"Beckham's walked in on me tied up a time or two," Katarina said with a wink.

"Can we get back to business?" Beckham said.

"Right. The spy's place was secure. We'd never even tracked it."

"So, like, is that what you do for Beckham?" Reyna asked. "Have you always been working behind the scenes?"

"Pretty much," Kat said. "Gerard and Philippé worked for Beckham in public, and Zoya and I did the things other people couldn't see."

"Like a spy."

Kat shrugged. "You could say that. We're a tight-knit group." She turned back to Beckham. "Anyway, I thought it might be that zealot group we'd had on our radar for a while, but it wasn't. This is an all-new thing. They use the tunnel systems to get around. Clever."

"Your assessment of the premises?"

"Secure," Philippé said from behind them.

Katarina agreed.

"Are they dangerous?" Beckham asked.

"Not in the least. Besides the stink-eye we got, they seem to want to be left alone. They're kind of doomsdayers. Stockpiles of enough shit to sustain a nuclear attack or, you know, vampiric control of the country. Whichever came first. Right now, feels like a coin toss."

"It keeps getting better."

"But can they house us?" Reyna asked.

"Oh yeah. They can probably house two hundred in a pinch. They agreed to let our people stay there as long as there were no vampires." Kat rolled her eyes to show what she thought of that.

They all stopped in front of the SUV. Reyna wrapped her pinky around Beckham's. He squeezed gently.

"This sounds like our best bet," Reyna said.

"Kat? Philippé?" Beckham looked at them with full trust in his eyes. She could feel the bond between them that had been shaped, molded, fired, and glazed over the years. Made from soft clay into a beautiful work of art that fire only solidified. She wondered what they had done to earn that sort of trust.

"I agree with Reyna," Katarina said. "The place is secure. We didn't know about it, so Harrington likely doesn't know about it either. It's better than the mansion."

Philippé grunted. Reyna supposed that was a confirmation.

"Okay."

And just like that Beckham was in on the plan to move the remaining members of Elle to the anti-vamp prepper facilities. They spent much of the rest of the day moving people. Meghan and Tye had checked out two other safe houses Zoya had discovered while they were gone and found another five people in one location, but everyone at the other had been killed.

Once everyone was finally settled, Reyna and Beckham followed them into the subterranean headquarters. Everett wore a smug look when he saw her.

"Stop that," she spat.

He crossed his arms. "Look, I held up my end of the bargain."

"There was no bargain."

"Oh right, that was in my head. I want to go to Visage and see if my brother is alive. And I want the help of someone who has been there." He snapped his fingers. "That's you. That's my bargain."

Reyna pinched the bridge of her nose. "We don't have the manpower or resources to break into Visage. How do you expect us to do that?"

"I'm a spy, Reyna. I can get us inside. But you know how to get around. You know where people are kept."

"I was a prisoner," she reminded him. "I didn't go out on strolls."

"Someone got you out, which means you have floor plans. Just think, you can make this altruistic, if you like. We can get everyone out of there. Even better, we can broadcast it and put a dent in Visage's credibility."

Reyna hated to admit that it was a good idea. But it *was*. She wanted to save the people who were like Jodie and had been under Visage almost all of their lives. The ones like her, who Harrington had used to feed from or experiment on. The ones like Beckham's sister, Bronwyn, and Everett's brother, Edmond, who Visage had kept for collateral.

"Let me think on it. We can't do anything until after the snow clears anyway."

Everett put his hand on her shoulder. She flinched and pulled away. Sadness crinkled his eyes for a split second before he covered it up. "I wanted to say I'm sorry. You know, for everything."

"I don't trust you, Everett. This is a huge step for me. I really think you're going to fuck this up. But do me a favor, okay?"

He looked at her warily. "What's that?"

"Prove me wrong."

She moved away from Everett, careful to avoid his friends, and went back to Drew's side. "Are you ready to go?"

"Go?" he asked.

"You and Laura can come back with us."

Drew sighed. "As much as I'd like to do that, Rey, I feel like I should stay here. I don't trust Everett farther than I can throw him and someone needs to be here to lead these people."

She swallowed around a knot in her throat. "Right. That makes perfect sense." Sometimes she wanted to be that little girl who threw herself into her brother's arms and let her cares fall away. But they both needed to lead this rebellion if it had any hope of getting legs again. "I'll miss you."

"Always, Rey." He drew her in for a hug and whispered into her ear, "We need to figure out what happened to Brian. The not knowing is killing her."

Reyna nodded. "I know."

"The stress is bad for the baby."

"How are *you* holding up?"

"I can take care of myself."

"Drew," she muttered. He'd always been the softer of her two brothers, trying so hard to be more like Brian, but it never took. "Gregory is gone. I know how devastating that is. I thought Becks was gone and it nearly destroyed me."

"I don't want to talk about it, Rey. Let's think about Laura, okay? I have to take care of her. Brian would want me to do that."

Reyna nodded sadly. Burying yourself in work, in a mission, in everything except the grief was a thousand times easier than facing it.

She saw resolve on his face. Grieve when the war was over. She hoped one day they would be able to live the life they'd always wanted. And not just endure the hardships they stumbled into.

• • •

By the time they returned to Washington's mansion, the roads were nearly impassable. The snow hadn't stalled even for a minute, and the forecast read white for days. A blizzard had struck and there was absolutely nothing they could do about it. The ragged group reluctantly left the heated vehicles they'd abandoned to Washington's garage and hurried through the rapidly building snowdrifts back to the nineteenth-century mansion.

Reyna shivered even when she was inside. A place this old didn't trap heat in the same way as modern houses. There were strange, chilly drafts. The massive fireplaces were built high to try to combat the heating problems that a house of this size had.

"This is an icebox," she murmured as she put her hands up to the fireplace. "Maybe we should have stayed in the city."

Beckham kissed her forehead and retreated upstairs. The rest of his inner circle followed him. Reyna almost headed after them, but one, she was too cold, and two, even though she and Becks were a team he enjoyed his privacy. They were his people. Not hers. Not yet.

The door to the basement creaked open and Jodie appeared, dashing across the sitting room. She threw her arms around Reyna. "Thank fuck you're back."

Reyna laughed. "Miss me?"

"A day felt like an eternity in this house with nothing but vamps and Gabe as a shadow." Jodie gave her a pointed look.

"Better to be safe than sorry."

"If you leave me with him again when he's feverish to be out with y'all, I might have to kill you."

"Seems fair."

Jodie sobered. "Tye radioed in when he got close enough. I heard what happened at the other safe houses."

"Yeah."

Reyna didn't want to think about that. Those bodies. All that blood. The message. She shivered and it had nothing to do with the cold. No, she definitely didn't want to relive that memory anytime soon. Harrington had done this on purpose and with her in mind.

"Stop that," Jodie ordered.

"What?"

"Don't 'what' me. I know you well enough to know when you're blaming yourself."

"Did Tye tell you about the message?"

"Yes. Harrington's toying with you. It's what he does. You know that."

"I do. But it doesn't change how I feel about it, Jodie."

"If anyone knows that, I do. I fucking had blood drawn today while you were gone."

"I know. I know."

"I'm tired of Harrington messing with us. He wants us to fall apart. We're not going to, okay?"

"You're right."

"Plus, Zoya said she'd help me find June."

Reyna's eye lit up. "She did?"

"Yep. She said she could take a look for me after she breaks through the last code for the final safe houses."

"That's great. I'm sorry I didn't think to help before this. There was so much going on…"

"Hey, whatever," Jodie said. She waved her hand dismissively. "You've got a lot on your mind. Like vamp boyfriend coming back to life, leading the rebellion, and I don't know, taking out Harrington?"

"I suppose that's true."

"Speaking of, how's vamp boyfriend?" Jodie waggled her eyebrows up and down. "He biting you? There better be some awesome sex."

"You are ridiculous."

"Come on. Don't hide the details. A girl is starving for sex here. Feed me."

Reyna pushed her gently. "There's sex. It's awesome. There may be some biting."

"Girl, yes."

Gabe walked into the sitting room. "What's all the excitement over? I thought we were in a sad state of affairs because we have to trust that motherfucker Everett."

Reyna blushed and turned her bright red face away from Gabe. Jodie laughed hysterically.

"What the hell did I walk into?" Gabe sank into an overstuffed brown leather chair. His dark red hair had been combed messily and his bright green eyes shined when he looked at the pair.

"Reyna telling me saucy stories," Jodie teased.

"Well, don't stop because I'm here."

"I'm pretty sure a certain vampire might kill you."

"I could take him."

Reyna arched an eyebrow.

"Okay, fine," Gabe said, looking sullen. "Let's get back on topic. *Everett?*"

"I know," Reyna said with a sigh.

"You trust him?"

"Of course I don't trust him."

"Yeah, get off her case," Jodie chipped in. She plopped down next to Gabe and punched him on the shoulder. "She's doing the best that she can. Give her a break."

"It's a huge risk. The only thing we know about this guy is that he's a spy. He turned you in to Visage. How do we know he won't do that to the rest of Elle?"

"We don't. But his brother is inside Visage, and he wants to work with us to get him out. To break everyone out. That's also something I want. As long as we have mutual interests, I think he's going to work with us. And really, what other choice did we have?"

"I trust you. It was a tough call, but we're in a tough situation."

"I'm hoping for the best."

"Me too."

Reyna pushed away from the fireplace. "I'll see you guys in the morning, once I've slept a solid twelve hours and washed this day off of me."

"Hey," Gabe said.

She glanced back at him.

"We believe in you, you know?"

She nodded. That was what worried her.

Reyna trudged up the flight of stairs and headed to her bedroom. But when she entered, it was clear that Beckham was holding court within their quarters.

She froze on the threshold. Barging into the room and acting like they owed her anything would never be the right move. Reyna met Beckham's gaze head-on. She tilted her chin up. She read the thoughts forming on his blank face. Ones she was sure only she could see. Things that said he was quite content for everyone else to get the fuck out right the fuck now.

"Let's reconvene in the morning," Beckham said. He nodded once at Gerard, who pulled out a phone and left.

Reyna hastily moved out of his way and into the room. The rest of Beckham's inner circle followed Gerard. Katarina winked at her as she closed the door.

Even though they were all gone, the tension didn't dissipate. He was the king of his people, and she was the queen of hers. Could two rulers come together like this? Trust each other? Not leave the other in the dark?

She felt at his mercy. He knew all of her thoughts, feelings, and actions. She hid nothing from him, least of all her heart. And sometimes she felt like he kept so much back. So much that was left unsaid.

"Come here," Beckham said.

She stepped across the room to him. He pulled the ponytail holder from her hair and let the dark strands fall loose around her shoulders. He tilted her chin up. Their eyes locked. His endless obsidian orbs swallowing her whole.

"You did good today."

She swallowed back the lump in her throat. "Then why do I feel so horrible?"

"Because trusting your enemy and seeing the death of your people is never easy. It shouldn't be. You should feel this, Little One." He ran his thumb across her bottom lip. "I spent countless years not feeling anything at all. A part of me knew that I should feel something for what I had done. For the wrongs I had committed. But I felt nothing. Feeling what you are feeling, feeling *something* is human. It is real. Do not wish it away. Get up, accept the pain, and keep moving forward. That is all you can do."

Then he covered her lips with his and there was no more talking that night.

CHAPTER THIRTEEN

Bacon.

The morning smelled like bacon.

Reyna followed her nose and grumbling belly downstairs and into the kitchen. Genevieve wore an apron printed with little kittens on it as she expertly handled the enormous kitchen.

"Morning," Genevieve said.

"Morning," Reyna said, bleary eyed.

"Breakfast is almost complete. Do you take tea or coffee?"

Reyna's stomach grumbled again. "Coffee."

Genevieve left the stove to pour her a mug. "Cream and sugar?"

"Please."

She mixed it to perfection and then handed it over. Reyna sidled up next to the oven, where all the heat emanated from. She drank the scalding coffee despite the temperature and let it warm her up from the inside out.

"I appreciate all that you're doing, but *why* are you doing it?"

Genevieve's eyes twinkled. "I enjoy it. Taking care of house and home was my calling long before I was turned and it has remained my calling long after my kids withered and died in their normal human lives."

Reyna's heart broke for her. She couldn't imagine what it must be like to live as a vampire for what would seem to be an immortal life and watch the ones you love die.

"How did you meet Washington?"

Genevieve laughed. "I grew up on a farm in this village. In my time, there were few vampires. They were still in the darkness. To many, including myself, they were myth and legends. Things to scare the children, you understand. I only discovered they were not myths the night that I was made. The vampire left me alone to starve or murder my own village from hunger. Washington found me. He taught me his ways. He kept me from destroying the family I loved so dearly. He's a good man."

"Did he know Harrington then?"

"William? Of course. He was always in and out of Washington's life. They were the closest of friends."

Reyna's stomach turned at the fondness with which Genevieve spoke of Harrington. "Was he always as he is now?"

"How so, dear?"

"A calculating and a murderous bastard set out to take over the world and leave humans subjugated to vampires forever?" she asked, unable to keep her vociferous hatred of the man from her speech.

"Hmm, he was always a passionate man. His mind was beyond reproach, but he did have a unique way of looking at the world," Genevieve mused. "He saw things like no other. As if the world was one of his precious chessboards. I know he has killed. All of us vampires have unfortunately. But he never went out of his way to do it. It wasn't his nature any more than Washington's. He didn't like to get his hands dirty, figuratively speaking."

Reyna thought over what Genevieve had said as she went about preparing plates of breakfast for everyone in the house that didn't sustain on blood. She couldn't see past her hatred of Harrington and what he had done to her, what he was doing to all the people she loved, and the direction took Visage. She would never forgive what he had attempted to do to Beckham. In that instant, he sealed his fate.

But maybe she needed to look at Harrington from another angle. If she ever wanted to destroy him, then she had to understand him. Know him like Washington and Genevieve had known him, how Beckham had known him, not just how she hated him.

"Genevieve," Reyna said, turning back to face her, "do you think you could tell me more stories about Harrington? From before Visage?"

Genevieve cocked her head to the side but nodded. "Of course. If you wish."

"Thank you."

• • •

Later, Reyna found Beckham standing stoically on the front porch. She wrapped herself up to the gills and followed him out onto the icy stone path. He looked pensive. This was one of those moments where she wished that she could read his mind. He'd had a life she could hardly fathom. She'd never known the real monster deep within. But she still loved him. Hopelessly loved him. Even with the monster chomping at the bit to be released again.

If she cared even a fraction less, then she wouldn't have fought so damn hard to keep him. She would be blissfully stupid in a warehouse outside of the city, dealing with everyday complications that meant the world to her then and hardly anything to her now.

But she hadn't loved Beckham any less. Not a modicum.

Even when he stood in the freezing cold as snow blanketed the earth and acted like the broody man he was.

"Are you going to tell me what you're thinking or should I guess?"

Beckham didn't respond.

"Oh, I should get creative, then. Friday afternoon after work, heading to the bar with your friends and drinking yourself stupid. No, summer days lying out in the sun and getting a tan." She chuckled at the idea of Beckham with a *tan*. Yeah, right. "Daydreaming about taking me to an exotic beach and never seeing the snow again. Or anything but the bedroom."

That got his attention.

"I prefer the night."

"And here I thought you preferred the bedroom."

"Reyna..."

"Could you clue me in on the staring? Why the somber aloofness?"

"I have been contemplating ways to stop Harrington."

"As have I. We already know how to draw him out and how to use his weaknesses against him. But I feel as if I'm missing something. Like Harrington is always one step ahead of us and I haven't figured out how to get a step ahead of him."

Beckham stiffened. "We already know how to draw him out?"

"Yes," she said softly.

"You want to use yourself as bait. Again." He said each word crisper and more biting than the last.

"If it comes to that."

"Your protection is my greatest concern. Even if you're his blood type, that does not offer you all the protections you believe it does."

"I know. You know there are ways to fix that," she said hesitantly.

His anger was swift and brutal. "No. Absolutely not."

"If I'm so soft and fragile as a human, then do the unexpected. Something Harrington would never expect."

"This isn't up for debate. I will not take your life from you."

"It's not *taking* my life. It's turning me into a vampire. Just like you."

Beckham snarled. "We don't know if you would even survive such a transformation. Or that you would be the same person you are now when you are on the other side. Most hunger for nothing but blood until they have their blood type matched. You have an incredibly rare blood type. Harrington has been looking for years to find a match. You may *never* find one. What would you do then?" His eyes were brutal with rage and vehemence. "You would eat. You would kill. You would be the very thing that you despise, and there would be *nothing* I could do to change that."

Reyna took a step back. His anger mounted at the mere suggestion, at the audacity of her even considering it. He didn't want her to change. That others had tried to turn and died. Washington had told her of a circumstance that had left her terrified of the prospect. And also incredibly disappointed to shut that door. Opening it was a last-ditch effort. It was a risk, but Beckham made it seem like a certainty.

"What happens in twenty years, Becks? Forty years? Sixty?" she threw back at him. "What happens when I'm a grandma and you're still thirty? Sure, I'm fragile, but I'm also dying. I'm dying every single day."

"That is *living*, Reyna. That is the way it is supposed to be."

"You're not supposed to go on without me," she whispered harshly.

"Can we make it through the next couple weeks, maybe *months* before we think about that? You're twenty-one years old. I'm not sacrificing you."

"One for a million. Seems fair to me."

"I won't entertain this any longer," Beckham said sharply. "There are other solutions to consider." He slid his hands into his pockets and paced across the room.

Reyna waited. He would tell her when he was ready. She shivered and licked her wounds. Bringing it up with Beckham again had been stupid and she'd known what his reaction would be. But she couldn't not say something. It would be a plan Harrington never considered, which made it a valuable one to keep in her back pocket.

He finally stilled and smoothed back his dark strands. "If you're considering sacrificing yourself as a viable option, then I think we need to train," Beckham said, resigned to the idea.

"Okay," she said curiously. "Back to the gym I go."

"No—we should train with this blood match. I can sense you better than ever before. I could sense you in the city. I can feel you right now. What we need to do is use this to our advantage. Our blood match is something that Harrington doesn't know about. He can't anticipate it."

"That's true," she said with a spark of hope.

"We should talk to Washington and get his view on it. He's the expert," Beckham said. "Once the snow finally stops, we'll get to the real work."

• • •

"What you're asking me is impossible to infer," Washington said. He looked up from the microscope he'd been peering into. "I've only ever seen one other blood match, and it was before modern medicine. I have no earthly idea what abilities you could have. The fact that you have any at all other than compatibility on a molecular level astounds me."

Beckham's nostrils flared. Reyna could see him holding in his anger. Washington was being purposefully obtuse.

They already *knew* that he hadn't worked with anyone else who was a blood match. But that didn't mean he didn't have theories. Washington had theories about everything.

"Hypothesize," Reyna said quickly.

"I'd need to look at your blood. When my lab was destroyed, I lost everything. I have a backup of the data I was working with, but not the actual samples. That would help me work toward a solution."

Reyna's eyes rounded and she gestured for him to continue.

"There are any number of abilities that you could possess working together. Before you I would never have guessed that you could sense each other across large distances. I wouldn't even begin to consider how that could happen. Perhaps some sort of biological transmission."

"We don't need to know how it happens, just what could happen," Beckham said.

"Knowing how something works is the first step to uncovering life's greatest mysteries."

"We're a bit short on time for life's greatest mysteries," Reyna reminded him. "We want to use this as a weapon. Something that will help us take down Harrington. You must have some ideas."

Washington frowned as if the thought of taking down Harrington repulsed him. Harrington was bad enough to work against him, but he still had trouble thinking about him dying.

"Off the top of my head, I would consider mind reading, emotional shaping, feeling, or projecting, enhanced touch, and sharing of each other's perceived strengths. The other option is that there are no other added benefits beyond what you have already discovered and you simply need to sharpen that quality. Attune yourselves to the other. I truthfully do not know but think that stretching your abilities is a worthwhile endeavor."

Reyna's mind whirred to life with all that information. Reading Beckham's mind might be awesome, but did she really want him to be able to read hers? And what the hell did *emotional shaping* mean? Could he make her feel a different way based on how he felt? And all she could think about were his strengths—enhanced sight, hearing, strength. Those would definitely help them out if she was in a bind.

"We'll give you the blood samples," Beckham said as if he had already worked out everything Washington had suggested. "Make Reyna's quick."

Reyna blanched. Oh right. The blood donation part.

She had two fears—needles and public speaking. She felt on a micro level like she was overcoming the public speaking. Talking to the group of Elle members was pretty much no sweat. She didn't know how she would do if she had to address an audience of strangers, and she didn't really want to find out.

But needles…

She didn't think she'd ever overcome that. She'd wanted to

vomit that time they'd taken her blood and she was selected to be Beckham's blood escort. And she'd never gotten over the trauma of Harrington drawing her blood and doping her with vamp venom twice a week for months. Not even something as simple as donating her blood to science was about to change how she felt.

Needles gave her the creeps. Plain and simple.

But Beckham held her hand and stroked confident whirls on each pad of her fingers. She ignored the jolt of pain as Washington pierced the vein. She counted backward from a hundred and tried to pretend like she was somewhere else. That sometimes helped. A little.

"I hate this," she whispered.

Beckham clenched his jaw and his hand tightened around hers. "Me too."

"Why are you so tense?"

His eyes flashed with annoyance. Not at her. But at the fact that she'd noticed.

"Oh," she whispered. "You haven't fed enough. You don't have to be here. You can go."

"I will not leave you."

"Beckham, if you are in need of sustenance," Washington said, "Genevieve brought over some blood packets. I know it's not your preference, but if you warm it up, it will do the trick."

"I'm fine."

"I would advise you to go now," Washington said. Anger tinged his every word as he spoke to Beckham. It was a tone Reyna had never heard from him before. "You are still weak from your healing. Reyna cannot sustain you alone. Nor should she. And you are endangering her by smelling her sweet blood while hunger pangs you."

Beckham stormed to his feet. "Do not presume to tell me that I am weak. Or speak in any way about my relationship with Reyna."

"Becks," she muttered, reaching for his hand and kissing it. "It's okay. We're almost done. Go eat and then come back so we can train."

A muscle twitched in his jaw. She could see him fighting with himself. With the need to protect her and with his mounting hunger.

Then he took one last look into her dark brown eyes and left the room.

"Is he going to be okay?" Reyna asked a few minutes later after Washington had completed drawing her blood. "I've never seen him so in need of blood. Even when I've seen him hungry, he wasn't like this."

"Vampire healing takes a significantly less amount of time than a human's. We can endure much more than your bodies can, but it also comes at a higher price. The worse the damage, the more it requires of the body to heal it. The more blood and the more time. If Beckham truly almost died and came back from the brink, a feat few vampires can achieve, then he needs more time. And he needs more blood."

Reyna's hand instinctively went to her neck. "He doesn't like to drink from me."

Washington sighed. "I understand his concerns, but convince him. I believe your blood match saved his life. That having your blood in his system helped bring him back. I can't prove it, but that's what my gut tells me. And if that's the case, then your blood may be the key to helping him finally heal completely."

Reyna nodded. She would convince him.

"There, I'm better," Beckham snarled as he walked back into the basement laboratory. "Let's collect a sample and get this over with."

Reyna exchanged a glance with Washington, who nodded at her.

They needed Beckham at full strength. She would be happy to give him more of her blood if it got him there. Now to figure out how to make that happen.

Chapter Fourteen

The snow fell ceaselessly for the next two days straight. Despite the wonderful reprieve from the real world, Reyna felt restless. It was too cold to go outside or really to venture far from a bed or a fireplace. And Beckham ignored any attempt she made of getting him to drink from her again. It was as if he knew what she and Washington had discussed. With his preternatural hearing, he probably did.

"Today is the day," Beckham said against her skin. He pressed a kiss into her shoulder blade. She yawned and rolled over to face him.

"For what?"

"The snow has finally stopped. The sun is out. We're leaving this house."

Beckham slipped out of bed. She tilted her head to the side and admired his naked body. The hard contours of his shoulder blades. The sharp line down his back. The little dimples in his lower back. The rounded, muscular ass. And those incredible legs. Her mouth watered at the sight of him. He was magnificent. Sculpted and hardened. A deadly Adonis.

She sighed as he slid into clothes, watching every inch of skin get covered. "You should walk around naked."

"I think you would not be the only one ogling as you just did."

"I wasn't *ogling*," she lied.

"You certainly were. I could sense every single time your eyes touched on me."

"Oh?" She leaned forward out of bed and pulled him back toward her. She was still naked beneath the covers and his pupils dilated at the sight of her bare breasts. "I can give you more than my eyes if you like."

He kissed the hollow of her throat. Her eyelids fluttered closed as a fang grazed the delicate artery. "Perhaps after we've put some work in."

He stood again and was out the doorway before she could even cover herself. She humphed noisily and then slid out of bed. She put on every single layer that she had in the bedroom before stuffing her feet in black furry snow boots and trudging downstairs.

Jodie laughed when she saw her. "You look like you're going to Siberia."

"I don't want to talk about it."

"Good news though. Zoya finally cracked another safe house. So we get to dig them out of the snow once we can dig ourselves out of the snow."

"That's excellent," Reyna said. "Any news from the anti-vamp cult?"

"Drew called this morning. Said Everett is being a pain in the ass and his friends are trying to convert the rest of Elle to their vamp-hating ways, but otherwise all is good."

Reyna blew out a heavy breath. "Well, just fucking great."

"Pretty much. The world is a toilet and we're all getting flushed."

"I love you."

Jodie winked. "I know."

Reyna found Beckham standing on the porch, looking out across the white expanse. She had no clue how she was going to survive this cold. At least Beckham had been right about one thing. The sun was out. Not that it seemed to make it much warmer, but it was better than the cloudy weather and the horrible biting wind that dropped the temperature a good fifteen degrees.

"Ready to go?" he asked.

She nodded. Though she was not looking forward to the cold.

Someone had come out and cleared the driveway so that it wouldn't completely ice over once they were free of this place. Reyna followed Beckham down the drive until he stopped at another path that someone had tramped through. She frowned but followed him off the road and through the snowbanks. She was still in snow up to her knees for most of the walk. They moved deeper through the woods until she saw a small cottage appear before them.

"What's that?"

"The original home on the property."

"Original? Like 1800s original?" she asked with wide eyes. Beckham nodded.

When they reached the tiny cabin, Reyna was surprised to find a fire already lit in the hearth. Beckham must have come out here earlier to build it for her. She smiled brightly up at him and hurried over to it. She was having trouble feeling her toes already.

The cabin had only one room, with marginal furnishings that centered around the hearth and a small bed in the corner. A thin layer of dust coated most everything. Light filtered in from the window at the front of the cabin and another small one by the makeshift kitchen area. Some off-white wax candles were burning throughout the room to give it more light. Reyna decided instantly that she loved the place. It was homey and comfortable and felt worlds away from the mansion.

"This is better," he said, lighting one more candle and setting it down on a rickety old table.

"Seriously, what is this place?"

"Before Washington built his house on the hill, he'd purchased the land from a farmer who lived with his rather large family in this cabin. He allowed them to stay on until they passed away or moved. He wanted it to be his permanent home. Not something most vampires at the time were afforded."

"Why?"

"The deaths are easier to conceal than in the city."

Reyna's stomach roiled. "Right."

"Genevieve is a descendent of that bloodline. She lived in it for many years after her children passed, but now has her own place farther removed from the memories."

"I couldn't imagine."

"I hope you never have to," he said quietly. "When I would reside on the hill, I would come down here to think sometimes. It freed my mind. I would like it to do so today."

"Okay. So how exactly are we going to train? I don't think this is like running on the treadmill or using a punching bag."

"I don't think so either. But when I was turned, I didn't have all the strength I have now. I developed my abilities. Honed them. It gave me an edge that others had no chance of surpassing as mindless drones. I want to try pushing our own connection in the same way."

Reyna suddenly bubbled with energy at the prospect. She liked getting more information about Beckham in this process. He wasn't usually so willing to divulge his secrets.

"Work it like a muscle. Even though it's not a muscle."

"Indeed."

Beckham stripped off his jacket and tossed it across the lone chair. He folded his arms across his broad chest. His eyes observed her in an all-too-familiar way. She'd seen him do it a number of times when she'd first started "working" for him. As if she were a puzzle he needed to solve, a question he needed an answer to.

At the time, she hadn't known that was a good thing. She'd felt like prey trapped in a predator's gaze. Maybe she still was. But now she liked it.

"I estimated you at six miles away from me when I sensed you in the city the day you came to get Jodie."

Reyna's jaw dropped. "Six miles?"

"I thought it might be because of the extreme situation I was in, but I've confirmed it."

"When did you do that?" she gasped.

"While you were sleeping."

"It's been snowing since we got back. You drove *six* miles away in this snow without anyone knowing?"

"Ran."

Reyna's eyes doubled in size. "Through the snow."

He nodded once.

"And really, six miles? How long does that take you?"

He grinned and lifted an eyebrow as if to say, *Wouldn't you like to know?* Secrets, secrets.

"I always topped out around six miles. We could stretch that, but I think our time would be better spent figuring out if there are other things we can do. Other advantages we have."

"I have a thought about that," Reyna said. "When we walked into the safe house, I was worried. But I noticed how calm and controlled you were. I wanted to feel that way and I kind of did. I don't know if I did it because we're connected, but it was like I tuned in to you."

"I noticed that."

"What are you feeling right now?"

He arched his eyebrow. "You tell me."

Reyna gritted her teeth and concentrated. She hadn't really *done* anything when it had happened last time. She had wanted to feel Beckham's confidence and she had. She'd wanted to be able to weather the storm and she had. She'd slipped right into it like pulling on her boots.

She assessed him. He looked calm. Not a bit nervous that she wouldn't be able to do it. The opposite of how she felt.

Mostly she felt out of her depth. When she felt him across a crowded room, it wasn't like she was looking for him. He was there. She knew precisely where he was, and she simply had to think about it and he appeared. No process to it at all.

Still, she reached out with her mind and felt for his emotions. She tried to nudge against what made Beckham *Beckham*. Which mostly meant standing there and staring at him in deep concentration, and nothing happened.

She blew out a heavy breath. "Epic fail. There's nothing. Maybe it was a fluke. Maybe I was calmer and more confident because you were there."

"I feel nothing from you. Though I can see frustration written on your face."

"Well, yeah."

"Again."

And again. And again. And again.

Nothing.

She tried every way they could think of. She could sense him standing there. Could count every breath. Knew when he opened and closed his eyes. Could tell where he stood in the room with her back turned and her eyes closed. But reaching beyond that was an exercise in futility.

Beckham was there.

He stood right there.

But he was a blank slate. As ever.

And she was as equally mystifying to him.

They moved on to trying to mind read. Reyna was excited about this one. Not that she wanted Beckham in her head, but she wouldn't mind unraveling some of his greater mysteries. But all they ended up doing was staring at each other for long stretches of time and asking, "What am I thinking now?"

"You want to eat lunch," Beckham said.

"Yes," Reyna shouted. She jumped in the air in excitement. "You got it. You finally got it."

"Your stomach grumbled."

She sank back into the chair. "I'm so transparent. You don't need to read my mind."

"At times."

"And you're so closed off, I'd probably get to read your mind and find locked filing cabinets inside."

Beckham's lips curved on one side in amusement. That was his way of saying, *Of course you would.*

"We should break for lunch. You need to keep your strength up."

"Me?" she asked. "Look at you."

He tilted his head to the side. "Are you suggesting I'm not strong?"

"I'm suggesting you're still not a hundred percent and need to eat more."

His expression said, *I can take care of myself.*

"I don't need to read your mind or grasp your feelings to know that you are still recovering. The little bit that you drank from me last week is nothing, Becks. We both know blood packets aren't enough. Maybe this isn't working because you're flagging."

Beckham snapped his eyes to hers. "Flagging?"

"Yeah."

His nostrils flared. "Are you trying to pick a fight with me?"

Reyna's lips quirked. "Yes."

"Explain."

"I thought I'd see if heightened emotions worked. But yeah, no luck."

He shook his head and rummaged through a bag that Reyna had completely ignored since they'd gotten there. It was full of food. She ate in silence, trying to figure out what the fuck they were doing wrong.

They spent hours staring at each other, boosting emotions and fighting, trying to get a reaction to make the powers work. When she opened herself up to sensing him, it was there. But beyond that was a brick wall of nothing. A wall of air that separated her from him. Imaginary and frustrating as fuck.

Somehow it was worse than exercising. She was warm in the one room and felt none of the calm thinking power that Beckham claimed the cabin gave him once upon a time.

All she felt was frustrated, achy, and tired.

"Maybe we can't do anything else," she suggested.

"Perhaps."

"This is all a waste of time. There are other things we could be doing."

Beckham shrugged one shoulder.

"Aren't you annoyed?"

"This was an experiment. As valid as any other."

"Ugh," Reyna grumbled. "Let's try again tomorrow or something, because I'm tapped out."

"I think we should keep—"

"I'm human, all right? I have limits."

Reyna couldn't help it. Her frustration was getting to her. She'd thought this would be an easy endeavor. That she'd magically be good at it, whatever it was. Like they'd been with sensing. But if she was capable of more, it wasn't going to come easy. Not by a long shot.

"We don't have much time."

"I know," she said with a sigh.

She turned and there he was. In her awareness, she'd walked right into his arms. They wrapped tight around her body, pulling her against him. She melted into the embrace. He held her as if she was adored, cared for, loved.

Her annoyance and frustration wasn't directed at him. That it shouldn't even be there. But she'd felt so useless for so long that sometimes it just exploded out of her. She loved that he knew what she needed.

His hands splayed across her back. She felt the urgency in his movements. And suddenly all the pent-up energy exploded between them.

Beckham pushed her back against the wooden cabin wall. He grabbed her hands and pinned them high above her head. Then captured her lips in a searing kiss. Her head spun with the intensity, the swift change of emotions.

"I need you," he growled into her mouth.

"Yes," she gasped.

He fumbled her jeans down and tore her panties off. He inhaled deeply at the strong scent of her arousal before freeing himself from his pants. She watched him stroke himself once, twice, three times, mesmerized. She wet her lips and he pressed forward to kiss her again.

His hands moved to the backs of her thighs and lifted her clean into the air. She wrapped her legs around his waist, and her hands left the cabin wall to fall to his shoulders. She felt his cock hard against her opening. She groaned in anticipation, wiggling her hips to try to tempt him inside.

But he held her hips steady and plunged into her when he was ready. Her head fell back against the wooden wall. She saw stars. Everything about it was wonderful and overwhelmingly perfect. She loved Beckham so much. And the way their bodies connected over and over again. Deep, hard, and unyielding.

An ache was building inside her. Starting in her core and moving out to her fingers and toes. Waves crashing within her.

Her eyes met his. She saw the same desire mirrored on his face. The same devotion and love. Then she turned her head to the side and directed his mouth to her neck.

She heard his sharp intake of breath. Felt the brush of a kiss over the artery. Her blood pumped energetically through her veins with the tempo of his vigorous fucking. Then she felt his fangs pierce her skin.

She gripped his shoulders as ecstasy shattered through her. She cried out in pleasure as her orgasm rushed through her body. Between his fangs in her neck and his cock in her pussy, she was a goner.

"Oh fuck," she groaned.

Beckham came a few thrusts later, roaring with pleasure as he released her neck and tilted his head back.

Her heart was thrumming violently. Her body rushed through with all the adrenaline and vamp venom. She felt alive. Alive and refreshed. Yet somehow exhausted.

And still so madly in love. Not just the love that she felt for Beckham, but the love he felt for her.

Here it was. Deep, undeniable, incredible, masterful love. Impossible and euphoric love. Hopeless, happy, desperate, perfect love.

She felt it all. Took it from him and gave him her own.

"Do you feel that?" he gasped out.

"You love me," she whispered.

"I love you." Beckham's eyes were wide with wonder. As if he couldn't fathom all the emotions ripping through him. "And you feel…so deeply."

She grinned. "Yes."

Beckham kissed her again through his awe. They had time for hypotheses later. Right now, they were feeling the full depth of love for the first time. And neither wanted to move from the moment.

CHAPTER FIFTEEN

"You're saying that you could actually feel Beckham's emotions?" Washington asked. He rubbed his hands together and looked giddy. "Not just felt an increase in your own emotions but distinguished your emotions from his?"

"Yes," Reyna said. "It was definitely different."

"What triggered this?"

A blush crept up her neck and onto her cheeks.

"Oh," Washington said. "I see."

"Also blood," Reyna added. "He drank my blood."

"Good. He needs to. Where is he anyway?"

Reyna waved her hand. "Preparing. Do you have any theories about this? Do you think it's the blood? Does it mean when he drinks my blood it's amplified?"

"It's possible. But of course many things are possible in this scenario."

"Yeah. I mean, the first time he sensed me was when Penny was having her mayoral banquet. He hadn't drank my blood in months at that time."

"But you also weren't that far away either."

"True."

"So, perhaps the blood does act as an amplifier. It also could be that your relationship itself amplifies the abilities you're developing."

"A blood amplifier," she mused softly.

"I've been investigating your blood match and how you each react to the other. It's quite extraordinary. Most blood when combined is like a blood transfusion. It either accepts the blood as the correct type or it rejects it. As you know, the correct blood type between a human and a vampire is important because it allows us to retain human consciousness. Some of us have the preternatural ability to do so already, but many of my kind were brutal murderers and the more who were made, the harder it was to conceal them." He tsked in frustration. "The interesting thing about your blood is that when the blood is combined, it neither accepts it nor rejects the other."

"How is that possible?"

"The blood is perfectly matched but instead of assimilating, it links."

"Links?" Reyna asked with a bewildered expression.

"Yes. One of your red blood cells attaches itself to one of his red blood cells. It creates entirely different blood."

"But what does that mean? What are the implications of it?"

"I've only had it a short while. I'm still amazed that this is even happening."

Now Reyna understood his giddiness. Washington discovered an entirely new form of blood and was on the way to a breakthrough in modern hematology.

"Do you think that our blood connecting in that way is part of the reason we can sense each other?"

"It's a distinct possibility."

Reyna's head turned toward the door before Beckham walked through it. It was a little freaky knowing exactly where he was before she actually knew.

He tilted his head to the side. She nodded, then he disappeared once more.

"Extraordinary. You knew he was there before he entered, didn't you?"

"Yeah. I did." She hopped up from the stool she'd been sitting on. "Thanks again."

Reyna left Washington in the laboratory with his experiments. Her mind was still filtering through all the information she'd learned. A blood amplifier. That was intense. It meant Beckham was going to have to drink a lot more of her blood to test this out. She didn't think he'd be thrilled with that.

Reyna pulled on her heavy winter clothing and then met Beckham at the back door. Zoya was discussing something with him in a low tone.

"Everything all right?" Reyna asked.

"We're ready to go," Beckham said.

"Sir," Zoya said.

"Just be careful."

Zoya nodded her head once.

Reyna followed Beckham out into the cold. "Are you upset that they're going to go check the camps?"

"No. My circle is perfectly capable."

"But you don't like that Jodie and Meghan and Tye are going with them?"

Beckham arched an eyebrow. "Just get in the car."

"They'll be fine. *My* circle is perfectly capable too. They're just taking some pictures. Why are you so tense?"

Beckham faced her fully. She nearly ran into him. He caught her by the shoulders and then tilted her chin up. "Tense is in my nature. You should calm down."

Reyna released a deep breath. "Okay."

Beckham opened the door to the van and she climbed inside. The engine was already running and Gerard sat in the driver's seat. Reyna crawled into the backseat and was surprised to find Gabe seated there already.

"Hey," he said with a wink.

Beckham hopped into the passenger seat. "What is he doing here?" he asked Gerard.

"Making contact with someone I think can help," Gabe said. "Plus, if I was in that house another fucking minute, I'd go insane."

"Who is this contact?" Beckham asked.

Gabe shook his head. "It's a guy who knows a guy. Last resort kind of person. He's the one you go to if you want information, and we need more information on Harrington. If anyone knows, it's him."

"Okay, let's get moving," Reyna said. Beckham and Gabe didn't get along, and they had places to be.

They pulled away from the mansion on the hill and down the road, which had been shoveled all the way to the gate and beyond. Reyna did not want to know whose unfortunate job that had been.

"We should move into the city. This driving an hour to do anything fucking blows," Gabe grumbled. "You're a bajillionaire, right, Beckham? Don't you have somewhere we can hide out?"

"If I had a place like that, we would already be there," he said calmly. He pulled out a phone and typed away at it. Just like old times.

Gabe grumbled under his breath. She heard a few choice curse words, but he dropped the subject.

The rest of the drive was mercifully silent. Gerard dropped Gabe off first, a few blocks away from his club, Five Points, which was a human night club and fighting ring. It also dealt in drugs and had for a while been a black-market blood bank. Being head of the Irish mob had its perks.

Beckham slid his phone into his pocket, relief evident now that Gabe was gone.

She wondered if she could sense that in him. She let it come to her in the way that feeling his presence came to her: gentle and effortless. There he was, sitting right in front of her. His emotions were locked down, but ringed with fading annoyance. She was right. He still didn't trust Gabe.

Reyna got lost in the feeling. She knew how Beckham felt about her. Believed him when he said he loved her. This was what he never unleashed. It felt like she was swimming in even the smallest emotional feeling.

A hand brushed against her knee. Her eyes jerked open. She'd been so lost in his emotions that she hadn't even sensed him tuning in to her.

"Don't do that," he said harshly.

Reyna retreated.

"Not here."

Reyna nodded. She put her own emotions away and locked them up in a filing cabinet like Beckham did. It was better to hold on to Beckham's calm and confidence.

Gerard parked the car on a slushy street. The city had plowed and de-iced the roads. Businesses were open. Things were returning to normal. It felt so distant from the country, where they'd been residing.

Beckham nodded his head at Gerard before slipping out of the front seat and helping her out of the back. They left Gerard with the idling car. Reyna linked arms with Beckham as they walked down the street.

"I didn't think I'd miss the city," she told him. "I always hated it after my uncle abandoned us."

"It's easier to be anonymous in the city."

"As if you've ever been anonymous."

He cracked one of his rare smiles. "I can blend into the darkness, Little One."

Reyna rolled her eyes at him and walked with him down the rest of the alley. He knocked on a side door. When nothing happened, he tried the handle and crushed the lock on his way inside.

"Wait," Beckham said, holding his hand up to her when she moved to follow him.

She stilled with her foot about to cross the threshold, and then she smelled it.

"Oh God," she whispered. "Blood."

The tangy rusty smell permeated the air. Even before she was all the way into the safe house, she could smell its pungent aroma. This was one of the larger safe houses. They'd been hoping to find upward of fifty people in this place. Reyna was terrified to see what waited for them.

Still, she couldn't just stand there. She steeled herself and hung on to Beckham's strong will. Then she walked forward, pulling the door closed behind her.

Bodies lay sprawled on the floor. So many bodies. Piled on top of one another and haphazardly arranged. As if someone had killed them, then thrown them aside like trash, again. In comparison, the other murders had been almost civil. Throats slit for a quick death and cryptic messages.

This was grotesque. Deep puncture wounds in their necks and arms and wrists. As if multiple vampires had been let loose in a feeding frenzy.

Reyna covered her mouth. "Oh my God."

Beckham didn't say anything. He strode into the room and observed what had happened. Reyna felt like her feet were buried in cement. Staring at all the dead bodies made her feel queasy. She would never get used to the blood and death. These had been people. Living, breathing people and vampires had mutilated them. They had no care for the lives they were living. Humans were food. Nothing more.

She forced herself to put one foot in front of the other and see what Beckham was seeing. With a quick scan of the room, she took in the number of bodies vaguely and the way they were arranged. She focused on the sheer number of bite marks.

"This is either a newborn or starved vampire. Or both," Beckham said, pointing out a young woman with eight visible bite marks on her.

"How...how can you tell?"

"Most vampires go for the throat. It's the easiest and most effective spot. Newly made and starved vampires have no conscience whatsoever. They're merely eating machines. They ravage prey until their system is full of blood. Then they begin to return to themselves."

"How horrible."

"Newborns usually snap out of it in a few weeks once they've eaten enough, especially if there are other vampires around. But starving vampires can be strung along like this— "

A scream pierced the air and Beckham stopped abruptly. Reyna's head snapped to the back stairs. She darted after Beckham, who moved at vamp super speed. She had made it to the top stair when she saw Beckham struggling with a stray vampire.

She looked beyond it and saw a group of Elle members protecting the children behind them with a human barricade. Her heart went out to them. How long had they been enduring this? Watching the others die one by one and not knowing how long it could hold the vampire off.

"It's okay. We're going to get you out of here," Reyna reassured them.

Whimpers and cries were heard, as relief flooded their systems. A few broke into tears as the fear relented. The children collapsed into waiting arms. A few whispered thank-yous were spoken.

Finally, Beckham restrained the vampire and Reyna reluctantly glanced away from the poor children. Beckham had his hands on either side of the vampire's face, prepared to snap the neck of the foul beast who had murdered so many, who had clearly been sent here by Harrington to finish off his dirty work.

But when she made eye contact with the vampire, she gasped.

"Beckham, no!"

His eyes locked on hers in confusion. The vampire snarled angrily, trying to break Beckham's hold.

"What?" Beckham demanded.

"It's…it's Brian."

Chapter Sixteen

Reyna's heart shattered into pieces. Her body felt as if it were going to collapse. The worst horror of all horrors stood before her.

Brian.

Her Brian.

Her oldest brother.

The protector of their small family.

She couldn't fathom what she was seeing. It was a mirage. She was lost in the desert desperate for a drink and imagining an oasis. Only the oasis was a rattlesnake ready to strike.

"No," she whispered.

She was amazed that words were even possible when all she felt was despair. Not just that Brian was a vampire. A vampire she could handle. She could understand becoming a vampire. She'd thought about it enough herself. She was dating one. Hell, she'd been employed by them, kidnapped by them, lived with them, loved them. Vampire wasn't the problem.

Starved. Newborn. Murderer.

The words obliterated all other thought. Her brother was a starved newborn vampire who had murdered all the people downstairs. If she and Beckham hadn't reached him, he would have killed the rest. Killed the children.

Monster.

She'd accused Beckham of it before. But this…this was what an uncontrollable monster looked like. Killing without purpose, unable to be reasoned with, or stopped without force. This was the vampires of nightmares she'd always been taught. And now, it was her brother.

"Reyna!"

Her eyes finally lifted to Beckham's. He must have said her name multiple times. She'd been adrift. Unable to process anything. Suddenly it all rushed back. She saw the people cowering in the corner and Beckham still working to restrain Brian and smelled all the blood.

"Call Gerard," he snapped.

"Just don't kill him."

"Do it."

Then Beckham smashed a fist into Brian's face and half-carried, half-dragged him back down the stairs. Reyna watched them leave, her heart in her throat.

But she needed to listen to Beckham's orders. They needed Gerard. She pulled out her phone and held her finger over the number three. He'd come get them just like Katarina and Philippé.

She slid the phone back in her pocket and then tried to channel Beckham's calm. But it was gone. Completely out of reach. As if her own emotions still roaring in her ears kept her from feeling him. She couldn't even sense him downstairs. All their hard work and in a time of crisis she felt nothing.

She tried to drown out the chaos. There were people here. People who needed her help. One foot in front of the other.

"Okay. Who's in charge here?" Reyna asked. She stepped forward. No one moved from their positions. "All right. It's okay. We're going to get you out of here. We have a safe place for you to go to. Other survivors are there."

Her phone buzzed. She checked her pocket and saw a text from Gerard letting her know he was out back.

"Okay. We need to get moving. The van is here to pick you up." Reyna counted off the number of people and prayed the van would carry everyone. "It's going to be a tight fit, so the children will have to sit on laps." She gestured for them to move forward. "Please, cover the children's eyes as much as you can. No one should have to see what we're about to pass, but definitely not children."

Each adult picked up at least one child in shaking arms and pressed their little heads into their shoulders. Reyna reached for the last little girl. The girl hugged onto Reyna when she scooped her up. Reyna rested her head on the girl's as she carried her downstairs with the others. She hoped that none of them tried to sneak a peek. This wasn't like seeing presents before Christmas. This was seeing death and destruction that would stay with you a lifetime.

They all hustled out of the house and into the frigid temperatures. Gerard was parked in back. Reyna hurried toward him and deposited the little girl into the backseat.

Reyna smiled sadly at her and then backed up as the rest of the survivors piled into the black van they'd selected from the garage for this very reason. One woman clasped her hand and murmured her thanks before getting inside.

Once the van was full to capacity, Reyna closed the sliding door and came around to the driver's side. "You know where to take them?"

"Yes. Where's the boss?"

"Dealing with another issue. Come back for us when you're done. If we leave before then, I'll text you."

Gerard nodded once, taking orders from her as easily as he did from Beckham. Then he left her standing alone in the sludgy, brackish water. She swallowed back the lump in her throat and promised herself she wouldn't cry. She couldn't lose it. She still had to figure out what the hell they were going to do about this. How they were going to deal with Brian being turned.

Harrington had done this.

And he had done it to her.

Once again, he had outmaneuvered her.

She drew her hands down her face.

With a shuddering breath, she returned to the safe house. Beckham had piled the bodies into a corner. Somehow, they looked even more gruesome that way. As if she and Beckham were moving furniture to clean the carpets. The blood was never coming out.

Brian was unconscious and tied to a chair. His head lolled forward against his chest. His emaciated figure shocked her. He'd always been a broad guy. Both he and Drew were made of packed muscle on wide frames. Even when they'd gone hungry, they'd never really been skinny. And she could see under his baggy clothes that he was wasting away to nothing.

"How is this possible?" she whispered. "It's been, what, three weeks? Just three weeks since he was captured?"

Beckham nodded. "It's the virus. Vampirism wreaks havoc on the body and completely re-forms it to be able to give us the strength, speed, and hearing. The first week is most important. You have to be fed, and fed regularly, while the body grows and mutates. You are burning energy at such a high rate that if not fed properly, the body eats away at itself."

She clutched at her chest. His body was eating away at him. Dear God, the pain he must've felt.

"How long do you think he's been like this?"

"More than a week at least. He was on his last leg. I've seen it before."

The way he said it made it sound personal.

"You've done this before?" she whispered.

He clenched his jaw. The only sign that he didn't like how easily she could read him. "It's a form of torture. We did it to our enemies or in interrogations. It's a power play." He paused and then continued,

"It's what was done to Sydney."

Reyna sucked in a harsh breath. "She came out stronger for it."

"That's why I respected her."

"She was uncommon?" Reyna guessed.

Beckham's curt nod was enough to confirm everything she feared. Sydney was the exception. Her strength was rare. It was more likely that Brian was broken and may never recover from this.

"What do we do?" she demanded, shucking off all the fear and moving into action.

"Blood. He needs a lot of blood."

"Where do we go? A blood bank? The hospital?"

"It'd be better to bring him back to Washington's, where we can monitor him."

"We have enough blood there?"

"Genevieve keeps us well stocked. You know his blood type?"

"Of course. He'll be okay on the drive back?"

"He'll be unconscious for a while," Beckham said with a hint of regret.

"You did what you had to. Now we have to do what we can to save him. Harrington won't win this."

Beckham didn't say anything for a moment as they both observed Brian. "Do you want to tell Drew and Laura?"

Reyna inhaled sharply. "No. No, I don't want anyone else to know what he's going through if I can help it."

"Okay."

Reyna loved that he didn't argue with her. He didn't try to comfort her. He didn't try to soften the blow. They both knew it was dire. There was no use lying.

Reyna called Gabe while they waited for Gerard to return with the van. He answered on the third ring. "What?"

"We have an emergency here. We found Brian."

"That's great, Reyna. Why is that an emergency?"

"He's a vampire."

"Fuck!"

"And starving and…he did some things he's not going to like if we can get him back to himself. We have to take him home to get him fed. Are you coming?"

"No. I can't. I think this is going to take a while anyway."

Reyna sighed. "Okay. Well, call when you want us to come pick you up after your meeting."

"Will do. Take care of yourself. I'm sorry about Brian."

She choked back her anger and tears. "Me too."

She hung up the phone.

"Gabe is staying," Beckham said. "That's probably for the better."

"He's going out on a limb for us."

"If I haven't heard of this contact of his, then he's not legendary."

"You think very highly of yourself."

Beckham brushed a kiss to her forehead. "With good reason."

Chapter Seventeen

When Gerard arrived, Beckham untied Brian and handed Reyna the ropes. Then he tossed Brian over his shoulder like he weighed nothing. They piled into the van. Beckham tied Brian up in the backseat just in case. Reyna kept glancing over her shoulder at Brian, watching him breathe softly. She wanted to brush his dark hair out of his eyes. Comfort him the way he had always comforted her. But it was a risk. She didn't want him to wake up and attack her, without even knowing who she was.

There'd been absolutely nothing in his eyes when she'd looked into them. He'd snarled and screamed like a monster completely lost to the virus. He hadn't even recognized her. She had been just another blood source. Not his sister. Not the girl he'd raised into a woman and fed and clothed and protected and taken care of for much of his life.

She turned away sharply as her heart ached for the brother she felt slipping away behind her. She hoped the long road ahead of them would be worth it.

Beckham dragged Brian's body into an empty bedroom upstairs. He upgraded from rope to chains to be sure Brian couldn't get free when he woke up. In fact, he seemed a little too comfortable with tying someone up.

"How many times have you done that?" Reyna asked.

Beckham clicked the lock into place. "Many, many times."

She sank into a chair against the wall and watched Brian until Beckham came back with a cooler full of blood. Reyna's eyes rounded.

"That's a lot of blood."

"He's going to need this and more. I sent Genevieve out again." Beckham set the cooler down. "A positive, right?"

"Yeah."

"How did he and Drew end up with such a common blood type and yours is so incredibly rare?"

"I ask myself that every day."

It was only a few minutes before Brian finally woke up. Reyna jumped to her feet as he roused. Beckham must have hit him really fucking hard for him to be out for over an hour. She didn't want to think about it. But at least he was awake.

He was no better than when they'd first gotten him though. He woke with a fiery vengeance. He snapped and snarled and yelled. He tried to kick and bite and claw his way out of the chair. But with the chains in place, he wasn't going anywhere. Especially not as malnourished as he was.

"You should go downstairs," Beckham told her.

"No, I want to be here for him."

Beckham's eyes were black and depthless. His hardened mask was in place. And for the first time since she'd found Brian, she delved into Beckham's emotions. He was practically projecting them into her. She could feel the hardened exterior, the savage beast within. She could almost taste the ferocity on her tongue. Feel the thing he had to become to handle this.

And feel that he didn't want her to become it. He was doing this to protect her. As much as he worried for her fragility, he didn't want this to ruin her fragile human heart. He'd promised to break it. But only him. Not this. Never this.

She swallowed and nodded. No words needed to be spoken. They were on the same page.

She stepped through the door and tried to close herself off to the sounds coming from the room down the hall.

• • •

It was hours before the others finally returned. Reyna had retreated to the farthest corner of the house. She was sure she could still hear Brian's screams. Or maybe that was just in her head.

"Hey," Jodie said, skipping into the room. "We had the best day. Wait, what's wrong?"

Reyna shook her head. She didn't want to repeat the words. She'd been trying to forget them all day. Despite the screams.

And there was another one.

Jodie's head snapped up to the staircase. "What the fuck? What the hell happened while we were gone?"

Reyna sighed and stood. She straightened her back. She could do this. She could survive it. "Brian."

"Brian? You found him?" Jodie's eyes lit up.

"Yeah."

"That's amazing. How did that happen?" Then she scrunched up her nose. "Is he okay? Why the screaming?"

"He's…he's not okay."

Meghan and Tye rushed into the room, followed closely by Zoya and Katarina, who had her swords drawn.

"It's okay," Reyna said. She held her hands up to keep them from charging forward to put out the fire. "Everything's under control."

Katarina whirled on her. "Where is the screaming coming from?"

"Upstairs. Beckham has…he has Brian up there." A flicker of recognition lit up in Meghan and Tye's eyes, but the expressions on the faces of Beckham's circle remained questioning. "My brother. My brother is upstairs."

"You found him?" Tye asked in relief. "How the hell did that happen?"

She didn't want to deliver this news. Not to the people in front of her. Not to Drew or Laura. Not to anyone. But she had to.

"He was turned," she whispered.

All the air was sucked out of the room.

"No," Meghan whispered.

Katarina slid her blades back into their holsters behind her shoulders. "Newborn?"

Reyna nodded. "And starving."

"Someone has gone out for blood?" Zoya asked.

"Yes."

"The boss has him chained up?" Katarina asked.

"Yeah. They…Harrington purposely starved him. We're not sure if he's going to come back from the point of brutality. He went so long without blood, Beckham is concerned that even the blood type cure might not bring him back to what he was."

Zoya and Katarina exchanged a glance. They'd been there when Beckham had used it as a form of torture. They knew the odds of Brian coming around.

"Why don't you have a seat?" Zoya suggested.

"I have the best recipe for Russian tea," Katarina offered as Zoya gently moved Reyna to the couch. As if she were a wild animal about to bolt.

"Russian tea?" Reyna asked in confusion.

"Vodka. Takes the edge off."

"This isn't good," Jodie muttered.

"Jodie, come help me in the kitchen," Katarina snapped. "Meghan and Tye, blankets and candles. It's going to be a long night."

...

Reyna fell asleep on the couch with her head against a pillow and her feet in Meghan's lap. Having someone to take care of had finally seemed to snap Meghan out of the daze she'd been walking in for the last couple weeks. She'd helped Zoya and Katarina nurse Reyna through the hours and hours of screaming and snarling.

Soft voices and the feel of fingers brushing her hair out of her face drew Reyna from her deep slumber. She felt half-awake and half-asleep. Somewhere in an in-between place.

"How's she doing?" Beckham whispered low.

"As well as can be expected," Katarina responded. "She is sleeping. That is best."

"How much vodka did you give her to get her to do that?"

"Enough." Katarina sighed. "Will the boy make it through?"

"He's going to need more blood. He's rabid. If I could get him to drink, then maybe he'll pull through."

"Did you ever think that we'd be the ones trying to save a rogue vampire?" she asked with a tinge of humor in her voice.

"Only one," he said fondly.

"You needed a good assassin. I was dying. And anyway, you're not saving this boy for your own sake. You're saving it for hers. Do you truly love her?"

Reyna felt Beckham's eyes on her. "I do."

"What does it feel like?"

"To feel?"

"Yes."

"Like indescribable pain and wonder." Beckham paused. "She's a weakness. I've never allowed myself to have one before. She's so fragile."

"She's not that fragile. She has steel for a backbone and she's as stubborn as you are. Stop treating her like she's going to break. She needs your strength, not your fear."

Beckham growled low at the comment. “I have to protect her.”

“I know.”

“She doesn’t want me to.”

“You’ll do your best.”

“I’d die a thousand deaths for her. No matter the cost, you protect her first.”

“Sir…”

“Her.”

Katarina sighed. “Okay.”

Beckham moved his fingers from Reyna’s hair and gently lifted her in his arms. She snuggled against his chest and promptly fell back asleep. Her brain convincing her that it had all been a dream.

Chapter Eighteen

Days passed and Brian got no better.

Genevieve brought more and more blood. Beckham and his inner circle spent endless hours locked in the room with Brian. Reyna learned not to ask how it was going. The answer was always a grim look and a shake of the head.

"What do I do if he doesn't recover?" Reyna asked Jodie one afternoon. They'd locked themselves in Washington's lab. He hated having them there chatting while he was working, but he relented when it came to Brian.

"He'll recover," Jodie assured her.

"Washington, are you sure there's nothing you can do?"

"I've already told you that this is beyond the matters of medicine. Brian has undergone a severe form of torture. It has reduced him to a wild animal. You are attempting to tame the beast within. Under normal circumstances the correct type of blood is sufficient to regain strength and mental cognition. This is not a normal case. He may never be the same again. I'm sorry, Reyna."

"I know," she said.

Jodie turned the computer to her. "My pictures aren't as pretty as yours, but *Perspective* is sure to make a splash now, huh?"

"Looks good," Reyna said.

On the computer was the website that Beckham had designed for her when he had first given her a camera. He'd wanted her to have a secure place to put the images she had taken and *Perspective* had been born.

Reyna scrolled through the images. Most of them were of the secure compounds Harrington had built. It showed the around-the-clock guards and barbed-wire fencing to keep people *in* rather than *out*. Someone had gotten close enough to see the holding facility inside where it looked like any other picture-perfect apartment building office space. They'd talked to a few people about the place, and everyone made it seem like a dream. Except that the people who went in never came out.

"We're going to need to go in there," Reyna said, glad to have something to take her mind off Brian. "Discreetly. We need pictures of the inside."

"Yeah. One problem."

"I know. If we send a human in, then they won't ever come out. I'm working on it."

"We could see if anyonc wanted to volunteer."

Reyna groaned. "I can't ask someone to do that."

"You wouldn't be asking."

"What we need is someone who Visage doesn't know, who will slip us information somehow. But I don't know who that would be."

"Or perhaps you could send in a vampire to feed," Washington said from the corner.

"A vampire Harrington doesn't know? Who the hell would that be?"

"Or one he does know like Penelope."

Reyna cursed. "She double-crossed us."

"What she did was horrible," Washington agreed. "But I think given a second chance she would make a different decision. It wouldn't hurt to send someone persuasive to ask."

"Beckham?" Reyna asked.

"She may be petty and opportunistic, but she has a soft spot for him."

Jodie held her hands up to prevent Reyna from venting. "Let's put fuckface Penny on the list. A backup, last resort, if the world is burning and she's the only double-crossing asshole left. Fair?"

"Fine," Reyna ground out.

The door to the basement cracked open. Philippé's stoic face appeared at the top of the steps. He grunted and gestured upstairs. Reyna was on her feet, running as fast as they would carry her. Her heart pounded in her chest as she came to a stop in front of Brian's door.

Her eyes adjusted to the low lighting almost immediately. And there was Brian seated in the same chair, with chains wrapped around his body. He held a dark mug in his hand, looking normal, and not like the monster who had flung blood all over the room, stained and shredded his clothes, and cut chains so deep into his wrists and ankles that he bled from the sores.

"Brian?" she whispered.

"Get out of here," Brian said, his voice low and deadly. Not the voice of her overprotective, caring brother. The voice of a killer.

"It might be harder for him to face you than us," Beckham warned her.

"Brian, it's me, Rey," she whispered.

"I know who you are," he said into the mug. "I said get out."

Reyna's eyes met Beckham's. He gestured for her to take another step forward.

"Are you…are you feeling better?" she continued. "Drinking again?"

"I've been well fed," he snarled.

"That's good. You need to keep your strength up. You lost a lot of weight. I didn't want to see you die."

Brian's eyes snapped up to hers. "I already died and now I'm in Hell."

Reyna swallowed. "You're not in Hell. You're at Washington's home. Beckham and I brought you here. Do you...do you remember us bringing you here?"

"I remember slaughtering all those people, if that's what you're asking."

Reyna winced. "That wasn't you."

"Who was it, then? I was there. I drank their blood. I killed them. I am a murderer."

"That was the beast within. They starved you on purpose and let the virus ravage your body. You weren't in control of yourself."

Beckham put his hand on her back. She sank into that embrace as if it was a life raft in the ocean.

"Just leave me," Brian snarled. He bared his fangs at her threateningly. He threw his mug across the room. It smashed against the wall and splashed the blood all over the room and onto both Reyna and Beckham. Reyna screamed at the outburst and took a step back.

"I said get out of here!" Brian yelled at her. "I don't ever want to see your face again."

"No, I won't accept that. I won't abandon you. Drew and Laura are still alive. You're going to be a father."

"I'm nothing," Brian said. He wrenched against his chains. His teeth snapped together. "Tell them I'm dead."

Reyna swallowed back the tears and then she ran out of the room. She shouldn't have come. He wasn't ready yet. She should have waited until he was one hundred percent better. Until he wasn't still so aggressive. But she had been so excited to see any progress.

She threw open the door to the room she shared with Beckham and headed immediately to the walk-in shower. She stripped out of her blood-soaked clothes, dropping them onto the floor with a squelch. Then she turned the shower on to the hottest setting and stepped into the spray. She scrubbed at her skin to get the blood off of her. No matter how hard she scrubbed—until she was pink and aching—still she felt dirty.

Beckham appeared at the shower door. He removed his many layers of clothes and then entered the shower.

"I can't get clean," she gasped.

"Let me." He took the loofah from her hand and ran it gently down her back, over her shoulders, and down her arms.

"Becks…"

"I know."

She threw her arms around him and finally let the tears fall hard and uncontrollably. Her body shook with the force of it. Heat flooded her chest and cheeks as her sobs took over. She felt ravaged from the inside out.

All the while, he stroked her back and held her firmly against him.

"Is he ever going to want to look at me again?" she said through the tears.

"I don't know."

"Oh God," she said. "What will I tell Drew and Laura?"

He tucked the wet hair back from her face. "The truth."

"What if I can't?"

"You can. They love him as much as you and will want to know."

"It'll break them."

"No. It will help you all to share the pain." Beckham tilted her face up to his. "Share it with me. I can handle it."

Her eyes, bloodshot, stared up into his as her emotions exploded outward. He clutched her harder as the pain hit him fresh. But in the process, she felt his resolve to help her. To love and care for her. And for the first time, she wondered if maybe she hadn't dreamed his conversation with Katarina.

"Grieve for the dead, not the living," Beckham said. "This is not the end. Just the beginning."

• • •

The next day, Gabe finally called to be picked up. And as much as Reyna wanted to stay behind, it had been five days since they'd found Brian. Drew and Laura had the right to know that she'd found him.

They met Gabe a couple blocks away from Five Points, the club run by the Irish mob of which Gabe was the leader. He hopped into the backseat and slammed the door shut.

"How was the club?" Reyna asked.

"Some fuck is trying to take over, and all hell broke loose when I was gone. I had to put a few people to fucking ground while I was there. Jesus Christ, you'd think it'd be easy enough to intimidate the fuckers. But no, they want to come at me like I'm fucking new here," Gabe barked.

Beckham cleared his throat. Reyna's eyes were round as saucers.

"It's fine," Gabe said with a laugh and a wink. Typical Gabe. "It's back under control."

"Did you say you put people to *ground*?" Reyna asked.

Gabe shrugged a shoulder. "All in a day's work. Didn't think I was all rainbows and sunshine, did you, sweetheart?"

"Going to find out how much of rainbows and sunshine I am if you call her sweetheart again," Beckham threatened.

Gabe ignored him. "Yeah, well, motherfucking contact won't respond. I keep getting rebuffed. I mean, it was a last resort to try to reach out to him anyway, but the dude could have had the decency to tell me to fuck off properly."

"We weren't expecting a miracle," Beckham said. He almost sounded satisfied that Gabe had failed.

"How's Brian?" Gabe asked.

Reyna winced.

"That bad?"

"Worse," she whispered.

"He's coming around," Beckham said. "Just not too happy with himself."

"I bet. He was a do-gooder type. Can't see him being okay with killing all those people."

"It gets easier with time," Beckham said.

"Sure does," Gabe said.

Reyna realized that she was in a car between two killers. Both had remorse for their past, but they still seemed unaffected when they had to kill to get business done. Reyna thought back to her brother's face, and she hoped that Beckham would be right. That this would all get easier with time.

• • •

"Are you sure we have to do this?" Reyna asked Beckham later when they were standing outside the anti-vamp cult room where the rest of Elle stayed. Beckham glanced at her. "Okay. We do."

She was not looking forward to it. Not even a little bit.

Beckham ushered her inside. Gabe was waiting in the car. They'd promised him they wouldn't be long.

The room they entered was massive, at least two stories up and round, with hallways branching out from it. It was full of people watching TV and hanging out. Her heart panged. It reminded her so much of the rec room at Elle.

"I didn't know you were coming by," Everett said, approaching from a hallway.

Beckham tensed next to her.

"And you brought him. You know this isn't a vamp-friendly place."

"Try to make me leave," Beckham said threateningly.

"Let's not," Reyna said, holding up her hands. "We're not here to argue with you. I need to talk to Drew and Laura."

"By all means." Everett gestured his arm. "But your escort stays here."

"If you think I'm going to leave her alone with you…"

Reyna blew out a strangled breath. "It's fine. You'll know if I'm not okay."

Their eyes met and she opened herself up to him. Let him feel the turmoil. He could sense her no matter where she went. She wasn't worried about being in this place. Just frustrated that he couldn't be here for this.

"Don't do anything stupid," Beckham said to Everett. "If you're capable of that."

Everett shot him a smug look and then directed Reyna down the first hallway on the left. The halls were narrow, with peeling white paint and muted tile. The dim lighting didn't help with the overall feel of the place. It certainly wasn't as nice as the old bunker, but it did the job. That was all that mattered.

"You don't have to antagonize him," she said.

"Why not? It's fun."

"You're an ass."

"Been called worse."

Reyna shook her head. She didn't want to argue with him. "How are things here?"

"Quiet."

"That's good."

"It is. I don't know how these people even got mixed up with Elle. They seem to want a normal life."

"We all want a normal life," she muttered. "We're fighting for a normal life."

"True. You're still going after Harrington, right?"

Reyna's eyes glanced down the empty hallway, wondering if anyone was listening. "Keep your voice down."

"I have feelers out. Other spies that I was in contact with."

"Are you serious?" she demanded. "You're on the outs. If they find where you are, they'll kill you. What happens if your negligence brings Harrington to their doorstep?"

"I'm being careful."

"You better be," she snapped. She sighed and sized him up for what he was telling her. "Can any of your contacts get into the camps?"

Everett shook his head. "None of them would risk it."

"Yeah." There went that idea.

"Well, here they are," he said, stopping in front of one of the nondescript black doors. "Let me know if you need me, Reyna." He placed his hand tentatively on her shoulder.

She jerked out of his touch. She still hadn't forgiven him for all he had done to her. Finding this place was only the tip of the iceberg as far as she was concerned. Everett had a lot more making up to do.

He held his hands up. "I get the picture. You can forgive murderers but not me."

"You turned me in. I was tortured. Then you help us with *information* at the last minute, which resulted in my brother being captured and tortured. Excuse me if I'm not running to make you feel better about the shit you've pulled."

"I didn't know about the stuff with Brian. I saw the trap for what it was. Would it have been better if I hadn't told you? Then no one would have gotten away."

"It was some well-timed information."

Everett sighed heavily. "You should trust me, Reyna. You're running out of friends."

"I appreciate what you've done, but it doesn't absolve you of everything else. We have a truce. Not a friendship."

Reyna knocked twice on the door to Drew and Laura's room. Everett blew out a long breath before disappearing back down the hall.

"Rey!" Drew said, flinging the door open and enveloping her.

"Hey, big brother."

"I didn't know you were coming."

"Well, here I am."

"Hey, Reyna," Laura said. She stood from the twin bed in the corner and came to give her a hug.

"It's so good to see you. How's my niece or nephew doing?"

Laura patted her belly. "Making mama sick as a dog, unfortunately."

"Sounds about right."

"Those new Elle people didn't help much. Shell-shocked. Going to need to get them some therapy. Even the children looked horrified," Laura said with a shake of her head. "I wonder what happened to them."

"I…I think you should sit down," Reyna said.

Drew raised his eyebrows. "What's going on?"

"Both of you."

Laura retreated back to her twin bed and took a seat. Drew looked uncomfortable and curious, then relented. He had a pallet against the opposite wall but took the chair in the corner.

"Tell us," Drew said.

Reyna took a deep breath and told them everything. Start to finish. She didn't want to tell them why the new Elle people were so shell-shocked or about Brian's feeding frenzy or how he was now. She especially didn't want to tell them that he didn't want to see them. Any of them. But she did. She told it all.

Then she held them as they cried. And cried.

As they begged to see him. And threatened her if she didn't let them come back with her. And cried some more. But by the end, she held them longer, hating that Harrington did this to her family.

And though Beckham told her not to mourn the living, she couldn't help but feel a piece of her brother had cracked away with his turning. And her entire family felt the reverberating repercussions.

Chapter Nineteen

A knock at the door finally broke them apart. Reyna rubbed her raw, red-rimmed eyes and then answered. Everett stood there, looking grim.

"What is it?" she asked.

"I have a rather annoying vampire demanding to see you," he muttered.

"Beckham?"

"Something important I presume, as he looks ready to tear me apart to get to you."

"Sounds like him. Give me a minute. I'll go."

She turned back to Drew and Laura and pulled them both in for hugs.

"Are you sure I can't come with you?" Laura asked.

"As much as I want you to, no. It's safer for you here while Brian is transitioning."

"I know you said that, but he's my husband. Wouldn't you be

there if this was Beckham?"

Laura had her there. Reyna would kill someone before they kept her from him. That didn't mean it was the right thing for Laura, or for Brian, right now.

"I'm sorry. As soon as he's in a better place. Any change at all. I'll bring you to the house, okay?"

Laura grumbled her disagreement, but Drew put his hand on her shoulder. "We'll be ready for that."

Finally, Reyna withdrew with an ache in the pit of her stomach and left them behind to deal with this together. Beckham was waiting for her right where she'd left him. He was pacing in frustration. He hated being barred from anything.

"What's happened?" Reyna asked.

He visibly relaxed when he saw her. "Just got off the phone with Gabe. It seems his contact has come through."

"That's good. When does he go?"

"Not him," Beckham said somberly. "Us."

Reyna tilted her head and narrowed her eyes. "What do you mean, us?"

"We're going to meet his contact."

"Okay but why?"

Beckham shrugged one shoulder. "Gabe told me to hurry."

Reyna would have laughed at how much that made him want to tear Gabe limb from limb, but she didn't think this would be a good thing. Gabe had made it sound like this person was dangerous. Not that she wasn't used to danger now. When had this become her new normal?

They returned to the car and found Gabe beside it, bouncing on the balls of his feet like the fighter he was. "Thank fuck. Took you enough time," he cried, his Irish accent bleeding through.

"Got here as fast as we could," Reyna told him.

"Look, this guy isn't someone to be messed with. If I'm saying that, then you can believe he's the real deal. I thought I was going to get the meeting, but he asked for you two." Gabe looked put out by that.

"Why?" Reyna asked.

"And how did he know about us? Did you tell someone?"

"Fuck no! But this guy, he just knows. He knows everything. That's why we're going to see the scary motherfucker."

Beckham looked skeptical. "When are we meeting him?"

"Tonight. But we'll have to get you cleaned up before you meet him. I don't know why, but that's what they told me."

"Fine. Done. What else?" Beckham asked.

"And you need payment."

Beckham's eyebrows rose. "How much?"

"Not that simple."

"It never is," Beckham muttered.

"Wait, slow down. What does he want?" Reyna asked.

"He trades for valuable information and priceless personal items," Gabe said. "I was going to give him the O'Connor family ring." He spun the giant ring around his right ring finger possessively. "But now you two have to find something to give him."

"I don't have anything," Reyna said. "I mean quite literally. Everything I owned—even my camera—was destroyed by Harrington."

"I've got enough for the both of us," Beckham told her. "I'll pick something up. Where are we meeting him?"

"He's going to send a car to collect you from this address," Gabe said, passing over the piece of paper he'd written it on and a key. "To open the building."

Beckham glanced at it and pocketed the key. "Fine. Anything else we need to know?"

"Yeah like the guy's name?" Reyna asked.

Gabe shook his head. "No idea. He keeps his identity secret. If he wants you to know, he'll tell you."

"Great," Reyna grumbled.

"This guy…I've only heard rumors, but usually there's some truth in every rumor. So just be careful."

"What exactly are we walking into?" Reyna asked.

Gabe shook his head. "I don't know much else about this guy. Just give him your payment and ask your questions about Harrington. We need something we can use to take him down, so be specific. Then get out of there."

Fear tingled down Reyna's spine at the declaration. Beckham seemed utterly unaffected by it, but what else was new? She didn't like that Gabe seemed freaked by this guy. What the hell could he do to someone like Gabe or Beckham? He couldn't be worse than Harrington. This guy might be cloaked in mystery, but he wasn't her first. She wouldn't quake in terror like she had the first time she'd met Beckham. She was a different person. She could handle this.

• • •

Beckham sent Reyna with Gabe to get her appropriately attired. He'd made a few quick calls and then suddenly she was being whisked away for pampering. Reyna couldn't understand the extravagance. They were undercover. They were trying to not be seen. And yet Gabe walked her through the back door of a luxury spa.

Beckham assured her that he still had some undercover connections, but she didn't see how having one at a spa was beneficial. She spent the next two hours in hair and makeup. When she had been living with Beckham, she'd been treated like a doll. And while it was fun sometimes, the endless makeup wasn't really her thing. She was more of a jeans and Chuck Taylors kind of girl.

But by the end, her dark hair fell long and luxurious down her back. Her skin glowed. Her eyes were lined and shimmery. She looked mysterious with her cat eyes, vampesque contoured cheekbones, and bright red lipstick. She looked like a whole new person.

"Wow," she muttered. "You guys are kind of geniuses."

The girls laughed and swatted her hand away from her hair. "Don't touch it," one girl said.

Reyna held her hands up. "No touching. Got it."

"Now for the real fun."

The woman marched her down the hallway and into a giant closet full of clothes, from the floor to the ceiling. Reyna's eyes bugged at all the gorgeous garments. For a second, she missed the lacy, silky, ridiculous clothes Beckham had once picked out for her. This was larger than her own closet had been, and it made her nostalgic for easier times. Who would have ever guessed that she'd be missing that life?

There was no way that Reyna could pick from the closet. So the women made her try on dozens of outfits before deciding on one.

Reyna's heart raced when she saw herself in the full-length mirror. She looked sexy.

A black dress hugged her features to her upper-thighs. Lace peeked out from the bottom of the scandalously short dress and ran up over her hips. The bustier top held her breasts up where they nearly spilled over the material, and fine spaghetti straps accentuated the entire thing. She had on red-backed black high heels and no underwear. The dress didn't allow for it.

Beckham was going to die when he saw her.

Gabe whistled low when she finally reappeared. "Holy shit, Reyna."

"Yeah," she said, running her hands down the sides of the dress.

"You look like a meal served on a silver platter." Gabe took a step back.

Reyna laughed softly. "I won't tell Beckham you said that."

"If he doesn't say the same, then there's something wrong with him."

"You're ridiculous. Is this going to be okay to meet your contact? I mean, is this too much?"

"Uh, no. That is the right amount."

Reyna smacked his arm. "You're trouble."

He bared a broad smile and winked. "That's my middle name."

"I won't tell Meghan you said that either."

He grinned. "That obvious?"

"Very."

"Well, don't let her know or she'll run the other direction." He winked at her and Reyna felt the tension dissipate. He'd helped her relax in his own way.

Gabe escorted her back downstairs and drove her to the address he'd been given for them to meet. It was in a nice part of town. Not too far from where Beckham's penthouse had been. Reyna hadn't been back to this part of town since that fateful night when she'd run out on Beckham after they'd had sex and he'd bitten her. All this time and she hadn't stepped foot near here.

She shivered as they stepped out of the car and Gabe hurried her inside. She'd put on a long black coat but was still cold.

Beckham was waiting for them in the entrance to the building, looking dapper as fuck in a tuxedo. She had no idea where he'd acquired a tailored tuxedo in a matter of hours, but she really didn't care. All she could do was stare. Seeing him in regular clothes for so long at the mansion had made her sensitive to him in a suit again. Or maybe she always would be. Because damn, he looked good.

He smiled at her approach and that made it all the better. "Little One…"

"Becks," she murmured.

"You need a minute?" Gabe asked with a laugh.

"You should go. We'll be in touch when we're finished." Beckham tossed the key to Gabe. "And lock up after us."

Gabe grabbed the key out of the air and then grinned wickedly as he strolled backward. "I'd take a look at what's under that jacket before you go."

Beckham's eyes were wide with hunger on her body. "Can I rip his throat out?"

Reyna laughed softly and shook her head. "You like him."

"Hardly."

Her hands went to her jacket, and she slowly unbuttoned the front. She let the front fall open and reveal her dress beneath. Beckham sucked in a harsh breath. A feral look crossed his face. She knew that look. It said, *Maybe we can skip this meeting*.

He took a step forward, bridging the distance between them. His hands went to her hair and she blocked him. "Uh-uh. Not the hair. My stylist would kill you."

"I'd like to see her try."

"All look and no play," she said teasingly. "You'll have to wait until after."

A growl ripped from his throat and Reyna tensed. Her body ignored the clear sign of danger and went straight to really fucking turned on. Worse yet, she wasn't wearing any panties.

His hand trailed down her front—over her breasts, down her stomach, and to the short hem of her dress. Her breathing hitched as he slipped his hand underneath the material and up between her thighs. Her core pulsed before he even touched her.

She wanted him.

God, did she want him.

"Look at that," he said. "Open to me."

A finger stroked across her exposed—and now wet—opening. She tilted her head back in ecstasy at the feel of him. Would it be the end of the world to mess her hair up? She could live with that.

"I love knowing when you want me," Beckham said against her ear.

"All the time," she gasped out.

He pressed a finger up inside of her and her body shuddered in response.

Okay, forget the meeting. Maybe they could reschedule. Or show up late. Neither of those things were possible and Gabe had gone to a lot of trouble to get this meeting, but her head was all fuzzy, and dammit, she wanted Becks.

He stroked inside of her once and then twice before removing his hand. She whimpered in frustration.

"Now who has to wait to play until later?"

"So cruel."

"You have no idea, Little One."

Reyna grumbled under her breath and snapped her jacket closed again. "Well, did you get the thing?"

"I have something I'd guess he would want."

"And that *is*?"

Beckham stilled her hands as she was finishing buttoning up her jacket and forced her to look at him. "Don't."

He easily unbuttoned the jacket again before sliding the material off of her shoulders. Reyna's breathing hitched at the movement. A small shiver ran up her body at the chill in the room.

Then Beckham removed a black velvet case from his own jacket and held it before her. She tensed, wondering what wonderful thing Beckham had believed to be a great enough price for their contact. He flicked the clasp at the front, then lifted the lid, revealing a dazzling diamond necklace.

Reyna's hand went to her throat. She'd never seen anything like it. It was absolutely the most beautiful piece of craftsmanship she'd ever seen. Five rows of diamonds created a choker with tiny teardrop diamonds hanging from the last row. Then a V of glittering diamonds festooned the choker with five pear-shaped diamonds hanging off the V, gradually getting larger the closer to the bottom, until the last diamond was roughly the size of a flat golf ball.

"Where did you get this?" she gasped, her fingers hovering an inch away from the exquisite piece.

"It was my first conquest on my way to becoming a lord." Beckham plucked the necklace from the box and gestured for her to turn around. "I always said that it was only fit to be worn by a lady worthy to be at my side." She lifted her hair out of the way.

He gently placed the necklace around her neck, the giant diamond settling right between her breasts. The choker clasped in the back. "And you are my lady, Reyna."

"You make me feel like one."

He placed a soft kiss on a part of her bare shoulder unobstructed by the necklace. Her heart fluttered at his words. She let her hair fall back down to cover the weighted necklace, which was sure to sink her.

"Perfect," Beckham said. He draped her jacket over her shoulders and offered her his arm. "Ready?"

"As I'll ever be."

Chapter Twenty

Beckham escorted Reyna out of the building and they found a limo idling outside. Unease settled in her bones as the reality of what they were about to do hit her. She didn't know who this guy was or what he would want or even if he would answer their questions, but they needed any help they could get.

She hated even more being put in a place where they had to wait and ask for help. She wanted to rush into the action and bang heads together. Figure out how to stop Harrington and just *do* it. Except that hadn't worked last time. It wouldn't work this time either.

She had to outmaneuver Harrington, which meant she had to do things he wouldn't anticipate. Barreling in and attacking him he expected. But her blood match with Beckham was not on his radar. The anti-vamp cult not something he'd ever consider. This new contact totally out of left field.

She could do this.

A driver got out from the front of the limo and came around to open the back door for them. He handed them each a black hood.

Beckham raised an eyebrow. "You expect me to wear this?"

"Not me. But if you want to meet your contact tonight, you won't argue."

Beckham snarled. Reyna put her hand on his arm. The last thing she wanted was for him to go full vamp on this guy. He was just the messenger. They would take it up with their stupid contact later.

"Becks," she whispered.

"We're on a tight schedule," the driver said, and gestured for them to get in the limo.

Reyna slid into the backseat, and after a few tense seconds Beckham followed suit. She took a deep breath, then slid the hood over her head. She shivered as memories of her kidnapping flooded her. The feel of the guy grabbing her arm. Him knocking her out. Blackness taking her over as she was dragged out of Everett's apartment.

"Oh God," she whispered.

Her breathing was uneven. She was pretty sure she was hyperventilating.

Logically this wasn't the same. Not even close to the same. She wasn't being kidnapped. She was willingly moving forward with this. Yet, her brain couldn't process the two things. It couldn't move past the horror and violation.

Beckham's arm swept around her shoulders, and he held both of her hands in his. "Breathe," he whispered. "I'm here this time. No one will take you from me. Not ever again."

"Becks," she gasped.

"I'll kill anyone who touches you. I'll protect you. You're safe."

"I'm safe," she repeated.

She took a strangled breath, and then let it out slowly. She did it a couple more times before she finally believed herself. With Beckham's arms safely around her the panic attack subsided. The residual effects of her PTSD drained out of her.

God, she hated this.

Beckham never released her. He held her the entire drive as they moved through the city and to their contact's headquarters. Even if she could have seen through this hood, the limo windows were tinted and night had fallen. Maybe Beckham would have been able to discern where they were going, but she sure couldn't.

It was forty-five minutes before the limo finally came to a stop. Reyna heard the window separating them from the driver slide down. "You can remove the hoods. We're secure."

They both tore them off. Reyna finally felt like she could breathe again and Beckham still looked pissed at the indignation of it all. She hardly blamed him. He wasn't the sort of man who took orders from others well. This should be interesting.

The driver came around and let them out of the limo. He walked toward elevator doors, which were built into the garage wall. Reyna and Beckham followed. When the doors dinged open, he let them inside first, then pressed a button.

"Have a nice time," he said pleasantly.

Beckham straightened and dropped all emotion from his face in the span of a second. She wasn't as good at that as he was. She'd hardened because of all the pain, but fear wasn't as easy to conceal as she would have liked.

When the elevator opened, a butler waited for them—trim build with dark hair and kind eyes. Her eyes moved beyond him to the entrance of the home. A large winding staircase led up several stories with polished hardwood floors, elaborate rugs, and grand artwork in gilded frames with a crystal chandelier dangling from the ceiling. Just the foyer was opulent beyond measure. She could hardly imagine what lay within the dragon's lair.

"Ah, Miss Reyna Carpenter and Mr. Beckham Anderson," the butler said. "What a pleasure to have you in residence tonight. I am Edgar. May I take your coats?" Reyna swallowed before taking her jacket off and handing it to Edgar, who hung them up in a closet. "Your meeting will be in the library this evening. Would you care for some refreshments?"

"No, thank you," Reyna said.

"Ah, well, I am certain you will want something while you wait." Edgar snapped his fingers. A woman in a black dress and white apron glided into the room. "Prepare a tray for our guests."

"Of course." She curtsied—actually *curtsied*—and then disappeared.

Beckham didn't blink. Reyna couldn't stop blinking.

"This way," Edgar said.

They headed up the enormous staircase to the second floor and turned to the left where giant wooden double doors stood closed. Elaborate whorls were carved into the frame in a design that felt almost alive with little strings of holly vines and berries. Over top of the doors held a bronze sign that read THE HOLLY LIBRARY. She and Beckham exchanged a look at the intricacy. Normal home libraries didn't have names. Who *was* this guy?

"Here we are." Edgar pushed the doors open and they followed into the most spectacular room she had ever seen.

"Oh my God," she barely breathed as she turned in a stunned circle.

"Welcome to The Holly Library," Edgar said with a small smile as if he knew what the weight of this room did to people. "He will be in soon. Make yourself at home and I'll have refreshments brought in."

"Thank you," Beckham said brusquely.

Edgar tipped his head at them before departing.

Beckham frowned. "I don't like this."

"I do," she whispered.

The Holly Library was the most beautiful place she had ever seen in her entire life. Bookshelves lined the walls and stacked high across the room going up as far as the eye could see until a glass opening revealed the moon beyond. While books covered every surface, it was the *vines* themselves that were fascinating. The name of the room made sense now considering holly vines covered the stacks and threaded down amongst the books. She didn't know how it was possible to keep them alive and not harm the books, but they looked well-tended. They looked loved.

As did the books. Tables full of them, half-opened and abandoned. Just more books and more learning and more information trapped in here. Enough for a hundred lifetimes. A thousand lifetimes.

Her mouth watered with the desire to reach out and take a book from the shelf and dig in.

"I want one," she told Beckham with wide eyes.

"I'll get right on that."

Reyna's high heels clicked on the hardwood floor as she walked mesmerized through the room. Her finger landed on a tome and a hiss sounded above her.

Reyna jumped back to see a black cat slink through the shadows. "Hello, friend."

"Careful," Beckham said. "Cats are tempestuous."

"It's not like I'm a bird," Reyna said, reaching her hand out. The cat batted it away and then dashed deeper into the dark. "Well, he can't be that bad."

"What makes you say that?"

"Cats choose their people," Reyna said as it if were obvious.

She should have felt like the dark depths of the library were cold and unwelcoming, but all she really felt was like she could get lost in here for a good long while and never come up for air. It was with great will power that she retreated from the confines of the stacks and returned to the center of the room where a chaise and two chairs were laid out before a large square coffee table. What an incredible place to call home. To get to cozy up in here anytime they wanted. To forget the world and all its troubles in a story. Was there anything greater than losing and finding yourself in the pages of a book?

Her finger trailed along the spine of a book on the opposite table as her mind wandered over the owner. A lover of books. A lover of knowledge. A lover of wealth, also, obviously. What would a man like this, with all his many secrets, be like?

"Good evening," a woman said, appearing at the entrance to the library. She whisked in a tray full of treats—little finger sandwiches, delicate desserts, and piping hot tea. "My name is Isolde. It's a pleasure to have you here. Please, have a seat. No one wants to wait without having a spot of tea."

Reyna took a seat as Isolde settled the tray of treats on the table, then poured both Beckham and Reyna a cup of tea.

"Thank you," Reyna said with a smile.

"Anytime, dear. It's wonderful to have you here. It's not often we have guests."

Guests? She'd been hooded to get here, and she didn't even know their contact's name. They were being pampered and treated with the utmost respect, but Gabe thought this guy was a scary motherfucker. What a strange duality.

Isolde bobbed her head at them before disappearing once more. Reyna reached for the treats on the tray.

"Don't eat that," Beckham said, taking the strawberry macaron from her hand.

"Ugh. Do not deprive me of macarons."

"I'll get you all the macarons you want when we leave. But you never go into an enemy's house and eat or drink."

Reyna sighed. She saw the logic in that. But strawberry macarons.

Beckham glanced at the watch on his wrist as they waited. And waited. No wonder Isolde had brought them something to munch on. Apparently, he liked to keep his *guests* in suspense.

Then suddenly the door to thc library opened once more. Reyna jumped to her feet and Beckham followed at a more resigned, leisurely pace. He was back in control. Ready to take on the world. She was anxious to finally meet this guy.

A soft breath escaped her mouth at her first sight of him. One look at him and it was obvious he was the most beautiful person she had ever seen. Not like the dangerous, scary goodness that Beckham exuded. This man had none of Beckham's bulk or menacing stares or looks. Nothing about Beckham that had made her fall in love with him.

But she could appreciate beauty when it was before her.

He stopped before them with his hands loosely in the pockets of his ten-thousand-dollar suit. He held himself as if he knew no threats in this world. As if he was the top of the food chain. Not a scratch could hurt him.

His hair was brushed back from his face. The black strands almost appeared midnight blue when they caught the light. His cheekbones were chiseled out of marble with a jawline as sharp as a razor blade. But it was his eyes that were the most striking. A dark, stormy gray that seemed to swirl to life when they were turned on her. She stilled as he assessed her, and she couldn't bring herself to utter a single word. Those eyes had known lifetimes.

He was otherworldly. Definitely not human. But no way was he a vampire either.

What is *he?*

"Welcome," he said, his gaze slowly shifting from Reyna to Beckham. "You may call me Graves."

CHAPTER TWENTY-ONE

Graves.

Reyna swallowed. It fit him perfectly. How many people had he put six feet under? If her time with other walking predators was any indication, the answer was many. Many, many, many…

"It's my pleasure to have you here tonight. It was fortunate that I heard your request. I apologize for keeping you waiting," Graves said. "I had other matters to attend to."

Murder or fucking.

There didn't seem to be an in-between for him.

"I see that you didn't partake of my refreshments." His eyes shot to the food and back. "Believe me when I say that if I wanted you dead, poison would hardly be my choice. I prefer something much more macabre."

"Poison is hardly the only possibility," Beckham said.

"I suppose you can never be too careful," Graves responded, his eyes alight with humor at Beckham's offense. He slid his hands out of his pockets to reveal that they were clad in black leather. Why would he need gloves inside?

Beckham crossed his arms. It was written in every line of his body that he wanted this over with. And something seemed to unspool in Graves at Beckham's annoyance. As if he was finally getting started.

"And you," Graves said, as he faced Reyna. "What did you fear from my tea?"

"Too much milk?"

A muscle feathered in his cheek. It was as if he was contemplating smiling.

He nodded his head once at her. "Humans." He turned back to Beckham. "I see why you like this one."

"Standing right here," Reyna said.

Graves arched an eyebrow. "Indeed."

"We've come with payment," Beckham interjected. "Are you willing to answer our questions or not?"

"Ah, straight down to business. Vampires always seem to despise the pleasantries," Graves said as if Beckham's behavior hardly registered on his radar.

"Pleasantries drag out negotiations."

"Are we negotiating?" Graves toyed. That hint of a smile playing at his features again.

"We should start," Beckham said impatiently.

"We didn't come to bother you," Reyna said. She took a step forward between the two men—monsters. "We were told that you had information that we needed about William Harrington. If you can help us, we would appreciate it. So, can you help us?"

"I can," he said.

Graves towered over her. He was eye level with Beckham if not slightly taller. He stepped around her body, his moody gray eyes considering her from every angle as he made a leisurely circle.

She stiffened at his nearness. Why was he looking at her like that? Was he purposely trying to provoke Beckham? Because she was certain at any moment he would come barreling into Graves's side. She didn't dare glance at Beckham, but she could feel his anger unfurling from him like wings.

"And what will you give me for my help?" Graves's voice slithered over her skin, crawling over her until she had to grit her teeth. Graves met her gaze and nodded once. "You have brought me something rather interesting?"

Beckham was steeling himself and his voice had regained its composure when he spoke. "We've brought payment."

"Wonderful." Graves strode away from them and, seemingly at random, lifted a book into his gloved hand. She wondered why he wore them inside. Everything else about him made him seem like a worldly gentleman, but the gloves didn't fit. He flipped to a page near the center and scribbled something in the margins. "Please sign here and here."

He offered the book to Beckham, who asked, "What's this?"

"Confirmation of payment. A receipt, if you will."

"No contract?"

"You will give to me that which I desire of your own free will," Graves said. "I haven't had to force anyone yet."

The way he glanced up at Reyna with that smirk on his lips said that perhaps he was not being entirely truthful. He wasn't forcing anyone, but there was more than pen and paper that was happening here. She didn't know what exactly she was expecting, what it was she was looking at.

"And what will this sign away?"

"You will speak of this to no one," Graves said.

"Fine," Beckham growled, as he vacillated before putting pen to paper. He clearly didn't want to put his signature in Graves's book. To leave behind a record of their presence here. But it didn't seem like Graves would let them off the hook otherwise. So Beckham signed.

"Thank you," Graves said, turning to Reyna. "And you, my dear."

Reyna took the pen in a shaky hand. Beckham's signature was

one of a dozen on the ledger. Not a single name was recognizable. It wasn't as if Harrington had been here and Graves would let them know. She sighed softly and then scribbled her name on the line.

The signature felt heavy. As if she had not just signed with ink but with blood. Like the weight of that signature was more than just her good word.

"Is it the signature that's important?"

Graves tilted his head at her. "No," he said slowly. "Did you feel something?"

She shook her hand out. "Maybe."

It had felt like…magic.

But magic didn't exist.

"Interesting," he said as he flexed his gloves. He looked as if he had more questions and was keen on asking them of Reyna, but then he decided against it. He snapped the book shut with a flourish and tucked it under his arm. "Now payment. You were informed of what I require."

"Yes. I've brought you the diamonds of the Lady Charisma. Before I became a vampire lord of the city, I toppled several other cities along the way. A domino effect, if you will."

"I'm well acquainted with your exploits," Graves said in a crisp, bored tone.

"This was my first conquest. My very first spoil of the war that I started."

"Hmm," Graves murmured. He gestured to Reyna. "And this is the necklace?"

"Yes."

"Gaudy thing."

Beckham bristled. "It's worth a king's ransom."

Graves replaced the book on the table before returning to Reyna's side. He seemed unconcerned with the worth of the diamond necklace or really with Beckham at all. He had his hands back in his pockets and he stood less than a foot from Reyna, staring intently at the jewelry.

"May I?" he asked Reyna.

"I can remove it," Beckham interjected.

"Now, what would be the fun in that?" he muttered under his breath. Then louder for Beckham's benefit. "Lift your hair."

Her eyes found Beckham's as she gently lifted her dark hair off her shoulders and held it to the side. Through his eyes, she could see the torment raging in him. How much he wished they hadn't come here. Neither of them had anticipated someone like Graves. Vampires were used to being the highest rung on the ladder. She didn't like finding out there was something more dangerous out there.

Graves examined the necklace with delicate fondness. Then he slowly, purposefully removed his black leather gloves. Reyna tensed at the deliberateness of the move and inhaled as his hands moved to either side of the diamond choker. The pads of his fingers skimmed the section around her neck, moved to the hollow of her throat, before slowly dragging down the V of the necklace. A finger circling each diamond as he dragged his way to the one dangling between her breasts, stopping just above.

"Yes, I think this will do," Graves said.

His hand moved back up the necklace, and he shifted around to stand behind her. Beckham's chest was rising and falling heavily. His hands were balled into tight fists. She could see that Graves wanted to toy with them, but she didn't understand why.

Then his finger touched her.

She couldn't suppress her gasp. Barely a touch—just his index finger against her shoulder blade drawing a line across her back to the clasp on the choker. And suddenly her cheeks were aflame, her body flushed, her heart beating furiously. Just one touch had made her skin tingle and her knees threatened to buckle.

If the signature had felt like magic, it was nothing compared to this. She had so many questions running through her mind and yet… she could do nothing but stand there.

"Ah," Graves said behind her. "I see."

"What the fuck do you see?" Beckham seethed.

Graves carefully unclasped the necklace and removed it from her neck. He took a step back and finally she was able to breathe regularly again. She dropped her hair down her back, feeling utterly exposed to him. It was as if one touch had bared her soul to him. It was unfathomable, of course. He hadn't *done* anything. But it was as if he had stuck his hand straight through her and rifled through all the locked drawers in her mind. And the only person she was comfortable letting inside was Beckham.

She was starting to wonder if coming here had been a big mistake.

He might be able to help, but the cost felt greater than any necklace.

Graves tossed the priceless jewels next to his book on the table as if it meant nothing to him, then carefully pulled his gloves back on.

"What did you do to me?" Reyna gasped out.

"I took your payment."

"I don't have anything to give."

"True. Material possessions. It is a good thing for your sake that I don't only deal in the material."

She furrowed her brow. "What does *that* mean?"

But a shiver ran through her at the words. Because she *did* sort of understand them. She had felt something different at his touch. As if he had taken something from her. But that had just been metaphor, right?

Graves chanced a glance at her and this time he *did* smile. Perhaps it was supposed to be intimidating, but it softened him slightly. Yes, a villain but it was as if he was letting her in on a secret. "You felt it."

"I…" Her hand went to her throat.

But it was Beckham who interrupted. "Are you going to answer our questions now or do you intend to keep putting your hands on my girlfriend?"

"Girlfriend." Graves frowned, sending his features into shadows. "Such an interesting term you picked."

"The term wasn't the point."

"I thought you'd prefer to go with *blood match.* Or perhaps *soul mate.*"

Reyna's jaw hit the ground. Beckham looked as shaken. How the hell could Graves know that they were blood matched? No one outside of their group at Elle knew that much. It was an incredibly small number of people they would trust with their lives. It wasn't possible unless…he hadn't taken it from *her*.

Now, *she* was seeing things in the shadows. He couldn't *read her mind*.

"How?" she murmured.

Graves waved his gloved hand in the air dismissively. "I suspected. But wasn't certain until I saw you together. It's been a while since I've seen one. They're always so temperamental."

"You've met another match?"

Reyna couldn't believe it. He might know more about what they could do or what they were capable of.

"Here and there. They don't normally last very long."

"Why?" Her eagerness overrode all logic.

"One usually kills the other," Graves said as a matter-of-fact. "Very *Romeo and Juliet* without all the family interference."

"Oh," Reyna whispered.

"Are they always vampire and human?" Beckham asked, clenching his jaw.

"The ones I've met. If they were two humans, they probably wouldn't have the sensory ability for it. It's something with the virus that triggers it."

"Have any of the humans ever been turned?" Reyna whispered as if it were some deep, dark secret.

"Reyna," Beckham snapped, drawing her back to reality.

Graves leaned back against his table and eyed them as if he suddenly understood everything. "You'd like to be a vampire?"

"It's out of the question," Beckham said. "That's not why we're here."

Reyna's mind filled with the ferocity of Brian and how he may never come back from that. With Beckham's help, she didn't think that it would happen to her. But the brutal truth of being turned had very recently been thrown in her face. It made her hesitate.

"Maybe," she finally said.

"This is not why we're here," Beckham repeated to deaf ears.

"Interesting," Graves mused. He tilted his head as he looked between them. "Do you think your abilities would follow with the change?"

Reyna nearly doubled over in shock at the words. It was one thing to feel like Graves had used some sort of unseen *magic* on her. It was another thing entirely for him to know that she and Beckham shared a sort of blood magic.

"What abilities?" Beckham asked.

"Magic," Graves said, waving his fingers at them.

"It's science," Reyna interjected.

"Blood science," Beckham added.

"Science and magic are only separated by a degree," Graves said dryly. "Monsters and men exist at the same time, but science hasn't yet made explanations for us all."

"Monsters?" Reyna asked skeptically.

Graves shot her an amused look. "Vampires, of course."

"Of course," Beckham said.

"So, did other blood matches have abilities?" Reyna asked.

"Oh yes. I can think of all sorts of things you two could accomplish together."

For a price.

Reyna could read it all over him. For more information about that, he'd need more payment. And as much as she wanted to know—she was dying to know—it made her nervous for what *else* he would ask.

She took a step back and reined in her eagerness.

She and Beckham could figure this out together. They could discover the rest of their blood match as a pair. They'd come this far. It was enough to know there were others. That people had gone through before what they were experiencing now. That there was someone else out there who had answers to this. Even if she'd have to pay the price later.

"We want to know about William Harrington," she managed to get out.

"Ah," Graves said. He almost seemed put out that they'd shut the inquiry down. Like he'd *wanted* to discuss magic and monsters, rather than speak of this one vampire currently attempting to destroy the world. "What about Mr. Harrington?"

"We want to kill him," Beckham said tersely.

"He's high on many lists."

"He's at the top of ours."

"What will killing Mr. Harrington do exactly?"

"He's up to something. Something big," Reyna said. "Surely you know about the feeding camps that he's calling housing. He's killing people and ruining lives, and he'll take over the world if he can."

"People go to those camps willingly. In fact, they go to Visage willingly." Graves's eyes bored into hers. "Surely you of all people know this."

"They go willingly because he has created a world in which people need him."

Graves nodded once. "Very smart of him."

"Smart," Reyna deadpanned.

"The strong will always lead the weak," Graves drawled.

"*He* is the weak one," Reyna snapped.

"You mean, you are his weakness." Graves arched an eyebrow. "Correct?"

She stumbled over her words. "I…"

"Enough," Beckham said. "Harrington is a very intelligent man. He knows what he's doing and how to spin things to his advantage. There's no dispute. I was at his right hand doing these exact things for years."

"And now you are no longer," Graves said.

"Correct," Beckham bit out. "However, we know that Harrington is working on something else big. Do you know what it is?"

"I do."

Reyna sucked in a breath. "You know what he's working on?"

Graves turned his gaze back to hers, his irises swirling dangerously. "I know much about William Harrington. He's a man that I keep tabs on for business purposes. I've never much cared if vampires spread like parasites on the surface of the earth," Graves said. "They can lay claim to the world they believe they own. It matters not to me. As petty as human wars."

Reyna saw then the machinations behind that beautiful face. Humans and vampires were ants to him. Moving around and waiting for someone to stomp on their ant hill. He wheedled away his time lording over it all and accomplishing his own obscure goals with none the wiser. A true master.

"Will you help us?" Reyna whispered.

Graves snapped his finger and moved away from the table. "Yes. I think I will."

Reyna breathed a sigh of relief.

"But there's a cost."

"We already paid," Beckham reminded him.

"That gaudy necklace covered as much as I've told you about your blood match anyway." Graves turned from the bookshelf he was inspecting. "We both know it really meant nothing to you."

Beckham balked at the accusation, but there was some sincerity to it. Material possessions mattered little to Beckham. He enjoyed living in luxury, but the objects were always replaceable. The only thing that truly mattered, that he fought for, was her.

"What's the price?" Reyna whispered, fear pricking her.

Graves looked at her from under long black lashes with his devious, wicked, trickster mind at work. For that moment, she wondered if he *had* read her mind and that the thing that was going to come out of his mouth was the one thing she could not give.

"A bite, if you please."

Chapter Twenty-Two

"No," Beckham said.

"Becks," Reyna muttered.

"I'm not going to bite her for your fucked-up pleasure of watching."

Graves turned his palms up and arched his eyebrows. "I haven't witnessed a bite between blood matches. This is *science*, if you prefer."

And Graves didn't care that Beckham was averse to biting her. Beckham had never willingly given in to his lust for her blood. Even while he was recovering, he couldn't bring himself to do it except while they were having sex. That's how much he feared the monster within. That carnal beast that threatened to break free to the surface. To end up in the same position they'd been in when he'd first bitten her. When he hadn't been able to stop.

She couldn't do this to him.

Not here.

Not now.

Not in front of Graves.

"We can't," she whispered.

"Something else," Beckham barked. "Ask for something else."

"Don't bite her, then. Just lose your war and any future with her." Graves stuffed his hands in his pockets. "Your choice."

Beckham moved so fast that he was just a blur. Reyna could hardly process it. One minute he was standing beside her, the next he was holding on to Graves's throat and glaring into his stormy eyes.

"I think I've had enough of you," Beckham snarled. "I should snap your fucking neck or rip out your throat for half of what you've done tonight."

"Becks," she cried. "Stop it!"

Graves didn't even look bothered by the fact that Beckham was attacking him. Reyna had never seen anyone look like that. It was unsettling.

Finally, he lifted his hand, held on to Beckham's wrist, and twisted it. Reyna winced. On a human that move would have snapped his wrist in two. On Beckham, it swatted his hand away as if he were a fly that had irritated Graves.

Beckham reared back in shock.

"Vampires," Graves said with a disdainful sigh. "You are tiresome. As if resorting to violence is always the answer."

Beckham looked as if he wanted to punch Graves in the face, but after that maneuver, he reassessed. Graves could handle a vampire. That was terrifying.

"I'd like to remind you that you came to me," Graves told them, irritation finally settling into his voice. "You offered me something that wasn't valuable enough for the information you requested and then threatened me in my own home." He stared at Beckham with malice on his face. "Now get the fuck out of my house."

Reyna jolted at his tone. Then she dashed forward between Graves and Beckham again before it came to blows. "He's sorry. I'm sorry. This isn't what we expected. You have to understand that we had no idea what to expect here. But we want the information." She placed her hand on Beckham's wrist. "We do."

"You know my price," Graves said. That flicker of amusement returning to his features. As if he had known that he had never been in any trouble here. "Either get on with it or leave. I don't have time for games."

Which was the opposite of true. Graves seemed to only deal in games.

Reyna faced Beckham. His mouth was set in a line of stone. His jaw clenched with barely controlled rage. His eyes, the window to his soul, screamed to unleash.

"Hey," she whispered. She brought her hands up to cup his cheeks. "It's okay. It'll be fine."

He clearly didn't agree with her, but she didn't care. What was one bite for the information they needed to stop Harrington? They'd deal with the consequences later.

"I'm here. I trust you."

"You shouldn't," he barely breathed.

"I do anyway."

Reyna swallowed and then gently pulled her hair back off of her neck. This time she had no necklace to obscure access to her throat. She guided his hands to her hips. His grip was tentative at first, then he seemed to remember the shape of her, sliding his hands up her sides to her shoulders.

Their eyes locked. Warm chocolate meeting the bottomless depths that had infatuated her from the start. She wasn't afraid. This was a pivotal moment for them, and she wanted to be here in the moment. She wanted him to know all the love that was in her heart. How little she feared him.

She took a breath and on release opened up that connection between them. Tapped into the blood match bond that allowed her to feel his presence and linked their emotions. As they linked, she didn't care that Graves was watching or that they had never done this before or about everything else they had to face. There was just her and Beckham.

"It's okay," she said again.

She angled her head to give him better access and held her breath. Somehow this turned her on. Maybe because he'd only ever bitten her while they were having sex. Although, everything about Beckham was a turn-on.

Not once in all the times that she'd been given the vamp venom had she ever gotten addicted. And Harrington had tried. But she was certain she'd been addicted to Beckham and the intensity between them long before he'd bitten her. Nothing else could compare to that. She doubted anything else ever would.

Beckham's lips grazed her neck. He trailed soft kisses up her throat. She stifled a moan and pressed her body into his.

The first prick jolted her. The pain as he pierced the skin of her neck. She shuddered at the feel. Then the venom flooded her system. A natural high from the bite. The fight or flight kicking in and adrenaline speeding through her, waking up everything.

When she'd first felt this, her body had immediately screamed, *Run. Run far far away. This man is going to kill you.*

Now she wanted more. More, more, more. More than she should give. Her body pulsed. Her core was hot. She squeezed her legs together.

Even when he went deeper, dipping into the artery and drinking of her blood, all she felt was desire. Her desire and his desire. Their love and heat and longing and want. So much want. Her blood, her body, her mind, her soul. They were one and the same. He would take it all. She would give it all.

Her fingers curled into the front of his tuxedo. She couldn't hold back her moan this time. She wanted. She needed.

Then she felt him pulling back.

She clamped down on him. "Please," she gasped. "More."

Beckham grasped her hips so hard he was going to leave bruises. Then he wrenched back, holding her at arm's length. Blood ran down his lips and over his chin. Her heart raced, beating a million miles a minute. She felt ravenous.

"More," she repeated.

And dizzy.

"Becks."

And she was floating on clouds.

"Reyna," Beckham said.

"Please."

"I'd kill you."

"What's the worst that could happen?"

Beckham growled low. "Come back to me, love. Come back."

She closed her eyes and felt herself swirling away. The bite shouldn't be this potent. He must have taken a lot to get to this point, and it was more potent with an emotional connection. But she couldn't seem to bring her logical brain around to caring.

Then Beckham's lips were on hers. Hot and enticing and demanding. His tongue tasted of tangy blood. Her blood. She gave in. She'd fuck him right here on this floor. What would be the harm? She wanted him. She wanted everything.

He wanted her too. She could feel it. Sense it. It overwhelmed her, it was so much. So much love and want. Fuck, the control the man had.

"Please," she repeated.

Then she felt something else. Her breath quickened. Her brain fizzled. Her body shook violently under it. And yet she didn't pull back. She didn't release him.

What was happening?

It was as if she pulled more than his emotions. As if he gave her *more*. Gave something she never thought possible to give.

Reyna felt as if she were coming out of dense fog. She hadn't been able to see an inch in front of her face and now Beckham was here. He was here and she could think properly. She felt no pain. She felt none of the normal side effects of the bite. It all vanished on the wind. Leaving her clear and levelheaded and confused as fuck.

Her hand jumped to her neck where deep bite marks should have been. But there was nothing. Not even a scab. Clear, perfect unmarred skin.

"What…what did you do?" she gasped.

Beckham looked as shocked as she did.

"Beautiful," Graves said. He took a deep breath as if he were inhaling the very essence of what he'd watched. "Wonderfully done."

They snapped their heads to the side to glare at Graves. Reyna had forgotten he was even in the room.

"What the hell happened?" Reyna asked.

"He healed you," Graves said.

"How?" Reyna couldn't fathom it.

"I transferred my vampire healing properties to you," Beckham said. "I could feel it happening."

"Indeed." Graves sketched a shape around them. "Your magic—sorry, *science*—was very clearly on display. It glowed red."

"Red?" Reyna asked in confusion.

"The power has a shape, a color, a scent to those who are attuned to it," Graves admitted. "You two are red. The power swirling around you when he healed you."

"Did you know that would happen?" Beckham demanded.

"I told you that I had not seen it done."

"But you knew it could happen."

He shrugged. "I know many things. I did not know the magic would be red. That is worth much." Graves rubbed his gloved hands together, his eyes alight with new knowledge. As if *that* was what sustained him and not the games he had wielded them through since they arrived. "Even better than I imagined."

"Red," Beckham muttered. His gaze shifted back to Reyna. "Incredible."

"Payment rendered," Reyna said a little breathlessly, her hand still on her throat. "Are you satisfied?"

"I'd watch it again for *science*," Graves said in an almost teasing voice. "Though I suppose you are not willing subjects."

"No," Beckham barked.

"So that will do."

Then he walked away.

"Where's he going?" Reyna asked.

Beckham shrugged. She could see that despite the amount of blood she'd just given him, he was flagging.

And so was she. She clutched onto Beckham's sleeve as her accelerated pulse started to recover. She couldn't believe that he'd healed her. She had never even considered that a possibility. All the things that he could have done when she reached out for him, and he'd made her whole again.

Maybe that was the point.

They were two halves of the same whole.

It made sense that if her blood could heal him, his vampire powers could heal her. Her blood match.

"I love you," she whispered.

He kissed her forehead. "I love you too."

Graves was gone long enough for them to worry. They lost the sound of his leather oxfords as he'd disappeared into the stacks.

Reyna was happy for the reprieve. She needed a couple minutes to recuperate after what had happened. By the time he'd finally come back, Reyna stood on her own two feet again. She felt good. Better than good. As if part of what had made Beckham so indestructible had been transferred to her.

"You required information about Mr. Harrington and what he's working on," Graves said. "William Harrington is building an army. As a matter of fact, he already has a sizeable one."

Reyna stammered over her shock.

Beckham simply sighed. "So it begins again."

"An army of vampires?" Reyna asked.

Graves nodded. "He's been turning people, setting a few of his vampires loose to feed the fear around the cogitare anemia. He's housing them in his new facilities and using the humans who enter as a feeding ground."

Reyna sighed. That much they'd figured out on their own. Well, everything except the army. "What are his plans with his army?"

"What are armies used for but destruction?" Graves asked.

"He's planning to take over," Beckham guessed.

"My sources point all the way up. Depose the human president and put a vampire politician in his place that he can use as a puppet. You can imagine where this goes. The facilities here in the city are the first wave. He intends to set them up all over the country. Humans are nothing but a food source. Vampires rule aboveground."

"Fuck," Reyna whispered.

"We suspected much of this. We've paid for more than this," Beckham said, taking a threatening step forward. "What's his next move? Where's he holed up? How do we get to him?"

Graves held up a hand. "I wasn't finished."

Reyna tensed. If an army and trying to take over the world wasn't the bad part…

Graves removed a small glass vial from the inside of his suit coat. Liquid sloshed around the inside. "*This* is what he's testing in the housing facilities."

Reyna stopped breathing. "What is it?"

"An antidote."

Chapter Twenty-Three

"Oh no," Reyna whispered.

The first time that Reyna had ever heard Harrington discuss the possibility of an antidote she had been sick to her stomach. The idea that vampires could go back to drinking from any human that they wanted regardless of blood type was a horrifying concept. The blood type cure kept them in check. Even if, as she had later learned, it wasn't as potent for every vampire, it still helped to drink the right match. But that would all go away with an antidote.

Reyna had stalled that research the day that she'd saved Jodie from Visage. A doctor had said that she was critical to the development of the antidote and Reyna had broken her out. They must have been further along or had used someone else's blood in Jodie's place. Now Harrington was using it in his feeding camps to build up his army.

She was going to be sick. Reyna covered her mouth and turned away.

"How does it work?" Beckham asked.

"One vial per human. It's injected into the blood system, essentially nulling the blood type and creating a universal host," Graves explained. "It lasts the length of time it typically takes to replenish the blood."

Reyna saw all of their potential plans unravel with the appearance of that one tiny vial. Jodie wasn't important. Reyna wasn't important. There was no reason that Harrington wouldn't drain her and dump her. No reason at all. He had no weakness.

Graves passed the small vial into Beckham's hand. "Because I'm feeling generous."

Beckham hastily pocketed it.

"And as for where Harrington is holed up, I'd start trusting your enemies."

"What does that mean?" Beckham asked.

"Don't you mean which one?" Reyna drawled in annoyance. She hated that he was being purposely obscure. They had *a lot* of enemies. He could narrow down the list for them.

"Start at the top of your list and work your way down," Graves said, and slid his hands back into his pockets.

Beckham glanced at Reyna. "Roland?"

"Penny," she spat.

Graves gestured with his gloved hand as if agreeing with them. "Now, it's been my pleasure to host you for the evening. I will have Edgar escort you out. I do hope that we meet again."

Reyna shivered at the words as he disappeared through the massive double doors.

Reyna met Beckham's gaze and lifted one shoulder. What the hell had they walked into?

Edgar entered the room almost immediately. "This way, please."

They walked in a daze back through Graves's unbelievable house, retrieved their coats, and were hastily pushed into the elevator. It spit them out onto the bottom floor in record time. The driver gave them back their hoods and they tugged them on once they were safely seated in the limo.

As soon as they left Graves's house, she had the distinct feeling like she'd dreamed the entire thing. It couldn't possibly have been real. It felt too unbelievable to even contemplate. And she didn't know what the fuck he was. Because he made it quite clear that he wasn't a vampire or a human. He didn't seem to like either group much. Whatever he was, it was powerful. That was for damn sure.

"What do you think he is?" she finally whispered into the silent limo.

"A bloody bastard."

"Well, yes. That much is obvious. But he's powerful."

Beckham's hand landed on her thigh. "I don't give a fuck what he is." His hand moved up higher and higher. "Or care to hear you talk about how powerful he is."

"Jealous?" she breathed.

"Infuriated."

He pressed her knee out wider and then wider still until she was spread open for him. His fingers continued up to the apex of her thighs, parting her lips and slicking through her wetness. She'd been hot all evening. On fire since the moment Beckham had seen her in her dress, and everything had only intensified through the night. Her body reacted instantly to his touch as he swirled a finger around her clit until she was quivering beneath his skilled hands.

Heedless of consequences, Beckham tugged both hoods off of their heads and slammed their lips together. There was nothing gentle in his touch. Just claiming her body as his own. Reminding her exactly where she belonged.

The tension had been palpable when they'd been in Graves's mansion. He'd tested their limits. Pushed them beyond what they had even known they were capable. He might be manipulative, arrogant, and conceited, but he'd played them like a fiddle. And now they both wanted to erase the memory with the feel of each other's body.

Beckham rocked her flat against the seat, splaying her out long. He hastily unbuckled his tuxedo pants and took his cock in his hand. A hand in her hair, lips melded together, bodies a furnace every place they touched, then his cock pressing against her waiting opening.

She gasped into his mouth. "Yes."

He thrust to the hilt, burying himself inside of her. She threw her head back as he filled her to the brim. She'd been on the edge all night. God, she needed this. Needed him.

"Mine," Beckham growled as he pulled out and pumped into her again.

She could sense that his anger about Graves had boiled over. This was a fervor that both of them couldn't seem to find release from. They belonged to the other and they needed that belonging right now.

"I'm yours," she repeated over and over again until her climax hit her like a tidal wave.

She cried out in the backseat of the limo as his own climax followed violently. As if his very roar of ecstasy could shake this world. And together they would remake it.

• • •

The rest of the ride was tense and silent.

Reyna had thought that, once they got that out of their system, things would go back to normal. But an uncomfortable strain echoed between them like a discordant song.

She'd never felt out of sync with Beckham. Even the days when she was terrified of him, where she had no idea what was going on in that limitless mind, even when she'd believed that he loved Penelope. They might have been on a different octave, but it was still in tune.

This stretched and expanded immeasurably.

All she had to do was reach out and touch his emotions to see what he was feeling. But she couldn't. No, wouldn't. Exposing herself to anything but his love was asking to push herself over the edge. He wouldn't be pleased and she couldn't blame him.

The limo finally came to a stop back at the pickup location. The driver opened the back door. "After you."

Beckham slid out of the backseat. Reyna took a deep breath and followed him.

"Thank you so much for coming. Hope to see you again soon," the driver said pleasantly.

Beckham inclined his head at the driver. Reyna threw him a half smile. She didn't have to tap into Beckham's emotions to know that seeing Graves again in this lifetime would be too soon. Reyna seconded that.

She followed Beckham through the double doors of the building. He'd already phoned Gerard to come get them when they'd gotten close. Gabe was waiting inside, pacing back and forth on the tiled floor like a caged animal. He'd changed into all-black attire. His red hair stark against the rest of his clothes. His jaw set.

His head snapped up at their approach. "About fucking time."

"Hey, Gabe," she said.

"It's one o'clock in the fucking morning. You were gone for-fucking-ever."

Reyna chewed her lip. She hadn't even realized how long they'd been at Graves's. Time had seemed to slow and stretch.

"Well, we're here now," Beckham said.

His eyes jumped from one to the other. "So, how'd it go? Did you get the information? What was it like? What was *he* like?"

Without even a single word, Beckham punched Gabe in the face. He fell back a few steps, spiraling his arms to try to stay on his feet. Then his hand went to his jaw as he cursed violently.

"Beckham!" Reyna cried, reaching out for Gabe.

"What the fuck?" Gabe cried at almost the same.

But Beckham wasn't even looking at them. He was far off somewhere else. His face cold and hard as stone. The mask she'd seen for so long before. Then he walked past them both.

"I just asked a fucking question," he grumbled. "What's with him?"

Reyna sighed. "It was tense and it's been a long night. But he shouldn't have taken that out on you."

"You think?"

Reyna's eyes were still following Beckham out the door to where Gerard waited. "We should probably get back."

"What happened that has him so pissed off?"

"We got what we were looking for," Reyna said on a sigh. "But there was a price. One neither of us wanted to pay."

"Must have really rankled him." Gabe followed her toward the door. "I'm dying to know though, what's the contact's name? Everyone is so secretive."

Reyna opened her mouth.

Graves.

She coughed. Nothing came out. She tried again.

Graves.

Gabe raised an eyebrow. "You didn't find out?"

She swallowed, shocked by the fact that she couldn't make herself say his name. She could think it. She'd been able to say it in his presence—hell, he'd commanded her call him Graves. But now she couldn't say it out loud. Had she said it out loud since leaving his house?

"He told us," she muttered. "But I can't say it."

Gabe's eyes widened. "What the fuck does that mean?"

"I don't know."

"Okay. What did he look like? Maybe I've seen him around."

Reyna opened her mouth to describe that midnight blue black hair. The stormy gray eyes. The immense height and expensive suit and the sheer magnitude of his beauty. And nothing.

She shrugged her shoulders. "I can't say."

"What the fuck, Reyna? Why not?"

"I don't know."

Gabe rubbed his jaw once before slipping the back door open for her. "What kind of guy can keep you from saying his name or what he looks like? Was he not human?"

Reyna chewed her lip. *No. Definitely not human.*

"Fuck me. You really can't say," Gabe said in shock.

"I really can't."

Reyna slid into the backseat of the van, carefully watching Beckham in the passenger seat. Beckham never looked back at her, and she felt almost as if he had a block on his emotions. She didn't dare try to discover them through their bond, but his anger was so evident. His shoulders tensed, his jaw set, his fingers typing rapidly on his phone in a way that felt all too familiar. And not in the best way. She didn't like that he was hurting or burying deep down whatever he was feeling. It was a defense mechanism, but it didn't make her feel any better.

It was a long and silent ride back to the mansion. The windows might as well have frozen over with Beckham's frigidity the whole way.

Once the van came to a stop, before she could say something or reach for Beckham, he darted out of the car. Beckham's circle met him in the garage, and they loped off without a backward glance. Reyna breathed out in frustration as he disappeared into the darkness. Gabe dropped a hand on her shoulder in solidarity and then they walked back to the house. They entered through the kitchen and Reyna made an ice pack for his face, which was already swelling an eye shut.

"Sorry again about this," Reyna said.

"Occupational hazard. Should probably check in with Meghan."

"Yeah. I'm going to look in on Brian."

"Be careful, okay?"

Reyna nodded and then headed up the stairs. A light was on at the end of the hall. The emotional roller coaster of the last couple hours hit her like a punch to the gut. She was exhausted. She wanted to clean all this makeup off and sleep for at least the next twenty-four hours. Deal with her brother and Graves and a vampire army and the fucking antidote another day.

But she didn't.

She walked down the hall to her own personal hell and pushed the door open slightly. She startled at the sight of Genevieve reading from Dante's *Inferno.* Brian was asleep. His chin resting against his chest as he remained chained to the chair.

"May not be the best choice," Reyna whispered. "Descending into Hell."

"Poignant," Genevieve said softly.

"How's he doing?"

Genevieve considered. "About the same. I believe he's more lucid with those he doesn't know. He's full of guilt and seeing your face reminds him of his humanity."

"Shouldn't we want to remind him of that?"

"Guilt can crush a person. It's best to start with people who understand. Let him come to some semblance of acceptance first."

Reyna nodded. "Thank you for looking after him. I truly appreciate it."

Genevieve got a far-off look on her face. "We've all been there before. It's nice to bring them around before they do worse. A chance most of us weren't offered."

"He's a fighter. He can come back from this."

"I hope so."

"You'll be here all night?"

"Yes. Until Katarina comes for a reprieve. But I don't mind."

"Again, thank you. I wish I could be there for him, but at least someone is."

"Get some rest, Reyna. Your brother just needs time."

Reyna took one last wistful look at Brian before finding her bed and promptly passing out.

Chapter Twenty-Four

Beckham didn't return that night.

Or the one after that.

A full week later and she hadn't seen a trace of him. No depressions next to her in bed. None of the O negative blood gone from the fridge. None of his musky scent. She couldn't even sense him, which meant he had to be at least six miles away from the mansion. Whatever he was doing, he wasn't nearby and he clearly didn't want to see her.

The whole thing was utterly frustrating. She hadn't done anything wrong, and she wanted him to come home to talk this out with her. But he wouldn't.

His inner circle returned routinely to help with Brian. Katarina had brought the antidote to Washington the next morning. When Reyna had asked about Beckham, she'd been tight-lipped and disappeared. Their loyalty ran deep. None of them would talk about it. Or where he was. Reyna respected that even if she despised it.

"He's going to come back, Rey," Jodie said as they walked the grounds.

The snow was melting, making the ground sloshy and uncomfortable. But it was better than being stuck in the house while Washington worked on replicating the antidote or hearing Brian's screams from upstairs or feeling the emptiness of Beckham's absence.

"I know. I don't worry about that. He's sending the circle back to take care of Brian. It's just me he doesn't want to see."

"Well, y'all went through some serious shit. That contact dude is scary," Jodie said. "I mean, you still can't say his name, right?"

"No. Well, I can say it to myself when no one else is around. I suspect I could say it to Beckham."

"Yeah, don't do that."

Reyna managed a smile. "Not high on the priority list."

"Maybe it's not even that he's jealous. Maybe it's all the feeling mojo and him healing you. He doesn't do well with emotions, right?"

"Yeah. Maybe."

"Washington went apeshit over that. I mean, fuck, girl, healing is a big deal."

"It is. I know. Beckham is feeling things for the first time. I know that must be intense for him. I wish he'd share it *with* me instead of running away."

"If that's even what he's doing," Jodie said.

Reyna shot her a look full of exasperation. "Anyway, I love him. He'll come back. It'll be fine. What's not fine is that there's a fucking blood antidote out there and Harrington is using it to feed his vampire army."

"Well, at least that takes me out of the hot seat. Washington was getting nowhere with my blood. So, it's on the back burner while he works through that vial you gave him."

"That's something at least."

"I wish we were having some luck with June. We've hit another dead end," Jodie said with a sigh. "It's so dire that Zoya and I have even been checking morgue registries. We haven't found anything there either. It looks like she's another missing person in Harrington's war."

"Ugh. I'm sorry, Jodie."

She frowned. "I didn't have much hope, but I wish I knew either way."

"Me too."

"Reyna!" Tye called from the back door of the house. He called a second time before she and Jodie made it to him.

"What's up? Did something happen?"

"It's your brother."

"Brian? Is he okay?"

"Sorry. Drew. It's your other brother, on the phone."

"Oh." She deflated slightly. "Okay. Yeah. I'll take it." She took the phone from Tye. "Hey, Drew. How is everything?"

"Everett left."

"Left?"

"Yeah," Drew said with a sigh. "He goes out sometimes to check on stuff and bring in supplies. But he'd been gone for over twenty-four hours and when we searched his room, we found his gun missing, a bunch of tech—microphones, cameras, that sort of thing—had been scattered all over, and he left a note."

Reyna grit her teeth. "What does it say?"

"He said to tell you that he was going to prove you wrong."

"Oh fuck," she whispered. She'd goaded him the last time they were together, when she had been grieving what had happened to Brian. She hadn't actually believed he would do something about it.

"I sent some people out to look for him, but everyone came back empty. I'm not too keen to risk perfectly good people on someone like him."

Reyna closed her eyes and pinched the bridge of her nose. What would Everett do? If she were in his shoes, where would she go with a gun and some tech? Her eyes snapped open.

"He's gone to do something really stupid," she whispered. "I told him to prove that I could trust him. I have a feeling it has something to do with underground Visage or with the feeding camps. Something to prove that he's on our side."

"Shit."

"I'm going to try to get in contact with him."

"I'll see if there's anything else in his stuff." Drew paused for a long moment. "How's Brian?"

Reyna winced. "He's…alive."

"That good, huh?" Drew asked. Reyna just sighed. What else could she say? "Okay, well, I'll hold down the fort here. Let me know if you hear anything or if anything changes."

Reyna cursed under her breath and tossed the phone across the table. "There's no point. Whatever the fuck Everett has done, he's done on his terms."

"Do you think he'll double-cross us?" Meghan asked. "He knows where the rest of Elle is. Does he know where we are?"

"I don't think so. He only knows about the cult HQ." Reyna grimaced. "I don't think he'll double-cross us, but then again, he's a spy."

"Fuck," Tye muttered.

Reyna stared around the room at the looks of confusion and uncertainty on their faces. "We should research another place to move people. I don't want to take a chance that anyone could be in jeopardy."

Jodie grinned. "I'll research with Katarina."

Katarina, who was the only member of Beckham's circle present, grinned back. "Come on, babe."

Reyna's eyes widened at their playful banter. Perhaps she'd missed a thing or two while she'd been busy worrying about Beckham.

"Oh," Reyna whispered, her breath catching in her throat. She could feel him. She could finally feel him. "Becks."

Everyone else glanced around as if expecting to see him standing in the entrance. But of course he wasn't there. He was still miles away, moving at vampire speed back to the mansion. She shivered. She hadn't realized how much she'd missed being able to feel his presence until it was gone. She hadn't even been actively trying to sense him and still it was like a radar that she couldn't turn off.

"Uh, Reyna?" Gabe muttered.

She stood. "I have to take care of this. Let me know how the research goes."

"Ugh, why are we always on research duty?"

"She did her part," Meghan reminded him. "You sent her into that place to get the antidote info."

"Yeah. Yeah. Still should have gone myself."

"And what could you give him that would have interested him?"

Reyna could only distantly hear them arguing, their definition of foreplay. Her mind was on Beckham and how close he was. She disappeared out the door, through the kitchen, and outside. By the time she walked down the few stairs, he was there.

She swallowed and took him in. Last she'd seen him, he'd been in his tuxedo and pissed beyond measure. Now he was in a solid black suit with a characteristic blood-red tie. He didn't look like he'd run here from more than six miles away. He looked refreshed but wary.

"Hey," she said. "You're back."

"Not for long."

"Oh?"

"I came to tell you I was going into the city."

Reyna's eyebrow rose. "And where were you before?"

He stared at her as if to say, *That's my own fucking business.*

"Fine. Don't tell me. I don't even know why you're here right now, then. Why tell me you're going into the city but not tell me where the hell you've been the last week?"

"I'm going to see Penny."

Reyna ground her teeth together and clenched her fists. "Are. You. Out. Of. Your. Mind?"

A muscle tensed in his jaw.

"Just talk to me. Tell me what you're thinking. Why the hell are you going see her? She double-crossed us. She almost got you killed. She tried to murder me."

"She might have answers."

"To what?" Reyna demanded.

"About Harrington."

"And you're, what, going to seduce them out of her?"

Beckham didn't even dignify that with a response.

"Becks," she said, exasperated.

"I came to tell you. I knew you wouldn't want to hear after I'd already gone. Now I'm going."

"Wait." Reyna snagged his arm. He jerked as if she'd burned him. She pulled her hand back in surprise. He'd never reacted that way to her touch before. Never pulled away from her like that.

Reyna straightened her spine. She wouldn't let him go that easily. And if he thought that she would, he was wrong. She didn't know why he even showed up like this if he was going to freak at one touch.

"I'm going with you."

"No."

"Oh, this isn't a negotiation," she spat.

"You're right. It's not." Beckham stalked across the field to the garage. He could have easily outpaced her, but he walked at an almost human speed.

Reyna trailed after him, jogging to keep up. "You disappear for a week because you're jealous or whatever and then think *I'll* somehow be okay with you going to see your backstabbing ex? Hell, no. This is not happening."

Beckham tugged the door to the garage open, ignoring her.

"Is this really about Graves?"

He growled low in the back of his throat. Yeah, his name was a bit of a trigger.

"I'm not going to stop talking about this. I don't even know why you're jealous. Everything we did was to get information. It's unfair that you're acting like this toward me, then going to see Penny."

"Reyna," he snapped.

"What?" she yelled back.

"Get in the car."

Reyna gnashed her teeth together. All she wanted to do was argue with him until he told her what the fuck was going on with him. But when had that ever worked with Beckham? When he put up a wall, he made sure even a wrecking ball couldn't fucking tear it down.

So she got in the car.

Chapter Twenty-Five

Asking Beckham to fill her in on the plan was about as fruitful as her stopping a bullet with her teeth. In fact, he wasn't particularly loquacious the entire trip. Not that he ever was. But even the air felt bereft between them.

They traded out their SUV for a shiny black sports car once they got into the city. Reyna didn't even have it in her to make a quip about it being inconspicuous before Beckham punched the pedal to the floor. Reyna quickly forgot her irritation as wonder took over. Just like the first time she'd ridden with him on his motorcycle, the sensation of flying resonated with her. The sheer power of the vehicle beneath her made her come alive.

"Where are we meeting her?" Reyna tried again.

Beckham took the next turn at top speed, the back wheels sliding across the road as if they were on ice. Reyna squeezed her seat to keep from slamming into the door. Questions seemed to be a no-go.

The sun had finally set by the time they swung into an underground parking garage. Literally swung. Beckham parked the car next to an elevator and sprinted around to her side to open the door. She stood on unsteady feet.

"Should we be worried about the cameras?" Reyna asked. "I can't imagine that Harrington isn't trying to track you or her."

"Took care of it."

"Of course you did," she mumbled. "You've already been here?"

In response, he gestured for her to head to the elevator. He must have spent his time away scoping this place out and possibly dismantling the cameras and security system. Making sure that everything was as safe as possible.

Reyna and Beckham stepped into the elevator, and Beckham pressed a button for one of the floors near the top.

"So are we going in with guns blazing?"

"Guns are pointless."

"Uh, right. I shot Penelope in the heart, and it put her ass on the ground."

Beckham's head snapped to her. "You shot her in the heart?"

Reyna grinned. "Yeah, I did, and I'd do it again if I had to."

"It won't come to that."

Reyna sure as hell hoped it did. Well, mostly she'd feel better if she was packing as she walked into this unknown situation.

The doors opened and Reyna saw a row of doors all marked with the floor number and a letter. Apartments. They must be going to Penelope's place. Reyna frowned, wondering which one belonged to her. She was certain that someone like Penelope Sky had a swank apartment. Even before she'd become the mayor, she'd lived a privileged and entitled life that Reyna had never been able to fathom.

"Stairs," Beckham ordered.

Reyna groaned. Her favorite.

There were five more flights of stairs to the top, which ended with a locked door. As she was well aware with Beckham's residence, the main way in and out was through the elevator. She wouldn't have even known if there had been stairs out of his place.

Beckham produced a key and it turned easily in the hole. Before he opened the door, he faced her. "Do exactly as I say and don't be seen or heard."

"Uh, you want me to just stand inside?"

Beckham placed a phone in her hand. "Record what you can."

"Won't she know I'm nearby?"

"She's not expecting there to be a human. I will keep her distracted."

Then he slipped through the door without another word.

Distracted. Great.

Reyna let the door slip closed silently behind her. Beckham moved down a hallway and then into an office space. He positioned her so she had a clear view of the living room, but she was in enough shadow that she wasn't visible.

Beckham pointed his finger at the ground as if to say, *Stay here.* She nodded her head in understanding. He gently tipped her chin up with his fist, his eyes penetrating deep into her soul. Then he was gone.

What the hell did *that* mean? After how he'd been acting, why was he being tender with her? The man wasn't warm to begin with. And considering he'd been a frozen iceberg since leaving Graves's place, she hadn't been expecting anything like that.

That man.

Reyna flipped the phone Beckham had given her over in her hand, pulled up the record feature, and waited.

She only had to wait a few minutes before Beckham entered and took a seat in an overstuffed armchair. He sprawled out, completely at ease in the place. Her mind drifted off to all the reasons he'd been here in the past. She truly hated to think about the fact that he and Penny had been together. Whether it was pretend or not, he'd drank her blood and had sex with her. Those things had happened in this apartment. And now he was here. Looking pretty damn comfortable. Her stomach turned.

Penelope entered the room wearing a sky-blue silk robe that was nearly sheer in the dim lighting. Reyna chewed on her lip to keep her disgust from erupting out of her and clicked the damn red button.

"I really didn't think you'd come," Penelope said. She held a glass full of amber liquid in her delicate hand. Faux delicacy now that she'd been turned.

Beckham shrugged a shoulder.

Penelope fidgeted. "Want a drink?"

"You know what I like."

Penelope grinned like a pleased little kitty cat and strode to a bar in her mile-high heels. She poured Beckham two knuckles' worth of whiskey and handed it to him. He took a slow sip before setting it down. So much for not eating or drinking from the enemy.

"I'm so happy to see you," Penelope said. "When you said you were coming…"

"You didn't tell anyone?"

"Of course not. I wouldn't do that. I wanted to see you and make sure you were okay. After you woke up at that morgue…" Penelope shuddered. "I've been a wreck ever since."

Yeah, and Penelope had helped put him there.

Reyna closed her eyes against the image of Beckham's head snapping to the side and him slumping to the ground. It was and always would be the most traumatic experience of her life.

Penelope continued when Beckham didn't respond. "But now you look so good. I've really missed you. It's been so hard doing all of this alone."

"Doing what alone?" he asked.

"Living this double life."

Beckham shifted forward. "I thought you ended that."

"Are you kidding? Of course not," she gushed. "I still want the same thing you do."

"And what is that?"

"Equality."

Reyna almost snorted. She was pretty certain that Penelope wanted far from the same thing as Beckham. Let alone equality between vampires and humans. She'd been made into a vampire as payment for turning Reyna in. Her priorities were seriously skewed.

Penny sank in the chair next to him. Her robe fell open and revealed inch after inch of perfectly smooth, long lean legs. "You have to believe me when I say that I'm still on your side. And I'm so sorry about what happened. I know I could never take that back, but it was never my intention for you to get harmed or for anyone to get hurt. I still want to see vampires and humans live and work together. It's even more important to me now that I'm a vampire."

"Really?" he asked, somehow managing to keep the incredulity from his voice.

She wouldn't have been able to. She leaned against the wall and waited to hear more of the bullshit Penny was spitting.

"Absolutely. Elle has been so scattered after Harrington destroyed the headquarters. God, I still can't even think about what happened to Sydney."

Beckham swirled his drink in his hand and pretended not to look interested. "Sydney?"

Reyna swallowed, terrified to hear the news. Oh God. No, no, not Sydney.

"Fuck, you probably haven't heard," Penelope said. She stood and walked away from him as if she couldn't bear to break the news to him. "She's dead."

No.

Reyna took a few deep breaths in and let them out. They always knew it was a possibility, but she still tried to slow her racing heart, and to stop the tears threatening to escape.

"In the fires?" Beckham asked. As always, completely unaffected by death.

"No. I guess they sent in a SWAT team to break the doors down to bomb the place. Sydney went to meet them, giving Elle members enough time to escape. She tried to stop the attackers, but they gunned her down until she couldn't move and then snapped her neck." Penny sighed. Her voice got really soft. "Harrington had a video and made me watch it."

Reyna put her hand over her mouth to keep back the choked sob. She hated to admit that she'd always held out some hope that Sydney would come charging out of the ether and save the day. That she had been waiting for her moment of glory. She was the indestructible leader of Elle. The voice. The original mastermind. It was impossible to think that she was gone. That she'd been gone for weeks, and no one even knew.

For a moment, the connection between her and Beckham opened up like a pinprick in the night. She wanted to reach for it, but a rush of feeling hit her head on. Calm. Ease. Comfort. Her heart rate slowed. The tears dried up. She could make it through this. With his touch on her heart, she could make it through.

Her entire body shuddered with the warmth of his embrace. As if he were right there holding her, calming her. Keeping Penelope from noticing that she was standing nearby.

The connection between them was a balm and then gone. She breathed out a soft breath and then released it.

"Sounds like his style," Beckham said passively.

"It was awful," she whispered. "And then I didn't know who to contact. All the comm lines were down. I couldn't reach anyone. Where have you been?"

"Around," he said evasively.

"Just around? That's it? I told you Sydney's dead and I've been trying to reach you or the rebellion and your response is *around*?"

"You almost got me killed, Penelope. What did you expect?"

"I know," she whispered, going suddenly still. Then Reyna saw her shoulders slump and start to shake. Oh dear God, she was crying. "That wasn't supposed to happen. I never would have jeopardized you. I thought we'd be together. That's what Harrington said. He used me, Beckham. And he's been trying to use me ever since."

"I know."

Penelope swiped under her eyes. "I'm sorry. Really, I can't say this enough. Tell me what to do. Tell me how to make this up to you."

"Do you think you can make it up to me?" Beckham asked. He stood and moved across the room with the purpose of a predator. She could see the anger in the set of his shoulders. She was sure that Penelope didn't miss it.

Penelope crossed the room to him, placing her hand gently on his arm. Her voice was low and husky when she said, "I want to try."

Reyna held her breath and she watched the tension visibly leave Beckham's shoulders. But his eyes weren't on Penelope. They were on Reyna. They were staring her down in the darkness. As if preparing her for what was to come. She didn't like that look one bit.

"I know you, Penny," Beckham said. He faced a distraught Penelope.

"Can we move forward? Figure out who we are from here?" She looked up at him from under her lashes with a coy smile on her face.

"There's nowhere to move but forward."

Penelope placed her hand on his chest, looked up at him hopefully, and parted her lips. Reyna felt a dragon crawling out of her chest about to breathe fire. Fuck this recording shit. She couldn't get through this. Beckham was doing this to get information, but fuck. He didn't *need* to do this.

She was about to take a step forward when he walked out of Penelope's touch. He returned to his chair and took another sip of his drink. "So if you're still living this double life, then you probably have information about Harrington."

"I don't want to talk about him. I want to talk about us."

Beckham didn't say anything for a minute and then his voice was low, "Has he hurt you?"

"Threatened," she said. "I'm fine. Roland deals with the brunt of it and I avoid that creep as much as I can."

"That's a smart move."

"Yeah. I stopped counting how many Permanents he's killed. He keeps Sophie for the sex and gets a second one for fun."

"That sounds like Roland," Beckham said bitterly. "And he's with Harrington? Do you know where they are?"

"Ugh, Beckham, I don't know. I try to stay out of the crossfire. That's an easy way to get shot." She spat the last word as if the very thought of getting shot was a trigger. "Let's talk about something else. Oh, I know." She clapped her hands together twice. "Do you want a treat?"

Before Beckham could answer, Reyna heard footsteps approaching from the direction they had entered. Reyna slipped deeper into the shadows of the office and angled her camera to follow the person. It was a man, probably a couple years younger than Reyna with pale skin and blond hair. He was pretty and distinguished in black slacks and an open-collar shirt.

He stepped into the room. "You called?"

Penelope giggled. "Beckham, this is my Permanent, Lance."

Beckham's face was passive, but rage simmered under the surface. "You bought into the system?"

"As if I had a choice," Penelope said. "Anyway, he's O negative like us. You can have a taste if you like."

"I'm not hungry," Beckham said casually.

"I don't mind," Lance said.

Beckham held his hand up before Lance could step toward him. The boy was smart enough not to push the subject.

"Don't be a spoilsport, Beckham," Penelope said.

"Miss Sky?" Lance said.

"What is it?"

"I wish to be polite to your guests. Should we offer some to the girl in your office as well?"

Chapter Twenty-Six

Shit, shit, shit.

He'd seen her. There was nowhere to go and nothing to do about this. She was totally fucking screwed. There was no way she could outrun a vampire. The only thing she could do was face what was about to happen.

She took a deep breath and exited the office, holding the phone close to her leg as it continued to record. Beckham had said stay in place, but they didn't have a contingency plan for Penelope realizing that she was there. And by the look on Penelope's face, she wasn't too pleased to see her. Considering the last time they'd been together Reyna had shot her, she didn't blame her. There was no love lost on her part either.

"Hey, Penny," Reyna said with confidence she didn't feel.

Anytime she'd been around really pissed-off vampires, things hadn't gone her way.

"You brought *her*?" Penelope asked, glaring at Beckham.

He released a breath. Decision made. "Yes. She's mine. So step away from her."

His stance shifted into predatory and he moved in a circle around Penelope, analyzing her like the threat she most definitely was.

"She's *yours,*" Penelope spat. "I cannot believe I fell for your bullshit. You came here under false pretenses."

"As if you have no ulterior motives."

"Right now I'm thinking about having my first kill," she snapped at him.

"If you touch her, it will be the last thing you do."

"And just think you'd die in that hideous robe," Reyna said with an unapologetic shrug.

Penelope's eyes were fire. "God, I hate you."

"Feeling's mutual."

"I was going to have Harrington kill you once you turned yourself in, but no, I'd rather do it myself."

Penelope rushed Reyna in a fit of anger, jealousy, and fierce rage. Reyna launched away from Penelope. At the same time, Beckham lunged toward her as he fully opened himself up to her. She felt everything all at once. An overwhelming melee of self-hatred. So much that she could hardly tell her fear from his fear, and her anger from his.

Beckham pushed her across the room. One minute she was standing in front of Penelope, about to get her head ripped off. Then the next she was standing across the room, out of harm's way.

Her head spun. Her legs felt like jelly. The entire fiber of her being was unsettled and discombobulated.

What the hell just happened?

She put a hand to her ears to try to stop the ringing as she regained her balance. She was so busy trying to stand up straight, she didn't see Lance until he was nearly on top of her.

"Stay away from Penelope!" Lance bellowed as he held a lamp over his head.

Reyna ducked with a screech. "What the fuck? She was trying to hurt me!"

"You're human," Lance said with wide eyes.

"No shit."

"You just…you didn't…"

Reyna ignored him and found Beckham circling Penelope. She couldn't believe he hadn't already ended this. It was as easy as subduing her and getting out. And by the way Penelope had talked about Reyna turning herself in, now would be the time.

"Becks, it's a trap. Let's go," Reyna called.

"You just realized that?" Penelope muttered.

"What did he offer you?" Beckham spat.

"You, of course."

"In exchange for Reyna, again?"

She shrugged. "Good deal to me. Even if you left now, you wouldn't make it out of the building."

"And you were going to turn me in?"

"Why not?" she asked with a maniacal laugh. "You never chose me. You always chose her. You both deserve to suffer."

"You're a monster," Reyna cried.

"Don't worry," Penelope told Beckham in a soft, sinister tone. "After I break you, we'll have a great life."

Beckham laughed. He actually laughed. "You could never break me."

"Would have been fun trying," she said.

"Becks, we have to go," Reyna said again, gesturing to the door.

Beckham moved as quick as lightning. Penelope tried to veer away from him, but Beckham had years and years of training on her as a vampire. She was no match for him.

In seconds, he had Penelope's back pressed into his chest. His hands on either side of her head.

"You were better than this," he told her.

"Beckham," she said, fear finally breaking through everything.

"Now you're just a loose end."

She didn't even have time to call out before Beckham twisted her head at an unnatural angle and let her lifeless body fall heavy to the carpet.

Reyna gasped as the phone slipped from her fingers. Beckham killed her. He killed her. Lance fell to his knees at Penelope's feet and began sobbing uncontrollably. His cries were loud and obnoxious, and at the same time she understood them. Death was the real monster.

Beckham didn't give Penelope another glance before lifting Reyna into his arms. "Hold on to me." Her body awoke at his nearness and she curled into him, wrapping her arms around his neck. "Head in." She did as he said and then he raced away.

Away from the living room with a dead woman and a forever broken blood escort.

She had to close her eyes as Beckham moved at superhuman speed. She couldn't concentrate on her own thoughts, let alone process what just happened. One minute he'd been seducing information out of Penny and the next she was dead at his feet. It had been so easy. So unbelievably easy.

Beckham set Reyna down inside the entrance to Penny's building, keeping her body obscured by the large metal door. "Don't move."

She couldn't argue. She could barely function after the way his speed muddled her. She latched onto the door handle and tried to remain upright.

Beckham glanced out the door to assess the situation and then slipped out. Reyna peeked through the opening and saw Beckham moving like a blur as he attacked Visage's men. An elbow to the chin, legs swept out from under, a rifle snapped in half, the butt of another gun smashed against a temple. Over and over every member of the team Harrington must have sent was taken down by Beckham's martial prowess.

If he'd been human, he'd already be dead. Bullets pierced his skin, lodging in his body. He never even wavered.

Soon his chest rose and fell rapidly as he stood over a plane of bodies. They lay like carrion awaiting the vultures. Beckham the unstoppable beast, riddled with bullets, and master over all. Nothing could touch him.

Reyna slowly inched the door open. "Are…are they dead?"

He shook his head sharply once to the right. His eyes were lost in the distance. A force raged through him that she couldn't possibly harness.

She chewed on her lip and waited for him to get under control. She could tell he needed a minute. Finally, his bottomless eyes turned to her and he extended a hand.

She moved toward him. The lamb stepping into the wolf's circle, expecting the slaughter.

"You fear me?"

"Never," she whispered.

Beckham snarled as if her answer infuriated him instead of soothed him. But he didn't give her another chance to respond. He scooped her back up and raced away from the scene. She tucked her chin in again and tried to ignore her brain rattling in her skull.

She couldn't even believe he still moved at top speeds. But a helicopter was beating overhead. Spotlights closed in around them. Other Visage vampires would be drawn to their trail. He couldn't stop. They couldn't stop. If caught, they were both dead and they knew it.

Just when she thought she might throw up from the sheer vertigo, Beckham dropped out of vampire speed and ducked into an alcove. The streetlights were smashed to pieces at their feet and the darkness enveloped them.

A helicopter circled nearby. They were so close. If they moved the spotlight one street over, she and Beckham would be seen. Beckham moved deeper into the alley, becoming one with the shadows.

She tightened her grip on him as fear pricked at her every nerve ending. She could feel his distress and the amount of pain he was in and thought she'd be sick. How could he endure it? He might think he was immortal, but eventually he'd have to stop. He was losing blood at too quick a rate. It oozed out of multiple wounds. Hot and red, pouring down his chest and arms. She was sticky with it.

"Becks, we have to get you help," she whispered.

"I just…need…to get the bullets…out."

"Where can we go?"

He shook his head. "The safe houses aren't safe."

"Can we get to Drew?"

Beckham clenched his jaw. "Too far away. I can't..."

He didn't finish the sentence. He wouldn't make it. Fuck.

"Okay. Okay. Shit."

"We'll have to find a place." Another helicopter shifted closer. Beckham moved deeper down the alley. "We'll be caught otherwise."

Then he sprinted again even though they didn't have time for this. They moved through the shadows, avoiding the police presence waiting for him to trip up. He stopped at what looked like an abandoned convenience store and barreled through the door. He finally put Reyna down on her feet.

"This will do," Beckham groaned.

Beckham leaned his weight against the door and pulled the shade down. Then he yanked the keypad from the entrance by the door. This wasn't the sort of place she'd think would have a security system, but better safe than sorry.

"Bathroom," he grunted.

They headed down the main aisle with a meager scrapping of various candy bars and an assortment of toiletries. The tile floors were rusted. The overhead light was missing the covering and one of the bulbs was burned out. This was the last place she ever thought she'd see Beckham Anderson.

They made it to the bathroom and she sighed. It wasn't warehouse gas station disgusting, but it certainly wasn't going to be sanitary for what they needed to do. Oh well.

"Sit," she commanded, pushing his ass down on the toilet seat.

The fact that he didn't argue showed her how much pain he was in. He unsheathed a wicked-looking blade and offered it to her. She looked at it in horror. Oh God, she would have to do this. Why didn't they have Meghan with them? A fucking nurse would help right about now.

"I should get ice or alcohol or...or something."

His eyes were dark as they stared back at her. "Just do it."

Reyna took the knife out of his hand. She had to do this. There was no other option. Reyna sliced down the front of his button-up and peeled away the material. Beckham grit his teeth every time it pulled on the wounds, but she didn't stop until he was shirtless. Six bullets were lodged in his chest. One had gone straight through his shoulder. Two more were in his arms. How the hell he'd held her with bullets in his arms was beyond her. She hadn't even gotten to his legs.

Beckham wasn't human. He could sustain much more pain than the average person, but he couldn't go on with this.

The first dig of the blade into his skin made her queasy. He didn't even flinch as she pushed the knife deeper into the wound. Lodging the point behind the bullet, she jerked it out of the hole. Blood gushed from the open wound, now no longer obscured by a foreign object.

A soft moan escaped Beckham as pain lanced him. Reyna rushed for a paper towel to staunch the bleeding, but Beckham stopped her.

"Finish it."

"You'll bleed out."

"I'll heal," he said.

Reyna gritted her teeth and moved on to the next bullet. She had to find a place within herself that didn't feel Beckham's pain, that didn't react to his short gasps, that didn't recognize the blood rushing down his perfect chest. She was calm, numb, empty. She had to be. Her emotions were always too close to the surface, and if she looked at it any other way she would break down at the sight of his suffering. It was easier to be present enough to remove the bullets but otherwise be absent.

She'd never been to this place before. Her courage had always sprung from her inherent hotheadedness. But now she needed steely inner strength.

All that mattered was Beckham. Everything else slipped away. She'd deal with her feelings about what she was doing later.

Her hands were steady as she dislodged a bullet from his arm. It had embedded into the bone and digging it out was a feat. It came free with a squelch and the bullet tinged on the ground. That was the last of the upper half. She stared down at his muscular legs, solid like tree trunks. Those beautiful legs with holes in them. She let the thought drift away and started in on his thighs.

Dig in, cut, pull, blood.

Again and again.

Her hands were coated with sticky red blood. Her body covered in a thin sheen of sweat. Her breathing even and measured. She didn't risk speaking.

The last bullet came out with a small pop. That was it. That was the end. Everything rushed back to her all at once. A rattling sound penetrated her sharp inhale. Reyna dropped the knife. It clattered noisily on the tile floor. The room looked like a fucking murder scene. Blood coated her clothes, coated Beckham's body. It was all over the floor and the walls and even the ceiling.

Reyna stood on shaky knees and moved to the sink. She turned the water to the hottest setting and ran her now trembling hands under it. She felt the burn but all she saw was blood. She washed her hands and forearms until they were raw, and still all she saw was blood red.

She faced him. "We need to clean you up."

A gurgling sound came from Beckham's throat. That was when she noticed what her brain hadn't been able to process before.

He wasn't healing.

Chapter Twenty-Seven

"Beckham!" Reyna cried. She lifted his chin and stared into his eyes. "What's happening? Why aren't you healing?"

"Slow. It's…slow."

"Why? Has this happened before?"

"When I healed you."

Reyna's heart was torn asunder. Using his healing abilities to save her made him weaker. It changed something in his vampire processes that slowed things down. Made him more human.

"You didn't heal me tonight," she whispered in fear.

He shook his head once and then coughed as pain shot through him. What the hell could have happened that would make him equally as weak as when he healed her at Graves's place?

Then it hit her.

"Oh my God," she whispered. "I moved fast. Like vampire super speed fast. Penelope's escort even thought I was a vampire." Reyna's hand went to her mouth. "You gave me your speed." He nodded.

"You need to heal. Drink from me."

She held her wrist out to him. He glanced at it. She watched him swallow once harshly. His fangs exposed over his bottom lip. She expected him to refuse, for them to argue about it.

Instead, he grabbed her wrist, sank in those fangs, and drank deeply.

"Oh," she gasped.

The blood flowed from her body into his. And like winter snows thawed into spring streams, the wounds began knitting together. Blood stopped flowing. It still coated his chest but was already drying against him. He looked strong, sturdy, and not at all like he was in danger of bleeding out.

Then the endorphins hit her from the bite. A freight train straight to her heart. The immediate rush a tidal wave as flight or fight kicked in. Even as she felt it, all she wanted to do was curl up into Beckham's lap and never leave. Never see him like that again. One death was enough for her for a lifetime.

Abruptly, Beckham wrenched back. Her blood lingered on his lips, dripped down his fangs. His black eyes were ringed with light as power radiated from his very being. Their blood sang as like responded to like.

Despite the carnage around them, all she could think was that she wanted to fuck him right here in this dirty convenience store bathroom. Life or death situations sure put things in perspective.

"You could have died," she accused.

"Unlikely."

She narrowed her eyes. "Your wounds weren't healing."

"They would have."

"Why do you have to argue with me?"

"I wouldn't have died. Something as simple as a bullet couldn't take me down. The sooner you realize that the better."

Reyna crossed her arms over her chest. "Well, since you're doing so well, why don't we talk about you ghosting me? Then you protect me with your life against Penelope. Say I'm *yours*."

"You are."

"I am," she said with a sigh. "I really am. I always have been and I always will be. But I cannot function with you leaving me out of the loop or taking your anger out on me with your silence."

So of course he was silent.

"I didn't like seeing you with *her* tonight," Reyna said, unable to speak Penny's name right after Becks killed her. "I hated it. But I'm not running away from you because I'm jealous and uncomfortable."

Beckham's nostrils flared at the insinuation. He stood, his immense height eclipsing the tiny bathroom. Suddenly he was towering over her, taking back the upper hand. Still, she refused to back down just because he was half-naked, covered in blood, and looked like a scary fucking vampire.

But when his eyes caught hers, something in them softened.

"When I'm with you, I feel. Intensely," Beckham explained. Reyna smiled at that. "The only time I have ever felt that intensely was when I killed."

Her smile dropped.

"Even when I was human, I didn't have this same passion. I was empty. You have more humanity in your pinky finger than I've ever had in my whole body. It's why I have protected you and coddled you and tried to keep you alive. I never wanted to see that light go out. I never wanted you to become the ruthless killer that I was. To lose the optimism that only someone so young and human could ever feel."

Tears pricked at Reyna's eyes, and she tried to tamp them down.

"It's hard to explain without telling you my whole past. My parents were young and came from nothing and I had my eyes on the stars. I left everything behind to become something great, but instead of going to space I ended up in business. I found that I was good at building things, destroying things." He looked at his bloody hands. "At dismantling the world and having people rally behind me as I did it. Except my parents. They never saw value in me. And in the end they were right."

"Becks," she whispered.

"No, Reyna, I became a vampire by choice. I thought it was the next great bid for power. The next step in taking over the world, which I did efficiently for years afterward." He met her gaze head-on. "And when I became a vampire, I wanted to bring pain to those who hurt me, who refused to believe in me. So how did I repay my parents? I tortured Bronwyn. She was young and innocent, and I was a sadistic vampire. I took everything from her that she loved, put her through immense physical pain, and shattered her mind. Then I fed her madness with brutality, taught her the ways of war, shaping her into a proper soldier. When she could take no more, right before her whole spirit would be broken, I turned her. Then I tested her loyalty by unleashing her on our parents. I thought their misery would be worse if she did it. I loaded the gun and pulled the trigger. She was the bullet that snuffed out their existence. She passed. I made her my own unfeeling second-in-command and gave her an army to feast on." He tilted his chin up. "And I enjoyed it. Reveled in it. It was all I was ever good at."

"That's not true," Reyna whispered.

"Oh no. It's as true as could be. Until you. You made me want to be better, but the truth is that I am not better."

Something cracked within Beckham. A chasm that was more than sixty years in the making. He was broken. He'd finally broken. He couldn't keep going with the crushing weight of his kills on his shoulders. And there were so many.

"You are," Reyna said. She put a gentle hand on his arm. "You are better, Becks. The fact that you feel this way shows that you're a different man."

"Did you not see what I saw tonight? I killed Penelope with my own two hands." He looked down at them covered in blood. "And I felt nothing."

"She was going to hurt me. Or you. And she had turned us in to Harrington. It was a trap, Becks."

"It could have been you," he said in a barely audible voice.

"Me?" she whispered. "You'd never hurt me."

"I would!" he roared. It exploded out of him as if he'd been holding on to it for so long. "I have."

"No. You have always been there and protected me and saved me. Even when I didn't want to be saved."

"Reyna, the only thing that I am is a killer. The night we saw that fucking bastard, I'd never *felt* so strongly in my life. All I could think the entire time driving back to the house was how to control my rage. I was so deep in it, I could've hurt you."

Reyna stared at him, stunned. "But I felt your emotions that night. I didn't feel anything like that."

"It was after the healing," he explained. "I was jealous and pissed, but I worried that if I stayed with all those emotions roiling through me, the only outlet I had was the only thing I was good at. So I left. I left to keep you alive."

"Oh Becks," she whispered, stepping into his space again. She put her hand on his cheek. "All this time I thought that you were mad at me. But really you were protecting me. Again."

"I'm not a hero."

"You're so very wrong."

Then she pressed her lips against his. His hands landed on her waist tentatively and grasped her with vigor as the kiss deepened. Beckham was broken. He feared himself so much that he'd disappeared to protect her. And he couldn't even see it. He couldn't even fathom that he was the good guy in this. So shattered by his past that a moment of vulnerability wrecked him and made him think he would revert into the only thing he believed he was capable of.

"You're not just a killer," she whispered against his lips. "You have subdued the monster and the reason you feel like this is because you are embracing the man."

He responded by picking her up, sliding her legs around his waist, and putting her ass down on the sink. Her hands went to his pants, jerking free the remaining tattered material. His cock lengthening in her hand.

"We are connected by more than our blood. We are united through our souls. You would sooner die than harm me. I believe that beyond words."

"I never doubted us. Just me."

Reyna sighed at the words. "No more doubts."

He stripped her from the waist down and plunged deep inside her body. Their souls connecting as all barriers disintegrated around them. Together they embraced the moon and landed among the stars.

Killer, savior, monster, man.

None of it mattered as long as he was hers.

• • •

After the sounds of the last foot soldiers disappeared from around the convenience store and Beckham had fully returned to health, they slipped outside and hoofed it back to the SUV. After Beckham checked it for a tracer, they left the city far behind.

Beckham threaded their fingers together. The stress of the evening evaporated. She leaned her head on his shoulder and closed her eyes. She listened to the rhythm of his heart and forgot the rest of the world. She'd deal with it tomorrow. Right now, she wanted this ounce of solace.

It was after midnight when they finally made it back. Her eyes were drooping and sleep was calling out to her. Had it only been a few hours ago that she'd gotten the call about Everett? When Beckham had returned and she'd convinced him to let her go with him to see Penny? Every day felt like a lifetime.

Beckham parked the SUV and they moved together into the kitchen. The light was on and Genevieve was humming to herself as she busied herself about the stove.

"Hey," Reyna said.

"Reyna."

"Who's with Brian?"

"Philippé took over for a while. I can go up there to check on him if you'd like."

Reyna nodded. "Please."

Beckham pressed a kiss into her hair as Genevieve disappeared. "Your heart breaks for him."

"He never wanted this. I don't know how he'll live with himself."

"The strong survive."

Reyna was surprised to find that her friends and much of Beckham's inner circle were congregated in the dining room. She and Beckham exchanged a glance.

"What's going on?" Reyna asked.

Meghan's eyes were wide with terror. They darted between Reyna and Beckham and back to the computer in front of her. Jodie chewed on her bottom lip. Katarina had been playing with Jodie's hair. Gabe had his arms crossed over his chest. Zoya was seated before the computer. Gerard was across the room, motionless as always, reading a book.

Meghan threw her arms around Reyna. "You scared the shit out of us."

"I did?"

"You're all over the news. The entire city was in an uproar looking for you."

"For me?" she asked.

"And Beckham," Jodie clarified.

"They're looking for the mayor's murderer," Meghan added. "We saw the video."

"Video?" Reyna asked, glancing at Beckham.

"You don't want to see it," Meghan told her. "It shows her neck twisted. You two running out of the room. It's being played on repeat despite the graphic material."

Gabe's eyes hit the ceiling. "Want to share with the class what happened before or after you, I don't know, lost your shirt?"

"No," Beckham said. "Any other questions?"

The room was silent. Not because no one had questions, but because Beckham was shirtless, still partially covered in blood, and prowling like an animal.

Doors burst open across the room. "I have it," Washington cried.

Reyna whipped around. She'd hadn't noticed that he wasn't among the rest of the crowd. He'd been locked up in his laboratory so long that sometimes it was easy to forget he was even there.

"Have what?" she asked.

He held up a tube of gold liquid and stared at it with a look in his eyes said that he'd just changed the world. What was to come next would raze to the ground everything they'd ever known. A cataclysmic event beyond which mere mortals could hardly comprehend.

"Golden Blood," Washington whispered.

"Come again?" Gabe said.

"What exactly is Golden Blood?" Jodie chimed in. "It looks like something I would not want to drink."

"The more I thought about it. The more I knew. The more you told me," he said to Reyna and Beckham, "the more I thought, how could two perfectly matched people possess such talents? How could the mixing of vampire and human blood like this heal? Or sense? Or produce such evocative shared emotions?"

Reyna shrugged. She had no answer to that. She'd just been rolling with it.

"How could he make *you* a little more vampire?" Washington mused, lost to his own epiphany. "How could she make *you* a little more human?"

Reyna's hand went to her mouth as she thought back to their time in the bathroom. How for just a moment Beckham *was* more human.

The stunned silence in the room only echoed her belief.

"I think I've done it…"

He passed Reyna the gold liquid, his newly deemed Golden Blood. "A cure for vampirism."

CHAPTER TWENTY-EIGHT

"A cure?" Beckham asked skeptically.

"That's not possible," Meghan whispered.

Everyone else stared at the golden liquid, stunned. Even Gabe didn't have a witty remark. The room was silent and shocked.

"I assure you it's quite possible," Washington said.

"And you discovered this in the last month?" Reyna asked. "I mean don't you need more time than that to make sure it works?"

"The last month?" Washington stared at her in confusion. "Oh heavens, no. I've been working on this for the better part of the last two centuries. But it all clicked when I saw how a blood match and the healing properties found in your blood reacted. It was a next logical conclusion to assume that you could heal more than just each other."

"But testing?" she pressed.

"Ah. Well, I've tested it on every kind of vampire blood I had on file here. When combined in perfect conditions, the virus that causes the disease was forced into paralysis and eventually killed. Essentially Golden Blood works as white blood cells attacking the foreign properties in the body. In this instance: vampirism."

Washington hastily took back the small tube from Reyna. "Though, it hasn't been tested on a vampire yet."

Reyna's eyes darted around the room. It was only Beckham who didn't shrink back from the prospect of having Golden Blood tested on him.

"Well, let's not all jump up at once," Gabe said sarcastically.

"It's untested," Katarina said. "Who knows what it could do to us? I'll take my chances as a vampire before that."

"We have to test it," Beckham insisted. "Think of the possibilities."

Washington's eyes lit up. "Imagine the number of people we could save. The number of lives we could change."

Beckham shot him an incredulous look. "Think of the weapon it could be."

Washington's face fell. "This isn't biological warfare."

"Isn't it?"

"No. Not everything created has to be a weapon."

"Fortunately for us the inventor doesn't have the proclivity to use it that way."

"We don't even know if it works," Reyna said.

"It works," Washington insisted.

"What we need is someone to test it on," Gerard spoke up from the corner. He gently placed a bookmark into his romance novel. "I'm not volunteering, but it'd be easy enough to find a vampire nearby to experiment on."

"Absolutely not," Meghan said.

"It is the most efficient option," Zoya added.

"That's unethical. It goes against all medical practice." Meghan's head snapped to Washington. "You can't do that."

"I agree with Meghan. I won't force someone," Washington said.

"For fuck's sake," Gabe said. "We have a couple of vamps here. One of you should step up."

Every vampire in the room glared at him. He hastily held up his hands and backed down from that notion.

"There's only one option," Gerard said. "We'll go now."

He nodded at Beckham before moving at super vamp speed out of the house. Katarina and Zoya followed close behind. Only Beckham remained.

"You're not going to let them do this, are you?" Reyna asked.

He stared at her. Fuck, he would let this happen. It made her sick to even consider it.

"Becks," she whispered.

"It's been a long night, Reyna. You should clean up and rest."

"Don't patronize me."

"In war, there are no rules."

"No. In war, we decide what rules to break. We decide how much of our humanity we will have left. We decide."

"Then you would rather choose to do nothing?" he asked. Not an ounce of offense or blame in his words. He was truly curious. In every world he'd ever lived, this was his reality. His life was a never-ending war of his own choosing, where rules applied to someone else and might was right.

"Not nothing. But we've only known about this for a few minutes. We can't expect there to be one answer."

"Find me another solution, then."

He affectionately brushed her hair back and then disappeared. Reyna cursed softly under her breath. The rest of her ramshackle team of Elle members stared wide-eyed at her.

"You heard the man. Anyone know another solution?"

"I hate to say it, but, this seems like the only answer," Gabe said, getting a good scowl from Meghan. "We have to test it. There's an army of vampires out there somewhere who want to take us down and rogue vampires going mad with an incurable disease. Would you rather have a weapon to stop them or not?"

"I would, but we could find volunteers. There has to be a better way to find someone willing to be tested on. So start looking," Reyna said, and strode to a computer.

She wouldn't believe there was no other option unless she had to. And she really fucking didn't want to have to.

• • •

Reyna jolted awake. She stared blearily around her and realized she'd fallen asleep at her computer. The screen was blank. She'd accomplished nothing. Great.

She rubbed her eyes to try to clear the haze of the evening. It was late. When she glanced at the giant clock in the corner, she realized it was just past six in the morning.

Jodie was passed out on the couch in the corner. Gabe, Meghan, and Tye had long ago gone to bed, by the looks of things.

Another string of curses came from the entranceway. Reyna stood and stretched her aching limbs. When she walked out of the dining room, she found Gerard and Zoya restraining a blond woman. She appeared to be in her late twenties. Tall, trim, otherworldly beautiful with blue eyes that nearly glowed. Reyna watched in horror as the blonde snapped her fangs at Gerard. He dismissed her as if she were nothing. And to him she probably was.

"What's going on?" Reyna croaked. She cleared her throat. "Who's this?"

Gerard shot her an impassive glance. "You asked for a vampire. I brought you a vampire."

"I didn't ask for anything."

"Irrelevant."

"What the hell is going on here?" the blond woman asked.

"I won't be a part of this," Reyna said, ignoring the woman.

"Then don't," Gerard said.

He muscled his way past her as Katarina and Philippé entered, holding an unconscious man between them. He looked to be in his forties in a battered button-up and slacks. Unlike the screaming blonde, he looked as if he'd come out of a gutter. Dirty and disheveled.

"Another one?" she whispered.

Katarina tipped her head at Reyna and smiled as she pushed past her. "Morning!"

Beckham appeared then. Coming out of the early morning light in a fresh three-piece suit. Not a trace of his near-death experience on him.

"Little One," he said with a smile as he approached.

"What are you doing with these people?"

"They're vampires. My circle found them. Do you have another solution?"

"Becks, please. This is *wrong*."

"I know," he said.

"If you know, then stop this."

"What's going on?" came a voice from behind her. It was Jodie. She glanced between Reyna and Beckham and Katarina's disappearing back. "You found someone to experiment on?"

"Beckham is going to put a stop to this," Reyna said.

"It's us or them. And none of my men are going to volunteer for something like this."

"So instead you're going to force people to do it against their will?" Jodie asked, her voice panicked.

She stalked toward them, stomping her feet with each step. Gabe, Meghan, and Tye were standing at the top of the stairs, staring down at them. Even Genevieve peeked her head out.

"I was taken at the age of twelve and experimented on by men who believed that this was ethical or just didn't fucking care. They wanted my blood and they didn't care what the fuck it did to me. If you do this, how are we any better than Visage?" Jodie asked with fire in every word.

"We aren't," Reyna said. "We do not need this cure to win. We can be better than them."

"I would keep you innocent of this if I could," Beckham said. "But sometimes we have to think like our enemies to defeat them."

Jodie reared back and slapped Beckham across the face. His head didn't move an inch. She wrung out her hand like a dirty dish towel as she yelped in pain. Reyna's jaw dropped.

Beckham took a step forward, like he wanted to say something, but thought better of it. Then he lifted his gaze over Jodie's head. Reyna could see the monster warring within him. How before he would have simply ended all obstacles.

"I can't…I can't let you do it," Jodie said, choking on unshed tears. "Innocents should not be the casualty of war."

"Beckham," Reyna said softly. "Please."

His gaze found hers and she could see him hesitate. How easy it would be to do this. How easy it would be to force people to do what he wanted.

But he had broken down to her in that bathroom after their escape. He had laid himself bare. He was not the same person who had been the prodigy nor the vampire sadist. He was something different. Something more. She knew he could be.

"Let them go," Beckham said.

"What?" Katarina asked.

"You heard me."

Philippé grunted and pulled the woman backward out of the house. Gerard shot his boss a confused look before following. As if his circle had never known him to show mercy. As if the thought of him showing mercy was abhorrent to them.

"Thank you," Reyna whispered.

He nodded. His gaze swept to Jodie. "Only volunteers."

Tears tracked down her cheeks and she swiped at them. "That's right. That's the right thing to do."

"The right thing to do," he said under his breath.

She wanted to open herself to him. To feel what he was feeling in that moment, but she wondered if he even knew. If all of this was so new as to be befuddling to who he was as a person. A crisis of character in fact. He'd changed when he came to Elle, but at his heart, he had still been the brutal overlord who got things done when it was necessary. This was something different altogether. And she loved it even more for it.

"I'm going to..." He gestured as his men and then disappeared.

Jodie fell into Meghan's arms as she continued to cry.

Reyna was glad for the change of heart. But she did wonder if they would lose the war because of this.

A few months ago, she wouldn't have even stopped to think about this, but now she had to be a leader. She had to win this war. And they had drawn a line in the sand for what they would endure. She needed a new way to find volunteers and they needed it quick. Or getting the vial in the first place would be for nothing.

Reyna pushed past Tye and Gabe as she went up the stairs. She should go back to Beckham's room and pass out. She hadn't gotten enough sleep and her emotions felt as if they'd gone through a blender, but that felt too accepting. As if she could just stay up a little longer then she could figure out this problem.

Her feet carried her the opposite direction until she was standing outside of Brian's room. Reyna took a deep breath and then entered.

Genevieve had ceased reading her book and was looking down at the words absentmindedly. Brian stared directly at Reyna. He was lucid, sharp, intelligent. It was clear that this much time feeding had helped. Yet he still appeared ominous. Not quite approachable. It was eerie.

"Reyna, now might not be the best time," Genevieve muttered.

"I want to speak to my brother. Alone."

"I said I didn't want to see you," Brian snarled.

"Doesn't look like I care what you want right now."

Brian snarled but Reyna held her ground. What the hell could he do to her? He was chained to that chair.

"Five minutes. I'll come back if I hear anything out of the ordinary," Genevieve said. She looked once more at Brian. "Behave."

He flashed his fangs at her in warning. She chuckled in response and then closed the door behind her.

Reyna grabbed Genevieve's abandoned chair and moved it so it faced backward across from Brian with enough distance to make her feel safe. She sat down and placed her arms on the back of the chair.

"Hey," she said.

"Leave."

"No."

"You're obstructing my recovery."

"Bullshit. That's what you are. You're bullshit."

"Get the fuck out of here," Brian snarled, pulling against his chains.

"Tell me what happened and I'll leave."

A low growl came out of him, but she was too numb about what was going on downstairs to care about his warning.

"I said tell me what happened," she repeated. "Or I'm going to bring Drew and Laura here to see you."

"No," he snapped.

"I know you want to see them. That you're feeling guilty about the devastation." She closed her eyes to stop the nausea that rose in her, thinking back on those scenes. "I saw it. I know. But I'm pretty much learning that we all have casualties to this war. And what happened to you was against your will. You were another experiment, another weapon in Harrington's arsenal."

"Don't say his name."

"Harrington? Yeah, I'm not too happy with him either. Remember when he kidnapped me? That wasn't great."

Brian's chest heaved up and down, but his eyes were on the ground. "He tortured me."

"I know," she whispered.

"He captured me that night, brought me to his facilities, stripped us naked, and tortured us near to death. He killed Xavier in front of us. He did anything you can imagine and anything you can't, to get information out of us."

Reyna swallowed. Poor Xavier. He'd been one of the few vampires of Elle that Reyna had known. Quiet but dutiful.

"Then he turned you?" Reyna guessed softly.

"Almost. Drained us near to dying, over and over again, then kept us alive, and then did it again. He did it all without the bites so that we never had a single feeling of euphoria, only pain. A few people died. A few people…killed themselves."

Reyna closed her eyes against the images that assaulted her.

"Then he turned me. Me and one other—Andrew. I don't know what happened to him. We were taken into different rooms and starved. I remember little of that time, only when I was unleashed on the safe house and you found me. Beckham stopped me." Brian released a harsh breath. As if finally telling his story had loosened something in him. He stared down at the floor as he said, "I heard you talking downstairs."

Reyna froze.

"A cure for vampirism."

"It's untested." She couldn't let that happen. Not when she still had never brought Laura or Drew back to see him. "What if something went wrong, Brian? I can't let you do it."

"I'm volunteering. You wanted a volunteer." He met her eyes. "Well, here I am. You don't get to make these choices for me."

"Please," she whispered.

"This is what I want." Something clicked into place at that. Brian sat up straighter. His movements became more fluid. Some of the madness left his face. "I'd rather die than spend another moment as a vampire."

Chapter Twenty-Nine

"Tell me about the side effects again," Reyna said anxiously. She paced back and forth in front of Washington's table, where he was removing another dose of Golden Blood. She couldn't believe this was happening. That Brian, her Brian, was going to take this experimental cure.

"Reyna," Washington said with a sigh, "I have already informed you that I do not know what could happen to Brian. I have no way of determining what could go wrong."

"Guesses?" she pushed.

"That is not how medicine works."

"Well, we're about to throw my brother under the proverbial bus. Give me something?"

"So that you can worry?" Washington set the tube down and faced her again. "If you persist in badgering me, I'll have you escorted out of my laboratory. Brian volunteered for this operation. That's what you wanted—a volunteer. It would be imprudent to reject the opportunity now."

"Fine. Fine," Reyna grumbled. Except she desperately wanted to reject the opportunity.

Reyna tried to sit and wait out the process as Washington added Golden Blood to a syringe. The needle made her mouth dry. It wasn't even for her, and it made her want to run in the other direction. She shuddered and hastily glanced away as Brian was escorted in.

It was the first time he'd been unchained and out of that room. His eyes took in everything like a sponge soaking up water. Reyna could see that his vampire abilities had manifested just in the way that he moved. Most vampires post–blood type cure had developed a human way of walking again. But Brian seemed to shift from one space to the next as if he couldn't quite control his speed. He prowled more like an animal than a man. It was disturbing.

God, she hoped this worked. She desperately wanted her brother back. Even though he'd never be the same.

Brian took a seat next to Washington, flanked by Beckham and Philippé. Reyna clenched the lab table as Washington prepped Brian for the cure.

"You understand that this is experimental treatment for the case of vampirism. Possible issues related to the cure are still uncertain," Washington said to Brian as he swabbed his arm with an alcohol pad.

"Yes," Brian said. "Just fix me."

"You'll feel a pinch and then a burning. That's normal."

"I've endured torture. Just get it over with."

Beckham raised an eyebrow at Reyna. She shrugged. He'd asked her for another solution.

It only took a second. Washington inserted the needle and pumped until the liquid was gone. He removed the needle, covered the drop of blood with a cotton ball, and then placed a Band-Aid over the injection site. A vampire with a Band-Aid. Now she'd seen everything.

"Did it work?" Reyna asked. She chewed on her lip and stared intently at Brian to look for any changes.

He hissed and clutched his arm. "You said burning. Not like I was on fire from the inside out."

Brian doubled over, clutching his stomach. It was as if he had a stomach bug and was about to spew everything he'd recently eaten. Except all he did was moan over the pain. It scorched through him as Golden Blood took root, acting as white blood cells fighting the vampiric virus that had infected his body.

Suddenly, he fell backward off his stool and collapsed onto the ground. His body seized once, twice, three times.

Washington rushed to him, turning him on his side to try to mitigate the problem. Reyna was there next. Her hand on Brian's shoulder. She didn't care that she was potentially in danger. This was her brother. She would not let this happen.

"What can I do?" Reyna gasped. "My blood?"

"No," Washington snapped. "I warned you it would be traumatic. Golden Blood has to get through his entire system. It's as painful to be remade human as it was to be turned."

Brian convulsed, yet was unresponsive while Reyna watched on helplessly. He had volunteered. This was what he wanted. But he must be in unbelievable agony. Suddenly he stopped, shifting onto his back and groaning.

His eyes fluttered open and he looked up at the ceiling. "Oh God."

"Brian? How are you feeling?"

"My skin is melting off."

"Did it work?" she asked Washington eagerly.

"Let's get him back up," Washington said. "I need to test his blood."

Philippé and Beckham helped Brian back into his seat. Brian shuddered against every touch as if he had an intense sunburn and his skin was on fire. Washington drew blood and went to work. Reyna remained at Brian's side, hoping and praying that this wasn't all for naught.

Finally, Washington loosed a breath. "It's eliminating the virus."

Reyna gasped. "It worked?"

"It appears that the first wave of the injection worked. His vampirism is being fought off, eliminated. It will take more observation time to determine how much of the other side effects of vampirism are eliminated, but at this time, yes, it worked."

• • •

Reyna stayed with Brian until Washington forced him to rest. The elimination of the virus would wreck him and leave him exhausted. He needed as much sleep as possible to process it.

Before she left him though, she got his permission to call Drew and Laura to tell them the good news. She was beyond ready to have something good to tell them. They'd both been worrying as much as she had. Laura had been a wreck, and Reyna was happy to tell her that they would bring her up to the mansion the next time they sent a car into town. At least this gave them hope.

"How's he doing?" Jodie asked.

"The cure is attacking the virus. He's sleeping finally."

"Good."

"How are *you* doing?"

Jodie shrugged. "A little numb. I thought experiments were long behind me. But it looks like the antidote must have come from my blood. Washington has been comparing my blood to the components, and it's almost a perfect match. So..."

"So they had enough to keep working with it," Reyna whispered. "I'm sorry."

"Yeah. It sucks that all of this is happening because of me."

"Because of them," Reyna said. "They did this."

"I know. Yeah. I just wanted to make the world a better place and find my cousin. Can't seem to make either of those happen."

"That's not true."

"I think June is dead," Jodie whispered. "I mean what other explanation is there?"

Reyna's heart broke for her. "That's not the only explanation."

Jodie opened her mouth to respond, but Tye came rushing into the room. "Reyna, come quick."

Reyna dashed after him. "Is it Brian? Is he okay?"

"It's an email."

"An email?" she asked in confusion.

He turned the computer and she glanced down at the inbox.

"It came in from Everett."

Reyna had a bad feeling about this. A chasm opened in the pit of her stomach and remained there as she clicked on the new email. There was no subject line. No text in the body of the document. Just an attachment.

"Is that safe?" she asked.

"It didn't pull up any viruses, but I can't be certain. We could get Zoya?"

"Get her," Reyna said.

Zoya appeared a minute later and gave the go ahead. "It's safe."

Reyna clicked on the attachment. A video populated. Jodie sidled up next to her. It was probably a bad idea, but she pressed Play anyway.

"Oh fuck," she whispered.

Jodie clutched Reyna's shoulder. "Holy shit!"

"Whoa…I…I…" Tye stammered.

"We need to get the others," Reyna said. Except she couldn't pull herself away from the video that was playing. None of them could.

"I'm going to kill that motherfucker," Jodie spat.

"Get in line," Reyna said.

"I will get Beckham," Zoya said.

Tye disappeared with her to get the others. Reyna couldn't stop watching the video. It was hours' worth of material. She could stay riveted to this spot for days probably.

"What's so important that you pulled us from the cure?" Katarina asked, storming into the room with her bright red hair flying. "Seems counterintuitive."

"Yeah. What's going on, Reyna?" Meghan asked.

"Everett sent us something."

Reyna positioned the laptop so they could all see exactly what was on the disturbing video. He'd said he was going to prove himself and he had.

"The camps," Meghan whispered.

"An inside look at the feeding camps. He turned himself in and somehow kept a video camera on him. I have no idea how he got the footage out to us, but it shows us everything we feared and were told in real time. Being sorted by blood type, the vampire army, being administered an antidote, the feeding frenzy, the general dehumanization of Harrington's supposed housing project. We need to get the footage edited and mass distributed as soon as possible. This is what we needed, to show the public the atrocities of Visage.

"Everett's inside that facility. I want to get him out. It was a huge sacrifice to be able to get this for us. I don't want that sacrifice to be in vain."

• • •

Reyna divided her time between looking in on Brian and helping with the time-consuming process of digging through Everett's video footage. It was an enormous file, and they'd had to process the most impactful parts first. They'd distributed it to the public only an hour ago. She felt buoyant that they were finally having an impact.

Especially with Brian.

After a few days of observation, he was eating human food again. The virus had completely detached from his blood. Though it wasn't fully gone; it still powered some of his vamp abilities. But hearing went first. One day he could hear whispers down the hall and the next he was back to normal hearing.

Reyna was almost giddy with excitement. She should guard her heart for the worst, but it was so hard to do that when she saw such marked improvement.

"Little One," Beckham said against her hair. She'd sensed him coming her way long ago, but it was nice to wait for him to embrace her before reacting.

"Mmm?"

"Give him some peace."

She'd been watching Brian sleep. He'd been doing a lot of that.

"All right. Fine," she said, turning into him for a kiss. "I'm just so pleased."

"We need to go back to the cabin. I want to test to see if I can give you my speed again. If I can heal you. What else we can do." Beckham kissed the shell of her ear. "A battle is coming. We should prepare."

"Ever the lord."

"This is simply the calm before the storm. The troops should rest, but never the general."

She glanced up at him, feeling her sense of ease evaporate. "How are we going to find Harrington?"

"Leave that to me."

"How are we going to stop him?"

"I have an idea about that too."

"Going to share?"

He kissed her lips. "Letting it percolate."

"Your ideas are coffee now?"

His laugh was a full-bodied thing that made her tingle in all the right places. "Oh, my love. Come. Let us practice."

Beckham had the decency to let her march out to the cabin rather than carry her. She wanted to be back at the house watching over Brian and waiting to hear the reaction from the public to the video that Zoya had uploaded. Instead, she was in the cabin, practicing Beckham throwing her his vampire skills.

Healing they had figured out. Speed he'd given to her at Penelope's. Hearing was next. Opening her up to their connection and pushing out the ability. It took a few tries before it worked, but she could only listen to the outside world for a minute before dropping the connection.

"Oh God," she gasped, falling to one knee. Beckham rushed to her side.

"What happened?"

"My ears. They hurt like a bitch. Ringing and pain." Reyna put her hand to her ear. Blood ran out of one of them.

"Did you have symptoms for healing or speed?"

Reyna closed her eyes as the pain receded and thought back. "Not much, just some pain as I healed. When you gave me the speed, I was disoriented and dizzy. Some ringing in my ears and it took a second to stand steady again."

"Of course." He nodded his head as if it all made sense. "You're getting my enhancements but without the virus changing your composition to be able to accommodate them. So your body is exhibiting physical side effects."

"What can we do about it?"

"Not do it anymore."

"No."

"Building up to it could take weeks, months, even years. We can't force this onto you. You could die."

Reyna groaned. "Then fucking turn me! Let's make it easier. If as a human I can't handle it, maybe I could as a vampire."

"That's not part of this discussion."

"Make it part of the discussion. There's a cure now. I could always turn back."

Beckham turned away from her. "I understand why you want this, but no. It's risky."

"Do you not want me to live forever with you?" she whispered.

"Do we have to decide about eternity in the midst of war?"

"When else will we decide?"

"Reyna, I don't know how many ways I can tell you that I love you. That I love you so much that I would never want this to happen to you. Look at what it did to your brother. Yes, he was tortured and starved, but *you* are the kind soul. What would the virus do to your heart? Would you still be my Reyna afterward?"

"Of course I would. We're blood matched. You're my soul mate."

Beckham shook his head. She could see the resignation in him. The sheer horror and discomfort that had settled onto him. "If it's the only way, Reyna, then I'll do it."

"You will?" she whispered.

"You can make your own choices. You trust me not to be a monster. Perhaps I could trust you not to be your own."

Reyna stared at him in shock. Not that he would allow her to make her own choice, but that he'd agree to *this* choice.

And it was the same moment she realized she could never do this to him.

Never.

Not ever.

It would break him.

For the man who had spent so long hating himself for his deeds, she would destroy him by doing this. He would see it as his greatest failure. Another chink in his armor that finally hit hard enough to shatter. He'd survived his parents and Bronwyn and hundreds of other deaths. But she could see in his onyx eyes that he would not be the same if she was remade.

She placed her hand on one of his. "We'll find another way, okay?"

He tilted his head in surprise but said nothing. Just drew her close and kissed her hard.

A promise, a recognition, an understanding.

They linked hands and began their trek back to the house. She'd try again tomorrow. Maybe she could figure out a way to take the abilities for shorter periods of times. Guard herself against the side effects. Be better at it now that she knew what she was up against. There had to be a way.

A hundred yards from the front door, Beckham abruptly stopped. "Do you hear that?"

She raised an eyebrow. “No.”

He held his hand up. “Two seconds. No more. Don’t hold on too long.”

Then he opened himself up to her. She reached for the ability to hear and suddenly she could. She gasped when she heard it and then dropped the connection. Her breathing was rough and her ears hurt a bit, but nothing as bad as before.

“A helicopter?”

“On its way here.”

Chapter Thirty

Beckham grasped her around the middle and took off. He dropped her on her feet once more at the house. "Get everyone to the garage and out of here before the whole house goes up."

"What are you going to do?" she demanded but he was already gone.

Reyna cursed under her breath and then dashed through the house. She was leading Elle. These were her people. She needed to get everyone out.

"Gabe!" she gasped, nearly running into him in the entrance. "Get to the cars as fast as possible. A helicopter is coming. We need to get out."

"On it. You need to get out too," Gabe yelled. Meghan came dashing after him. He grabbed her hand and rushed for the door.

"I need to make sure everyone is out first. I'll meet you there." Reyna pushed through the kitchen and found Tye and Jodie packing a backpack. "You two need to leave. Now!"

Katarina flew into the room. "I've got them."

"Thank you. Now get out of here. I need to get Brian."

Katarina nodded at her like a soldier, then all but hoisted them into her arms and dashed from the room.

Reyna felt a wind kick up next to her as more of Beckham's circle cleared the house. But she saw no sign of Brian. No sign of Washington. The helicopter was getting close enough that she could vaguely hear it with her normal ears, and that was *not* good. She didn't want to end up like Sydney, a captain going down with her ship. She wanted to save everyone.

She pushed forward deeper into the house. "Brian! Washington!"

Washington appeared then at the top of the stairs. "Reyna, over here."

She hurried to him and he foisted a cooler into her hands. "What's this?"

"You must save the Golden Blood, Reyna. The fate of the world rests in your hands. I have to finish the backup of my life's work."

"Washington!" she cried.

"I'll follow." Then Washington ducked and ran back down into his laboratory. The helicopter blades were getting louder. And she was stuck with a fucking cooler full of the cure for vampirism, without her brother or the love of her life.

She vacillated forward and back, forward and back. Brian or the cure. Brian or the cure. She cursed this fucking war and then rushed ahead with the cure in her arms. She would *not* leave without her last charge.

"Brian!" she cried again, almost to the bedroom stairs.

Genevieve rushed down the stairs then, helping Brian out of his room. "I have him."

"We'll never make it," Reyna said. "You're going to have to take him yourself, Genevieve."

"What about you?"

"Save my brother. I'll follow behind you."

Genevieve gave her a sad smile and then lifted Brian into her arms. She dashed out of the house then. Reyna sighed with relief. She hadn't seen Beckham. Washington was still downstairs. The helicopter was too close. She had no choice. She had to get out of there. She had the cure. If she didn't leave now, they'd have a problem.

Adrenaline pumped through her veins. She cleared the back door as an SUV tore out of the garage and barreled down the driveway. Reyna kept moving. Her feet couldn't carry her fast enough. She glanced once over her shoulder and saw the chopper was nearly upon them.

"Fuck, fuck, fuck."

She was to the garage when Beckham whizzed toward her.

"Beckham!" She reached her hand out toward him. Tried to grab on to him, but he wasn't close enough.

"Reyna!" he cried.

"Please," she gasped, stretching her hand out farther toward him. *I don't want to die.*

It was the last thought she had before the first bomb dropped.

• • •

Silence.

The moment before it shattered was almost worse than what came after.

It was like standing in a bubble.

And then the bubble burst.

The bomb dropped on the mansion that stood as a beacon on the hill for more than two centuries.

Boom.

Sound rushed back in, louder than anything Reyna had ever heard before. Stone blasted apart, fire flew like a volcano from the top, and the world as she knew it stopped.

The blast rushed outward. A sonic roar crashing against her skin. She felt it in every inch of her body. Top to bottom. Inside and out.

She was lifted off of her feet. The force of the eruption kicking her high into the air. Her hands released the blood cure on instinct.

She tried to gasp around the pain, but she could do nothing. Nothing but flail midair as pain lanced through her and she descended into freefall.

Everything kicked into slow motion and all she could think was this was the end.

She was going to die.

After all of this, she was going to die from a fucking bomb.

She tried to save the world. Tried to right the wrongs. She wasn't the best leader, but she was at least trying.

And Beckham…

Oh Beckham.

She hadn't even gotten one last kiss. She'd barely seen his beautiful face. And what would happen to him if she was gone? Would he ever again risk everything for others? Would he ever open himself up? She didn't want him to become the beast again. She wanted him to be hers forever.

She wanted to feel him.

One last time.

She reached out for him. Felt his presence adjacent to her. He was getting closer. Then she felt different.

Solid.

Hardened.

Powerful.

Her fragile human body was no more. Instead, it was replaced with the strength of a vampire. Strength to withstand a blast a human never could. Strength to endure. She was as hard and impenetrable as a diamond. Forged of steel rather than muscle and sinew and bone.

Her body collided with the ground a full fifty feet from where she'd last been standing. She skidded, shredding the jacket and shirt she'd been wearing. Her back scraped against the ground with grass and dirt and little stones penetrating her skin. She moaned as she came to a stop.

The connection dropped. And suddenly her muscles remembered every ache and pain and sore in her body. She coughed and hacked and tried to roll over to ease the pain. The back of her head felt like there was a knot the size of a golf ball where she'd banged it against the ground. Cuts and scrapes and soon-to-be-bruises covered her body. Every single part of her was on fire.

But she was alive.

Miraculously alive.

"Reyna!" Beckham yelled.

She opened her watery brown eyes and stared up at the vision of a man before her. He towered over her, not a cut on him. His dark eyes filled with fear. And God he was beautiful.

"You saved me," she croaked.

"You're alive." He fell to his knees before her, desperate. "You're alive."

She choked back her next reply and tried to ease the pain in her skull.

"Don't speak. I'll heal you."

"After," she gasped. "Save your energy."

His emotions were rampant and effusive; she could feel them without even reaching out.

"This is going to hurt," he warned.

She gritted her teeth and tried to keep from screaming when Beckham picked her up. Her back felt like a tattered mess. She could smell her blood mixing with earth. Feel the well of wretched pain intensify.

"The cure?"

Beckham's eyes darted around. He must have located it, because he grabbed the small cooler, and with it and her tucked beneath him left the scene behind.

• • •

Reyna blacked out at some point, because when she woke up, the rumble of an engine was beneath her. She reached out for Beckham with her senses and felt him hovering over her.

"Becks," she whispered.

"Oh Little One, if not for the slow beat of your heart, I would have feared for your death."

"What happened?"

"Everett was captured. Visage sent a video of his murder to your email and a bomb to the mansion."

Reyna winced. "Everett is dead?"

"Yes. I watched it."

"Was it painless?"

Beckham said nothing, which was answer enough.

"He was tortured for our location," she gathered.

"Yes."

"How did he know where we were?"

Beckham shook his head. "I don't know. I thought we were careful."

Tears came to her eyes. "Fuck, fuck, fuck."

"We have to get the rest of Elle out of their locations in case he gave them up too."

"Have you reached out to Drew?" She tried to sit up, but pain lanced through her and Beckham gently pressed her back down.

"Yes. He's aware. He's rallying everyone into action to get them out as soon as possible. They have a system in place. They're moving quickly."

"Where are we going?" Reyna asked. "Without the cult-y place and the mansion?"

"I have a place."

"You have a place? We stayed at the mansion and left them at the cult and all this time you had a place?"

Beckham sighed slowly. "It's temporary. I stayed there when I was healing. I wasn't sure if Harrington knew about it, so I've been having it monitored. It can't house everyone, so it won't work long-term."

"I thought you stayed in a safe house when you healed."

"Of sorts." He placed his hand on her shoulder. "Now rest. I'm going to need to feed before I heal you so I don't weaken. We reached Meghan and she's going to look after you."

"Do you have blood there?"

He kissed her temple and said nothing else. She sighed and let it go. What he drank was his business. He needed to be a hundred percent and get her back to a hundred percent, because the time was now. They'd waited long enough. They'd planned and schemed and used every advantage they had. No one else would be kidnapped or tortured or experimented on or killed. Harrington had to be stopped.

...

"Hey," Meghan said softly. She was running her fingers gently through Reyna's unbound hair. "It's time to wake up."

She opened her eyes and stared up into her friend's face. "What happened?"

"I had to sedate you. I got the shrapnel and debris out of your body, but it was painful and tedious. Beckham did the rest."

Reyna found Beckham standing on the other side of the table. She eased up into a sitting position.

"Let's not do that again, okay?" Reyna said.

Beckham grinned. "I'll put it on the list."

"How do you feel?" Meghan asked.

"Better. I'm not even sore. How long was I out?"

"About an hour."

Reyna rubbed her eyes and then swished her legs off of the table. She jumped down and stretched out her sore limbs. She felt none of the pain from the explosion. Her hand went to the back of her head. No goose egg. They'd put her into sweatpants and a black T-shirt. Her old clothes were probably long gone. Destroyed in the blast.

"Oh, the cure."

Meghan winced and sat back. Beckham gestured to the cooler sitting on the floor. Inside all the tiny vials of liquid were shattered. Glass lay at the bottom with a few dribbles of the gold liquid mixed with some kind of ice to keep it cold.

"No," she whispered. "All of it's gone?"

"It must have shattered and drained before I got to it."

Reyna put her head between her knees. All of that work. Everything Washington had done to get them a cure—a weapon to use against Visage—and now it was gone.

"And Washington?"

Beckham shook his head. "He never left the mansion."

"We're so fucked," Meghan said.

"Was there a backup? He said that he was going to try to back it up," Reyna said.

"It's gone, Little One."

"No," she whispered. "It can't be. He said…"

Meghan shook her head. "I checked. Zoya checked. It looks like it's gone. He didn't finish in time."

"All that research. Everything he'd been working on just gone. No cure. None of the research on our blood match or on Jodie's blood." Reyna closed her eyes for a minute, took a deep breath, and then straightened. "But we can't change what happened. I think we knew all along what we needed to do. We were trying to find an edge to use against our opponent. Well, we found onc." Shc faccd Beckham. "We're blood matched. If that doesn't throw his chess game out of whack, nothing will."

"What are you suggesting?" Meghan asked.

"I go in and face Harrington alone. I'm the only one who can get close enough."

"Are you serious?" Meghan gasped.

"He might have an antidote, but nothing can substitute for the real thing. And it'll be a point of pride for him that he has me after I've evaded him for so long. I can do this."

Reyna braced herself, expecting the worst from Beckham. His

silence was weighted. It typically held more power than most people's words. His first priority was her safety, but if there was only one way to save the world, she'd take it. One more life for millions.

"You're right," Beckham said, staring down at the floor. Then he finally met her gaze, and she felt calm resolve resonate from him.

She blinked twice. "Come again?"

One side of his lips upturned as if he found her surprise humorous. But he nodded at her as if they were on the same page. As if he understood where she was coming from and what this would cost them both.

"You really think I can do this?" It was different hearing it from him. She'd been expecting a fight. He'd always fought her on anything that could harm her. This acceptance was new. It was powerful.

"You can get close to Harrington," he said, taking her hand. "That much we know for a fact. No one else is going to get that close. And we'll need that advantage if we want to end this."

Her heart stuttered at his words. His confidence.

He opened himself up to her and their connection bloomed into life. She felt his fear. It was there of course. But also his deep love, his careful calculation, and his determination to succeed. He believed in her. He really did.

"Plus," he continued, "I'll be there with you every step of the way. I trust you."

A slow smile stretched across Reyna's face. Trust. What a magical word.

And with that he leveled the playing field.

Soul mates and blood matched and finally equals in every way.

CHAPTER THIRTY-ONE

"All right. All right," Gabe called from her left. They'd managed to get a lot done in the week since the explosion. And it was finally time to put that plan into action. "Shut up and let Reyna speak."

She turned her eyes to Beckham and swallowed. "Speak?"

"You're taking them into war. You have to rally them," Beckham said.

Reyna's eyes darted to her friends. Meghan and Jodie gave her an encouraging nod. Gabe winked. Tye smiled. They were all counting on her.

"Public speaking?" she hissed.

"Want my advice?" She nodded. "Don't faint."

"I hate you."

He grinned. "Knock them dead."

Reyna hooked her foot up on the stool and climbed onto Beckham's sleek kitchen table. Her knees felt wobbly as she faced the crowd of people.

Her two fears: needles and public speaking.

She'd had to face one repeatedly. Seemed as if it were time to face the other.

"Hey. Hey!" Reyna raised her voice.

She waited for the room to quiet down. It took a while, considering how many different groups of people were congregated into one space.

She could see Drew standing in the crowd. All of the Elle members had been relocated, and the remaining Elle sleeper agents had been brought in. The anti-vamp cult looked pretty pissed to be standing so near Beckham's circle, who had apparently called in some favors. Now the vampires were a solid thirty strong. All in all, she was looking at her own little army. A terrifying thought, to say the least.

She cleared her throat and tried to recount all of the reckless ideas she'd implemented since becoming Beckham's blood escort. It was a long list that culminated with this moment. And if she had been able to get through all of that, well, public speaking shouldn't be that bad. *Shouldn't* being the optimal word.

"Thank everyone so much for coming," Reyna said, her voice barely above a whisper.

A groan of dissent came from the crowd. She was losing them already. She needed them to rally with her to do what must be done. But they'd already decided. They were going in. She could do this much.

"I said thank you for coming," she shouted into the crowd. The silence was swift and secure. Her stomach flipped. Sweat accumulated on her brow. But she continued. "Many of us here are from different walks of life. We have different beliefs. We have different values. We want different things."

The crowd was nodding. Her nerves settled with Beckham at her back. Her hands still shook slightly but she balled them into fists.

"Our differences aren't what brought us together. Our differences aren't the thing that make us want to fight. It's how we are similar. We all want to save humanity. We all want a shot at a life after this that isn't controlled by Visage. That isn't controlled by anyone."

More nods. A deeper silence. Her heart was in her throat.

"At the beginning of this, I was no one. I was a person desperate to help provide for my family. They're the ones that I was always fighting for. They're the ones who I wanted a better life for. I joined Visage under good faith, and they took that faith and shattered it." Her chin wobbled slightly and she felt Beckham's reassuring gaze on her shoulder. "They put their foot on my neck and said stay down. But I refused."

"Yeah!" someone shouted from the crowd. And then more and more were cheering at her proclamation.

"I still refuse!" she called back. "I refuse to stay down, to stay silent. I rose up. I became something powerful. And all of you here today are just as powerful." She pointed into the crowd, made eye contact with as many people as she could. They were here. They were with her. "So leave your differences at the door. Because today we don't fight just for ourselves, we fight for humanity, for equality, for freedom."

A cheer rose up from the crowd. Reyna's eyes swept the room. A smile tugged at the corners of her lips. These people were going out to fight with her. They trusted her to make this work. It was daunting, but also incredible. So many people from so many places, all here, now, willing to work together.

"Today we take back our world!" she cried as she pumped her fist into the air and grinned at the sea of people cheering with her.

So much excitement as they all went into battle. Her heart hardened against the consequences. She couldn't think about what could go wrong or else all she would do is fear that she had made the wrong choice moving forward. And it was clear that there was really only one choice: the right one.

Beckham held his hand out and she hastily jumped off of the table.

"Incredible," he praised. "No one could feel your anxiety but me."

She blew out a breath. "Good."

"Hey, good speech," Drew said, throwing an arm around her. "When did you learn not to throw up when you addressed a group?"

"Very funny."

"I'm proud of you."

"Thanks," she said with a smile. But her eyes flittered over Drew's shoulder. "Where's Laura?"

Drew cocked his head to the side. She followed his gaze and found that Brian and Laura had snuck into the room to listen to her speech. They'd had a tear-filled reunion once Reyna and Brian had made it to Beckham's place. Brian was on the mend and Laura was there every step of the way to help.

"Come on," Drew said.

They moved across the room where Brian had an arm around Laura. She was beaming and he gave her a tentative smile as if he wasn't sure this was reality. His eyes were shadowed, memories of his time as a vampire and the torture he'd endured from Harrington would follow him forever. As it would follow Reyna too. She understood that look.

"What a speech," Brian said.

"You did really great," Laura said. "Though, I wish none of you had to go."

"I know," Reyna said. "But we do. We have to end this."

"Give him an extra bullet for me," Brian said fiercely.

She nodded and then pulled Brian, Laura, and Drew in for a hug.

"I hate to say this, but I have to go," Drew said. He ruffled Laura's hair affectionately. "First wave and all."

"Thank you for taking care of her," Brian said, holding his hand out. They shook, an unbreakable bond forged between them, and then Drew left.

Reyna kissed Brian's cheek and left him alone with his wife. They needed time together, and she needed to be here for the army.

Drew filed out with the rest of the Elle members, as well as the heavily armed anti-cult crew. Reyna had had more than a few choice words with Everett's friends about joining the team, but ultimately none of them wanted to see Everett's death be in vain. Luckily, they had guns galore and knew how to use them.

Beckham's circle spoke furiously to him in a corner for a few minutes before splitting into teams with the other vamps and exiting the room. Beckham nodded once at her and then followed them out to supervise.

Reyna turned then to her own team—Gabe, Meghan, Tye, and Jodie.

"Like old times, huh?" Reyna asked.

Jodie threw her arms around Reyna. "We've got your back."

Meghan smiled brightly. "I'm ready."

Gabe winked and slung an arm over Meghan's shoulders. Tye crossed his arms and gave her a cool nod. These were her people. Her team. She wished that she could tell them how much they meant to her, but she could see in their eyes that they already knew.

Tye tossed the keys in his hand. "I call getaway car."

"Shotgun," Jodie yelled as she pushed past Meghan and Gabe toward the car.

Reyna took a deep breath, and glanced around Beckham's safe house. He'd been right when he'd said it wasn't big enough to house everyone. The place was smaller than the mansion. But it was enough as a base for those who were staying behind. Genevieve had agreed to remain and guard the place along with Brian and Laura. Reyna was relieved by that at least.

Beckham reappeared in the doorway then. "Are you ready?"

She swallowed and nodded. "Yes."

He crossed the threshold and pulled her into his arms. "I love you."

"I love you too."

She melted into his touch. Their bodies becoming one. She needed this comfort. To know that she was loved as she went out to take on the world.

"We can do this together," Beckham said.

"You're right. We should have always done it together."

"Just don't hesitate. You'll only get one opportunity."

"I know. We've gone over this."

He tilted her chin up to meet his deep obsidian eyes. They were the hardened eyes of a warrior, with the fierce determination of someone who had gone into battle time and time again and come out ahead. His experience far outweighed hers. The thrill of battle was a drug to him. It was all over him. If she reached for his emotions, she could revel in it like a pill for her anxiety.

But she needed her anxiety. Her stress. Her total awareness of every fucking thing that could go wrong.

She'd gone into battle once already against Harrington.

She'd lost.

Beckham had died.

If she wasn't aware of that, then she would be going into this with false confidence. She was terrified. And she needed to be. The last time she'd faced Harrington she'd been cocky. Young and inexperienced, not yet completely weathered by the reality of her world. Somehow still completely naive to the ruthlessness of William Harrington. She wasn't walking into this half-cocked. She had a plan and a team and backup. She was about to walk out onto the chessboard and play the hardest game of her life.

Beckham brought his lips down to hers. The kiss was short and soft and raw. Jarring enough to drag her back to earth. He brought his hand to her heart, where it beat steady.

"Just remember, I'm always right here." He moved her hand up to his heart. "And you are always here."

"Always," she repeated.

He nodded. "Good. Showtime."

A voice cleared behind them. They found Genevieve standing in the hallway that led to bedrooms. "Excuse me. Would you mind if I had a quick word with Reyna before you depart?"

"Of course," Beckham said deferentially. "I'll wait in the car."

"I won't be long." Reyna crossed the room to where Genevieve was standing. "What's going on?"

"I have been a vampire for a long time," Genevieve said. "I was not long on Mr. Washington's property before I was turned. He treated me with kindness and respect even before I became one of his kind. What you are doing today is what he always wanted."

"I know," Reyna said, choking back the sadness over his death. She couldn't even believe it was possible. The man who avoided war found that it caught up to him after all.

"Believe me when I say I understand your need to even the score. I'm not sure I would have ever said this before Roger…died," Genevieve choked on the word and Reyna squeezed her hand. "I know that William and Roger were close, but William never deserved his friendship. Roger gave everything to his research. He did everything he could to help William's condition. And William truly was a wonderful man," she said breathily, "until you had something he wanted. And *you* are now what he wants." Genevieve grasped her hands. "Think first of yourself, dear. You have to make decisions that you can live with."

"I know what I can live with."

"Choose justice." Genevieve's hands tightened around hers, pressing into her palm. "Do the right thing when the time comes."

Reyna closed her hand into a fist. "I will."

"You reminded Roger so much of his Elisa. He'd only ever trust you with this."

"I'll make him proud."

Genevieve nodded, releasing her. "I know you will."

Chapter Thirty-Two

Reyna bounced from foot to foot in the back of the black van. Zoya had hooked it up with several video screens so they could see everything playing out. Nearly everyone was wired with a tiny camera and they broadcasted everything live. Anyone who wanted to see the realities of Visage now could. People had called Everett's video propaganda, but they were listening after video of his murder was released and they were enraptured now that Elle broadcasted live for the first time ever.

From Reyna's vantage point, she could see what she now called the storming of the camps. It was frantic and manic and totally incredible. Guns going off to stop the vampires from obstructing their entrance. People rushing forward through the front. Mayhem as they moved deeper through the trenches.

Humans poured from the front entrance as they escaped their vampire guards and made it out. And all of this was just the first couple minutes.

Madness.

Panic.

Distraction.

That's what Reyna wanted and needed.

"Your cue," Zoya said as a flare erupted on one of the screens.

"We're sure he's in there?" Reyna asked.

Beckham nodded. "Affirmative."

Gabe slid open the van door. He jumped down enthusiastically. "I'm fucking ready for this shit."

Meghan shook her head. "Only you are this happy about it."

Jodie cocked the gun in her hand and shrugged. "I don't know. They gave me a gun. I'm pretty stoked."

Tye jumped out of the van and adjusted the many guns strapped on him. Philippé stepped out with them, leaving Gerard with Beckham. Zoya was on comms and Katarina had gone in first.

Beckham grasped Reyna's chin and faced him again. "If anything goes wrong, I'm coming in after you."

"It'll go to plan."

"It never goes to plan."

"Okay. Yeah. It never goes to plan." Reyna ran her hand down her ponytail and shrugged. Her nerves ate at her as she played the plan over and over again in her head.

"Don't do anything reckless." She arched an eyebrow. "Anything more reckless than normal." Then he kissed her. This was fierce and loyal and demanding. His emotions exploded through her all at once. She could sense him, feel him, taste him. It was so intoxicating that she thought she'd never be able to walk away from this. Never be able to go into that pit of Hell. Not if it meant she did it without him.

"You won't," he said, reading her thoughts. "I'll be with you every step, remember?"

"Good," she gasped.

"You're bloody coming out of there."

Adrenaline pumping through her veins and pushing her into action. "You bet I am."

• • •

Reyna followed the vanguard of her army.

Gabe paved the way to a back entrance into the camp. They'd scoped it out yesterday to check for guards. There were two on the door at all times and a rotating round who patrolled the perimeter. Despite the fact that Reyna hated the idea, Beckham had contacted Roland to get inside information—schematics, blueprints, passcodes, everything that would help. They'd debated it for a long time, but it was the only way that they knew they could get to Harrington. It was a risk. The biggest risk Beckham might have ever taken. But at the end of the day, Roland wanted to depose Harrington as much as they did. The enemy of my enemy was my friend, even if she hated him. She hoped the bastard played his part.

Tye discreetly cut his way through the fencing with a laser that Katarina had provided. It took a full minute while they waited anxiously before they could slip through the hole he'd created. Reyna ducked over to the other side, with Gabe flanking her rear.

The distraction had done its job. All the guards were missing from the back door and the patrol was gone. That didn't mean they wouldn't meet someone on the inside, but for now they were in the clear.

Reyna hurried after Jodie and Meghan to the back door. She plastered herself against the wall. Her breathing heavy and terrified.

"You're doing great," she heard Beckham's commanding voice in her ear.

She pressed her finger to the tiny earpiece. It was amazing to be able to hear him. Though she wanted to rely more on sensing him. She opened herself to him and sensed him in the van. Good. Close enough. Not too far away.

"Enter the passcode and follow the hallway to the left."

Reyna repeated the instructions. Gabe was already a step ahead of her, entering the fifteen-digit code. The lock gave with no resistance.

"Here goes nothing," Gabe said. He yanked open the door, holding the gun aloft in front of him. He shot the vampire in the heart who was waiting on the other side and quickly the second one. The bullet was enough of a distraction for him to jump in with a large knife and lop off both of their heads. He checked the rest of the hallway with a nod. "Empty. We're clear here."

A sinking feeling set into the pit of her stomach. Even though this was exactly to plan, she still felt like Harrington knew they were coming. Except he *couldn't* know they were coming. There was no way he'd predicted this. Still it felt like he was clearing the path for her to walk into another one of his traps. Had Roland given them up? Given them all the information that they needed to hang themselves? She'd have to do something he wasn't expecting.

"What's this mean?" Meghan asked. Her red box braids were in a high bun on the top of her head, and she held a gun in her hand. Jodie came in behind her, looking around wide-eyed.

"He knows?" Tye guessed.

"If he knows and he wants to see me, well then, let's make that fucking easy for him."

She strode forward and did the thing that Beckham had told her not to do. She abandoned the plan.

...

"You are not walking to the left, Little One," Beckham said in her ear.

She sighed. Yeah, she wasn't. "He knows we're here. Roland must have told him we were coming. We have to go with Plan B."

The silence on the other end was enough for her to know he was not pleased. Five minutes in and already shit was breaking down. But that was okay. She could roll with the punches. It didn't change what she needed to do. Nothing did.

"Where the hell are you going?" Gabe asked, jogging to catch up with her.

"You can't walk in there," Jodie said.

"I appreciate it, but clear the way for me."

"But…" Meghan began.

"That's what I need from you," Reyna said. "I'll be fine."

Meghan looked skeptical. Jodie snorted. Philippé said nothing of course. But none of them contradicted her and they all ran ahead to clear the hallways as she walked through the first floor of the feeding camps like a woman on a mission. She passed dozens of closed doors that led to holding facilities. The nicer ones. The ones they kept the new prisoners in before they got them doped up on vamp venom and forgot to care that they were living or eating or breathing.

That knowledge made her grit her teeth. She needed to save these people. Give them back the lives they deserved and not the one forced upon them by Visage through poverty and desperation.

A set of double doors stood closed at the end of the hallway. Two dead guards were lay on the floor in front of them. Philippé and Gabe stood by impassively. Meghan's gun was aimed on the vampires. Her hand was steady, but she'd rather heal than kill. Jodie and Tye returned a minute later from connecting hallways.

"Clear," Tye said. "What's our next move?"

"Help get others out this way," she told them.

"What about you?" Jodie asked.

Reyna kicked one of the vampires out of her way with the edge of her black boot. "I have an idea."

"Little One, do you know what you're doing?" Beckham's voice crackled through her earpiece.

Yes. Yes, she did. She needed to do this her way and on her terms. She stepped over the second vampire and pushed the double doors open with both hands.

"Did someone throw a party without me?"

About a hundred pairs of eyes snapped to her and her grand

entrance. She'd entered the main holding facility for the humans. Medical equipment lined the walls and rows of chairs filled it to its entirety. As with most things from Visage, the room was strangely sanitary. No one would guess that they were dosing humans with antidotes and feeding a vampire army out of a place like this. But it didn't surprise Reyna. Not when she knew about Harrington's idiosyncrasies.

"Get her!" someone cried as a group of vampires lunged for her.

Philippé and her friends kept most of them off her, but one got through and grabbed her upper arm with enough force to bruise.

"I'm here to see the boss. It's time that we had a face-to-face."

The vampire snarled, "You're not seeing anyone."

"Ouch," she yelped. "That hurts. I'm needed in one piece. You do not want the boss to get mad at you."

The vampire released her abruptly. That had struck a nerve. Seemed Harrington had instilled some discipline into his army.

"I'm Reyna. Perhaps you've heard of me." She snapped her fingers in the vampire's face, twice. "Let's get a move on."

The vampire looked to his buddies in confusion. She blew out an exasperated breath and tried to walk past them. But he grabbed her by the wrist and yanked her to him. She was only an inch from his face and nearly gagged.

"Dear God, did you stop brushing?" she gasped.

"What is wrong with you? Don't you fear me?"

"Not in the slightest. I contend with the heavyweights, not a grunt."

The vampire snarled and reared back as if he was going to sink his teeth into her.

"I wouldn't do that if I were you. Harrington would probably kill you if you drank from me. I'm Reyna fucking Carpenter. Now bring me to the boss before I get pissed off."

The vampire was so confused that he actually did what he was told. He probably thought this was a joke and seeing Harrington would be worse for her in the long run. She couldn't really argue with that. Harrington was never someone she wanted to see, but sneaking into his private area was not how she wanted to have this confrontation.

She wanted to play chess on her board, not his.

No traps except the ones that she set.

The henchman vampire dragged her around the action and up a wide set of stairs to the observation deck. Sickeningly, there was a platform to watch what was going on below. To check to see who was feeding and when and change people out when necessary. Reyna was sure a lot more sinister shit had gone on down there, but she didn't really want the details. The ones she envisioned were bad enough.

She stumbled over a step and was nearly dragged up the rest of the way, but hastily regained her stride. The vampire was faster than her, and he didn't care for how fast her human legs could carry her.

They made it to the landing, and Reyna hazarded a glance behind her. She shuddered at the glimpse of the pandemonium below. So many casualties. She prayed that it soon would be over.

"You want to see the boss?" the vampire snarled at her.

"No, I asked you to take me to him for no fucking reason."

The vampire laughed viciously, and it sent a shiver down her spine.

She sensed Beckham's unease about the situation from a mile away. It was hard to separate it from her own terror, which she was harnessing like a whip. But she couldn't back down now. She was clutched in the jaws of an alligator, waiting for it to bite.

"You asked for it."

The vampire pushed open the door to the observation deck and tossed Reyna to the ground.

"Boss, brought you a present."

Reyna groaned on impact as the metal flooring collided with her body. That was going to bruise.

"Excellent," a female voice said from above. "Dismissed."

Reyna's head snapped up at the sound. The sound she only heard in her nightmares. The sound that haunted her like a ghost.

"Bronwyn?"

Chapter Thirty-Three

Well, fuck, Harrington was stupid enough to let *Bronwyn* out. The last time Reyna had come face-to-face with her, she'd been smartly locked away where she couldn't hurt anyone but herself. She'd been uncontrollable. She was still the only other vampire who had ever bitten Reyna.

Reyna felt her muscles freeze as she stared up at Bronwyn from where she'd landed on the floor.

"Fuck," Beckham spat into the earpiece.

Oh shit.

Beckham hadn't seen his sister in fifteen years. He'd mourned her death. He'd hated himself for what he'd done to her. Now here she was. And his first look at her was through the camera attached to Reyna, on a tiny screen in an SUV. She felt his emotions like a roller coaster through his controlled exterior.

He was wrath.

He was regret.

He was vengeance.

He was murder.

Reyna shuddered under the weight of his emotions. How much he wanted to rush in and murder Harrington for what he was doing to Bronwyn. For using her again. For letting her out. For hiding her from him.

"Don't," Reyna gasped. "Please don't."

She was speaking to Beckham through the earpiece, but it was Bronwyn who heard her.

"Oh my pet"—Bronwyn lifted Reyna's chin up at a sharp angle—"we meet again."

The same danger that Reyna had witnessed in her eyes the first time they met hadn't lessened an ounce. Why wasn't she contained? She was a danger to everyone around her.

A shudder ran through Bronwyn. "Don't like the smell."

She took a step back and snarled. Her head whipped to the side, and she grabbed onto a metal table, and her nails dug points into it as if it were aluminum.

"So wrong," she spat. "Yellow and purple and the stars are listening."

She teetered from foot to foot a second before grasping Reyna by the front of her T-shirt. Bronwyn glanced at it and grinned like a cat.

"*L. L. L,*" she singsonged. "All wrapped in a bow."

Reyna had momentarily forgotten that they'd spray-painted the Elle logo onto her shirt, a cursive *L* in yellow with a circle around it. Her jacket had fallen open when she'd been dragged up the stairs and now it was visible.

"Bronwyn, please, I know that you're in there."

But she had retreated back into whatever place was trapped in her brain. "Up!" she shouted.

"Please," Reyna begged.

Bronwyn flashed her fangs and then grabbed Reyna roughly by the shoulders. She hoisted her off of her feet and then dropped her back down, jarring Reyna's teeth. Beckham cursed violently in her ear, a constant stream of profanity and anger. She prayed that he didn't react exactly how Harrington wanted him to. That he didn't come barreling in here and confront Bronwyn.

Bronwyn hummed a nursery rhyme to herself as she patted Reyna down. "Don't need these," she said as she discarded two knives strapped to Reyna's forearms.

She found a third blade holstered down her back, then the two guns attached to her thighs, and a lock pick in her pocket. Bronwyn casually tossed the items into a container. Then continued her perusal.

"Oh bad toy. Bad, bad toy." Bronwyn found the earpiece, popped it out of its place, and then smashed it under her foot. "No other toys allowed."

Reyna blew out slowly. It was okay. She hadn't thought that they'd let her keep the earpiece. It'd been nice while it lasted.

Then Bronwyn ran her hand over the video camera. It met the same fate. Finally she found another smaller knife in her boot and a tracker. Reyna winced at the loss of that. Not that she wasn't a beacon already for Beckham, but they'd hoped that would be of value if they took her too far away.

Too late now.

She hated the loss of Beckham being able to hear and see what was happening to her, but at least they had each other. She tried to broadcast clearly to him that everything was okay. Or as okay as it could be. She could still sense that he was in the van, but for how long?

"Any other tricks up your pretty little sleeves?" Bronwyn asked. She made a predatory circle around Reyna. "I like the way the music sings in battle. It suddenly all makes sense. All the other noise is gone and I can finally hear."

"This makes sense to you?"

Bronwyn tilted her head to the side. "Battle is what I'm built for. Can you hear it?"

Reyna tried to listen to what Bronwyn was talking about, but there was nothing different. Just the din noise in the background of fighting. Fighting that she needed to stop.

Bronwyn's hands were in fists in front of her and they started to shake. Her head swiveled side to side as if she listened to a song only she could hear.

"You need help," Reyna said. "We can…we can get you help."

Bronwyn hummed louder.

"Beckham would help you."

Her eyes snapped open. Something like lucidity came back in her black eyes. Her black bob swished around her chin at a haphazard angle. Her spine straightened to her considerable height. For a second—a small second—she almost looked human.

"Nooooo!" Bronwyn screamed. She put her hands on her head and shook back and forth. "No. Not then. Death and death and death. And say hi to mom. Cut and slice and burn. Murder. Turn it around. Show me how. Do it again. And again."

She mumbled again and again until she crouched in on herself, all sanity forgotten. Reyna swallowed, torn between leaving Bronwyn behind and escaping now that she had the chance. There was no way to reach her, and it was hard to see her like this.

Reyna took a breath and then darted for the door. She almost had her hand on the handle when Bronwyn realized what was happening. Suddenly Bronwyn was upon her, dragging her back.

"Bad pet. Not how we act."

Reyna cried out as pain lanced up her arm from Bronwyn's grip. Blood seeped out of her veins as Bronwyn's nails dug deep into her skin. Shit. Her blood. It was going to cause a frenzy if other vampires smelled it. It was so sickly sweet that it attracted them like moths to a flame.

Bronwyn stared down at the wound as if she didn't know how it had gotten there. Then she threw Reyna's arms away from her.

"Rotten! Trash! Sick!" Bronwyn gagged as the smell of Reyna's blood assaulted her. "Make it stop!"

Reyna clamped down on the wound. She couldn't exactly ask Beckham to heal this. They couldn't show their hand to Harrington.

But fuck, it was going to drive Bronwyn mad. Fuck it. She'd have to wait. She'd have to endure a little longer.

Bronwyn had stopped shrieking and was staring at Reyna from a crouch on the ground. "You hear them too."

"Yes," Reyna lied.

"I was built for an army. Battle is my lullaby. Murder is my fairy tale," Bronwyn muttered.

"You don't have to be."

"I haven't had an army in a long time. No battles. No murder. Just voices. So many voices."

"I'm sorry." Reyna's heart broke for the girl that Beckham had shattered into so many pieces she could only find herself surrounded by violence and death.

"Why are they so loud around you? They should be quiet. I can hear the battle cries below. The sweet scent of destruction on the wind."

"I remind you of him," Reyna said.

"No," Bronwyn said. She straightened again and stared at her. "No."

"You can smell Beckham on me. You can hear his voice in me. You can feel your brother when you are near me. The voices are louder because of him. He did this to you."

"Stop," Bronwyn commanded.

"He did and he's so sorry. He wants to help. He still loves you."

"I said stop!" Bronwyn counted loudly as if it would drown out the memories that Reyna brought back to her.

"You can't change the past, but you two can have a future."

Bronwyn ceased counting. Her eyes slid to her like a viper ready to strike. Then she sprang toward Reyna. She grasped her by the throat, crashing her body back against the table she'd indented earlier. Bronwyn held her aloft with her feet dangling off the ground.

Reyna gasped and choked. She struggled to free herself from Bronwyn's solid grip, but it was useless. She couldn't budge her. As she kicked and clawed at Bronwyn's hands, she realized that she might die. That she might have finally underestimated Harrington's ferocity.

"Bronwyn!" Beckham snapped from the doorway.

Time slowed to a standstill. Bronwyn released Reyna, letting her fall into a heap on the ground. Reyna gasped for breath, coughing as air filled her lungs again. Her awareness of him registered and healing flooded in. Her wound knitting back together in a rush.

Bronwyn faced her brother. Every movement rigid and deliberate. "Beckham," she said softly. A child's voice. One who hadn't seen her brother in fifteen long years. And hadn't seen beyond the monster within him in much *much* longer.

"I'm here, Bronwyn. I'm finally here."

"You let them take me," she accused.

"I believed you were dead." He took a step toward Reyna. "You were my second, my *sister*. Do you think I would not have torn apart the world to get you back?"

"You left me to rot."

Another step closer to Reyna. He circled Bronwyn, getting Reyna out of danger.

"I mourned you."

Bronwyn laughed. A discordant, high-pitched squeal.

"Fifteen long years and I missed you every day."

"You do not feel," Bronwyn accused.

"You know that's not true."

"Stop."

"What I did to you, it was wrong. I'm so sorry. You are still my sister."

"No!" Bronwyn assessed the situation as Beckham finally put himself directly in front of Reyna. "You are not a person," Bronwyn said, tilting her head sideways. "And she is not leaving."

"Your quarrel is with me," Beckham said instead. "One last battle for the ages, B?"

"The girl stays."

"Nonnegotiable."

Reyna glanced between Beckham and Bronwyn. When Reyna

had first met Bronwyn, it had been such a blur. She hadn't even known until weeks later that she was Beckham's sister. Now seeing them so close together, it was obvious.

"Reyna, go. Now," Beckham barked.

"But what about you?"

"I will take care of this. Be ready."

Reyna gritted her teeth, took one last look at the stalemate between siblings, and sprinted toward the door. She hated leaving Beckham behind, but what could she do? He was supposed to be in a van a mile away. She'd been so fucking freaked out by Bronwyn she hadn't even felt him moving closer toward her. And then he'd healed her, which meant he could be weakened. Fuck, fuck, fuck.

No, she couldn't think about that. Beckham could handle himself.

Reyna didn't stop sprinting. She knew where she was going. She'd studied the map well enough to have a mental guide for which way to go. It would be easier with Beckham directing her, but she'd done her homework. Still worse the way to Harrington's office was empty of people. He wanted her to find him. But there was no backing down. Not with battles raging behind her. She had to finish this. That was the only way. Cut off the serpent's head to scatter his army.

When she reached the last hallway, she skidded to a stop.

"Bonjour, ma cherie," Roland said. His thick French accent sweeping over the words as his eyes did the same to her battered body.

Reyna put her hands on her knees to catch her breath.

"Did you believe you could stroll through these walls unnoticed? Barge in here and save the day?"

She had no response for him. She wanted to spit in his face. He was waiting for her. He had clearly double-crossed them. But at the end of the day, it didn't change anything. She still had to see Harrington.

"You've played your part. Now your fight is up. Surrender and he may be merciful."

"Yeah. Sure. Okay," she said sarcastically. "Has that ever actually worked on someone?"

"Or I could kill you right here."

"Now we're talking." She stood up and began to stride toward him. "You're standing between me and that door. Either get out of my way or do something about it."

"You have no weapon. Beckham is occupied. It is just you—a weak, defenseless human—against two of the most powerful vampires in known existence. What do you seek to gain from walking into that room?"

"Justice," she spat in his face. She would not back down. She would not walk away. She could speak Roland's language. She knew what made him tick. "Now open the damn door."

He laughed seductively. "I love when you order me around."

"Liar."

"Oh yes, I'd prefer to rip your throat out to shut your loud mouth, but watching you walk to your own death will do just fine."

Then Roland turned the knob on the door and held it open for her.

"After you."

Chapter Thirty-Four

"About time," Reyna said, and then entered the monster's lair. She held her breath as she walked inside. She couldn't believe she was here. That she was actually doing this. It was impossible to think that she was face-to-face with her kidnapper and torturer again. That she could look at him and not see the man who had turned Brian and set him loose in a room full of people. That she didn't see Beckham's murderer.

Harrington was sitting behind a glass desk in a glass room. The walls were opaque so that he could see out, and undoubtedly her exchange with Roland, but no one could see inside. Clever, creepy, and voyeuristic all at once.

How little Harrington had changed.

"Ah, my little queen," he said. "Welcome."

Reyna shuddered at the nickname.

"William," Reyna said. She held her chin high on the offensive. "Nice digs."

He gestured for her to take a seat. "I thought you might like it."

Yeah, not happening. She stood her ground.

She heard Roland enter behind her and the door quietly closed. He stepped around her, taking a position of power to the right of Harrington. She nearly rolled her eyes. Bastard.

"It's so clean," she commented.

His eyes narrowed briefly and then relaxed. "I prefer my life orderly. It has been a sticking point between you and I."

"Right. Because I'm so out of order."

"You are a complication," Harrington said, gesturing forward.

He didn't get up out of his seat. She tilted her head to the side in contemplation of what that could mean. Then she assessed him. His color had worsened. His eyes were sunken in. His shiny hair was no more, replaced by an oily, thinning mess. His hands were gnarled and sickly. He looked the way he had the first time she had met him all those months ago at Visage. He looked like he was dying.

Her eyes snapped up to his. And it was there that she saw the masterful mind who had always outwitted her. He held his supreme intelligence deep in the windows of his eyes. Yet his body was failing him.

"I don't believe that I am the only complication," Reyna said.

"Ah. Yes. Things have changed, you see."

"Your blood match died?" she guessed.

"She did. She was quite old. A frail woman. She couldn't keep up with the demand."

Reyna clenched her hands into fists at her sides and then released them. Such careless and thoughtless murder.

"And the antidote doesn't quite work like you hoped," she added.

"It nourishes the body, but not the illness," he admitted freely. "Rh null negative blood is so rare, and the components counteract the vampiric disease I have been carrying with me all these years. It turns out that I can re-create a universal donor and still not get it right."

"Too bad you killed Washington, then," she said callously. "He could have fixed it."

Shock registered on Harrington's face. "Roger is dead?"

"You dropped a bomb on him."

"He got out."

Reyna narrowed her eyes. "He stayed behind."

"What a horrible loss."

"Oh yeah, a 'loss.' Not another one of your murders."

Harrington waved the comment away. "You and I both know that to get to the top there must be casualties. You've certainly sacrificed enough people to get to where you are."

Reyna wanted to stab him for what he was insinuating. She was nothing like him. She was not casually sacrificing good people to get ahead. She felt every single loss like a shot to the heart.

And he felt nothing.

"All I'm hearing is that you need me again. Big surprise."

"I've always needed you, Reyna. It was you who did not realize that you needed me."

She laughed. "I don't need you."

Harrington pressed a button on the glass desk and suddenly the windows changed to televisions. Every single one of them showed the battles being fought below them. Beckham and Bronwyn fighting in the observation deck. Meghan and Gabe back-to-back, taking on a pack of vampires. Drew leading a team of anti-vamps into a nest. Tye fighting, fighting, fighting, and finally failing. Succumbing to the vampire before him. Fangs piercing his skin and drinking his precious blood. Spilling it on the already red floor of the main room.

Reyna gasped as the vampire heartlessly dropped Tye's body and moved on. Her hand went to her heart. Death. So much death. She had known there would be casualties in this war, but she hated seeing it happen. Hated being forced to watch.

"See. You do need me, my little queen," Harrington said. "I can make it all stop."

"As if you would."

"I simply wanted you to play the part of a queen on the board instead of a pawn."

Reyna ran her hand across her braid in frustration. "The game isn't over yet."

"Almost," he agreed. "But I did know that you would show eventually anyway. Incredibly predictable. Haven't we already danced this once?"

"Can you dance right now?"

He blinked at her. "You want to save your little friends, I presume. They are the reason that you're in my office. Your little rebellion has failed. The *L* on your shirt means nothing. You have accomplished nothing. Except to kill everyone that you care about. Is that what you want? To be the last of your kind?"

"No."

"I didn't think so." Harrington leaned back in his chair and steepled his fingers in front of him. "You are as self-sacrificing as you have ever been. You would do anything to save your friends and your precious Beckham."

"God, you really love to hear yourself talk, don't you? Couldn't you have curbed that desire since we last met?" Reyna cursed and crossed her arms. "You're right. Okay? I would do anything to save them, but I'm not here to be self-sacrificing. I'm here to kill you."

Harrington laughed and Roland joined in along with him. Apparently, she was a fucking riot.

"Kill me," Harrington said, patting his chest. "Oh Reyna, you always do surprise me."

"You couldn't lay a hand on him before he'd snap your neck," Roland threatened.

"Except he needs me. So, we both know he's not going to kill me."

"Ah, but you are easily incapacitated," Harrington said. "You're a human."

Reyna held her breath. She needed to stay in control. She needed to get this over with. She didn't want to stand here and give him more time to figure out a different way to stop her. Her eyes flitted to Roland's. He was another complication she'd have to figure out.

"Come quietly, Reyna, and I can make this all stop," Harrington offered, holding his hands wide.

He believed that he was being benevolent. That was the real kicker. He was so past recognizing his own evil that he believed that the ends always justified the means. And in this case, he would do *anything* to get Reyna. He would do anything to take Visage to the next level, and if that meant subjugating every human in the entire world, he wouldn't even think twice.

"I won't lose," Reyna told him, lifting her chin. "I won't surrender."

At some point, the scales had tipped. His ego had gotten in the way. He'd won so many times that he didn't believe himself capable of losing. So when he looked down with a little huff of laughter she wasn't surprised that all he said was, "Such a disappointment."

Reyna rolled her eyes. Same old, same old. "I think I finally understand you." She dropped her hands at her sides and took a step forward. "All this time I spent trying to anticipate your next move, all I did was learn your board. I see past the big bad monster to the man beyond the mask."

"Go on," Harrington said. He waved his hand in front of him and then leaned forward earnestly as if he were placating a child.

"You were Washington's best friend. You nurtured your friendship until you could use him. He created your blood type cure and asked for nothing in return. You rewarded him with a bomb on his house. You had his Elisa murdered in cold blood for being a visionary and then stole her ideas for your own aims. You were a thoughtful, intelligent man. Yet you discarded everyone you deemed unimportant. You treated Beckham like a prodigal son and yet you had his sister chained up for more than a decade to use against him. You held me against my will. I bet you even have someone that Roland cares about locked away somewhere."

Roland narrowed his eyes at the insinuation but didn't press the issue. It was good enough that she had him thinking.

"*Brava,*" Harrington said. "You have a warped view of my history."

"I'm not finished." He arched an eyebrow. "You are manipulative, destructive, highly intelligent, and most of all, single-minded."

"Single-minded?" Harrington laughed. "Shall I bring out my chessboard for you, my little queen? I can assure you I have many aims."

Reyna shook her head. "No. This is where you are different. This is where you fail time and time again. The only thing you have ever cared about in all of your days as a vampire is your own blood."

Reyna held up the cut that Bronwyn had given her and dug in until it flowed freely again. "*My* blood."

"Hardly."

Roland hissed behind Harrington as he drew in a deep breath, but it was Harrington whose eyes were glued to her arm. To the blood he so craved.

"Which makes it a weakness. One you have attempted to cover the severity of for centuries."

Harrington scoffed as if what she said had no merit. But it was his reaction that proved it did.

"Your very rare blood type coupled with a blood disease is a weakness." Reyna took a step to the side, slowly circling him in the way she had witnessed Beckham do to unnerve others. She'd had long conversations with Genevieve about Harrington, listening carefully to everything she knew about the man. Taking it in and absorbing it for this moment. "You were a sickly child."

"You know nothing of my childhood," Harrington quipped.

Reyna smiled darkly. "Your family assumed you'd die young. They cared nothing for you. Kept you in a bubble away from the other children. Your only saving grace was that you weren't poor. So you were given free rein to read." Harrington narrowed his eyes. "You gathered enough information to free yourself. And in doing so, you became a vampire. Irony of all ironies, you're still a sick, twisted, worthless bastard."

"Are you finished? I've had enough of your babble."

"You treated Washington like the brother you never had and Beckham like the son you couldn't have. Except you can't let anyone close to you. Not for real. And when they get close, when they start to figure you out, you revolt, which only makes it worse. Because the truth is, William," she said coolly, "you're just a sick, lost boy who's hoping no one will see it."

"Enough!" Harrington roared, jumping to his feet.

"Hit a nerve?"

"You are grasping at straws. You know nothing of my childhood or the life I've lived."

"I don't have to know. I know *you*."

Harrington's eyes blazed with fire. He was furious that she was using his past against him. She could see on his face that he despised her for it.

"It changes nothing," Harrington said, slowly sinking back into his seat. "You've left me no other choice."

"There are always choices. Why do you have to do this? We can make the world a better place together."

"I see you believe that. But what you don't realize is that I am already creating the utopia I so desire. And with you feeding me, I will rule everything."

"All you want is someone to love you. To see you for who you are and not be afraid. Can't you consider another route?"

Harrington met her gaze head-on. Then he pressed another button on his desk. "Bring her in."

A door behind her swished open. Reyna swiveled in place, careful not to put her back to Harrington. Fear crept into her heart. Whatever Harrington had prepared for her couldn't possibly be good.

In walked Jodie.

Held captive by a vampire.

"Now, let's reconsider your position," Harrington said.

CHAPTER THIRTY-FIVE

"Release her," Reyna cried. She pointed her finger at Harrington threateningly.

He raised an eyebrow. "It's your move."

Reyna's head whipped back to Jodie. The vampire was about her height, with black hair tucked into a hat so low over her eyes that Reyna couldn't see her face. She held Jodie with an arm around her neck. Jodie's skin was pallid with terror. Fangs were only inches from her exposed neck. Reyna's blood ran cold. Terror was blatant on her face. Reyna itched to do something dramatic. To throw caution to the wind. But she couldn't. Not if Jodie's life was in danger.

"I said release her!"

"And you thought I didn't have you figured out? Will you let her die for you? Will you be able to watch it while I have her cut to pieces in front of your eyes?"

"You'd never stomach it," she shot back at him.

"The floors are glass. I can have them cleaned."

Reyna's own stomach roiled at the thought. He was serious. He would do this to Jodie. All they'd sacrificed and now she was again at his mercy.

"Surrender to me, Reyna. I prefer to have you coming willingly."

"You think this is willingly? It's coercion."

"We both do what we must."

She looked back and forth between Harrington and Jodie. A tear flowed down one of Jodie's soft cheeks.

"Don't even think about it, Reyna," Jodie said.

The arm on her throat tightened as a warning.

Reyna felt a sense of déjà vu. She was once again standing on that patio on New Year's Eve, watching Beckham die before her eyes. Harrington was no longer strong enough to do that. He was sick again. But that didn't mean he wouldn't have someone else do it. Maybe even Roland.

"I can't let him kill you," Reyna told Jodie. She choked on the words.

"He'll kill me anyway." Jodie yelled.

"You won't kill her," Reyna snapped at Harrington. "Give me your word."

"Done."

"You will let her go and never look for her again."

Harrington grated his teeth together but then nodded. "As you wish."

"Your word."

"You have my word."

"Whatever that's worth," Reyna muttered.

She wavered. There was no right choice here. Giving herself up to Harrington meant he would live forever. He would run this planet into the ground and ruin everything she had worked for. But if she didn't, he'd kill Jodie and take Reyna prisoner *anyway*.

There had to be a third option.

She couldn't, no, wouldn't stand by and let him win again. She could see three steps ahead of her. She could stop this.

"Admit it, my little queen," Harrington taunted. "I am always and will always be one step ahead of you. You are a worthy opponent, my dear, but I have lived hundreds of years longer than you. I can see the long game. All the things that are a mystery to you."

"No," she whispered.

"Oh yes." He slowly rose to his feet, pushing the chair out of the way. He shifted his weight onto his cane. It was almost painful to watch him shuffle his feet across the floor until he came to the front of his desk. "You could never beat me."

"I will."

She had to.

She had to beat him.

This couldn't all be for nothing.

"There are no moves that I haven't anticipated. You have nothing left to play. I've taken all of your players captive. It is just you and me. And there is nothing that you can do to stop me now."

Reyna closed her eyes and blocked out his words. "You'll let them all go? You'll make the killing stop?"

"If you come willingly, I will stop everything. But you can never run away or plot escape. You will be delighted with your new position at my side. You will do what I say."

"Reyna, no," Jodie spat. "Let me die. What is my life worth anyway?"

"Everything."

"Nothing. I'm nobody. No one will even miss me."

"I would," Reyna yelled back. "I would miss you. I would miss everyone out there. You all came here for me. You believed in me. And in the end, I failed. *Again*."

"Reyna, please don't do this."

"While this is all touching," Harrington said, "do be quiet. We're negotiating."

"Are we negotiating?" Reyna asked, whipping around to face him. Her heart was caught in her throat. "Or are you attempting to steal my freedom?"

"I will give you all the freedom you desire."

"You and I have different definitions of freedom."

"I weary of your prattle." He looked up at the vampire holding Jodie. "Cut off her finger."

"No," Jodie shrieked. She tried to wrestle herself free, but there was no luck. She wasn't stronger than a vampire. "Please, no!"

The vampire unsheathed a blade from her belt. She peeled open Jodie's fist and held her index finger in her hand. The blade moved to Jodie's finger. A trickle of blood ran down her hand. Jodie began to cry. Seeing her friend break down did her in. She couldn't endure it. Even if Jodie could sustain the pain, Reyna could never watch her go through it.

"Wait, no, stop," Reyna cried. She rushed a step toward Jodie. "Please don't. Just let Jodie go and I'll come willingly." She brought her hand to her mouth and turned wide eyes on Harrington. "You don't need her."

"I had a feeling you would think that way."

"Let her walk out of this building and then I'm yours."

"Wonderful," Harrington said as if she had agreed to a business deal rather than given up her soul. "Come to me first and then I'll release her."

Reyna's eyes flickered between Jodie and Harrington. She nodded her head. What other option was there?

"You will be happy with me. Together we're going to take over the world. You can stand at my side while I rule. Come to me, my little queen." He gestured for her to approach him.

Reyna took a step forward and then another. Her steps were heavy and reluctant. She couldn't make herself take another step. She couldn't do it.

"This was one step on the path to total domination. Vampires are in the light, but soon we will own the world. And I will do anything to make it so. Subjugate the humans, infect vampires with a blood disease, kill everyone who stands in my way. Be on the winning side of history. Stand by me."

Reyna glanced once more at Jodie. "I'm sorry. Please forgive me."

"Reyna, no. Don't do this!"

"Just get on with it," Roland said dryly from behind Harrington. He crossed his arms in irritation.

"Come here, Reyna," Harrington coaxed. "Take my hand. Nothing and no one can stop me now."

Reyna chewed on her lip and then opened herself up to Beckham. She wanted to sense him, know him one more time. He would be furious with what she was about to do. She took another step forward and placed her hand into the devil's grasp.

Harrington's smile widened in triumph. "Check."

"And mate," Reyna replied.

Then she grasped for Beckham's powers, pulling them all into her like lightning into a conduit. Speed, strength, hearing. All of them at once, making her as unstoppable as the person before her believed that he was.

Her hand grasped at her ponytail holder, yanking it loose. Braided up into her ponytail was a small hidden vial that Genevieve had placed in her hand before she'd left. The last of its kind.

"This is for Washington, you bastard," Reyna said.

Then she jammed the needle into the carotid artery in his neck and released the plunger.

Golden Blood flooded his system.

Chapter Thirty-Six

Harrington collapsed forward onto the glass floor. His cane clattered next to him. "What did you do to me?"

Roland took a step forward, but she glared at him, and there must have been something in her face to stop him in his tracks.

"What did I do to you?" Reyna repeated. She grinned devilishly. "I cured you."

"Cured me," he spat out.

"Oh, not of whatever has been ailing you for hundreds of years. Just of the virus you've been carrying around to keep yourself alive through it," Reyna said. "A cure for vampirism."

Harrington screamed as the Golden Blood whisked through his system, eating away at the virus that had infected him for centuries.

"Impossible," Reyna heard Roland mutter behind her. He tensed, and it seemed as if he wanted to move against her, but stayed back, clearly not certain of the new abilities she'd demonstrated.

"Oh, it's possible," she said to Roland with a glare. Then she turned back to Harrington. "Washington finally perfected it and we tested it. And you just got a dose."

Suddenly he began to convulse rapidly. The seizures hit him fresh, rocking through his mangled body. Reyna adjusted him onto his side the way that she'd seen Washington do for Brian.

"Uh-uh, we're not ready for you to die yet," Reyna said.

"How can this be?" Roland asked. He sounded disgusted and terrified. He was the last person alive to want to take such measures.

Reyna ignored him. She stood and wiped her hands off on her pants. She sent a signal to Beckham that all had gone as planned and he could come upstairs when he was ready. She was anxious to find out what had happened with Bronwyn and hoped that her using her abilities hadn't weakened him too much before it was resolved. She'd delayed and stalled and made Harrington talk out of his ass for as long as she could stomach it.

Now that Harrington was officially going through the transformation, she tipped her head at Jodie. "Katarina, you can release Jodie now."

Roland scoffed as the pair pulled apart, moving into a defense stance. Katarina tugged off her hat, revealing her freshly dyed black hair. The disguise had been good enough to fool the guard Katarina had traded places with in the hallway. Neither Harrington nor Roland had recognized her, as she kept her hat low and hid her face.

"That hurt," Jodie accused, holding her hand to her mouth.

Katarina laughed and smacked Jodie's butt. "Good acting though, babe."

"Acting," Roland said in monotone.

A choked sob came from Harrington, still rolling around on the floor. It would take a couple more minutes before the cure went through him. Though it was a guess. They hadn't tested it on someone as old as Harrington. The virus had its claws in him. It could take longer presumably.

"Roland, why don't you move away from the desk?" Katarina said in a low, dangerous tone.

"Ah Katarina, don't use that tone with me." His eyes flicked to Jodie and back. "I see you're slumming now."

Katarina bared her fangs in anger. "Watch what you say and step back against the wall."

Roland laughed. "You're no match for me."

Then he was gone. His movements so blurred, so quick that Reyna had no time to react. She couldn't even reach for Beckham's powers to try to get away from him. And having seen Beckham and Roland fight, she would need his powers for a lot longer than she could hold on to them. She'd need them as a surprise, and she'd used that surprise on Harrington.

Fuck.

In a blink, Roland had his arm around her neck with her back pressed against his chest. His mouth dangerously close to her ear.

"You double-crossing bastard," Reyna spat at him.

Roland laughed in her ear. "Tell me, Reyna, how did you move that fast?"

"Trick of the trade."

"You've turned?" Roland guessed.

"Do I look like I've turned?"

He pressed himself further against her and then sniffed his way from her neck up into her hair. She shuddered at the forced touch.

"I can still smell you. I can still hear your pattering heartbeat. I don't understand."

"Good. I like when you admit you're an idiot."

"No matter." Roland's grip on her tightened. "I acquired Beckham's trust and led you here. I was waiting for you to make your move and expose yourself."

"Reyna," Katarina said from the corner. "Stay very still."

"Keep out of this," Roland spat at her.

Jodie slowly eased out the door. It was clear she was going to get help, but who could help Reyna out of this? Even Beckham couldn't move fast enough to stop Roland from snapping her neck. She had to do it. She had to make him stop.

"Why are you doing this?" Reyna asked. "You helped us. You gave us the information to stop Harrington. You were on our side."

"You're the key, Reyna. If I control you, then I control Beckham. I can take Visage. I can put him in his place. I can rule."

She sighed in exasperation. "God, get an original idea. Harrington already tried that one. Look how well that went for him."

Roland snarled low and then did the unthinkable. He reared back and sank his fangs into her neck.

Reyna screamed as he pierced the tender skin. His venom flooded her system. It felt like black sludge in her veins in comparison to Beckham's sweet euphoria. But it rocked through her nonetheless. Adrenaline raced through her. Flight or fight started and all she wanted to do was flee. She struggled against him, attempting anything to dislodge him, but he had her in his grasp.

She was the sheep.

He was the wolf.

Nothing she could do would stop him.

Then he pulled back, gasping in pleasure. "Sweet nectar of the gods," he groaned. "No wonder he has held you to himself."

Reyna reached out, dizzy and disoriented, for Beckham, but she felt nothing. She felt like ice. Roland couldn't have taken that much from her. It wasn't possible.

She tried again, grasping for Beckham to heal her. She felt a flicker of his location. The sense of where he was somewhere below her in this enormous compound. But that was it. Either he was too weak to heal her or she was too weak to reach him.

She slumped forward in Roland's arms.

"Let her go," Katarina snarled. "You're killing her. What is wrong with you?"

"I wanted to taste her, as I have wanted to for too long."

Reyna coughed and tried to hang on to coherent thought. She straightened and opened her dark eyes. She could do this. "Do you know what happens if you kill me?"

"I take over the world."

"Beckham kills you. No if, and, or but about it. You will be dead within twenty-four hours. If you go through with this, you die." Reyna's head lolled. "Beckham will kill you. He will hunt you down and end your worthless existence. You think you're going to get Visage out of this bargain? Now that you've tasted my blood? If you kill me?"

"That's your version of things."

"If you let me go," Reyna continued, "you'll get a head start. We can go back to being enemies tomorrow."

Roland laughed. "We never stopped being enemies, ma cherie."

"At least that we can agree on."

She closed her eyes, ignoring the pain from her neck, and felt for Beckham. He was closer than before. Much closer. He was coming for her. She didn't want him to come in here. Then he would be in the same position she had pretended to be in with Jodie. She needed to get Roland to release her before Beckham came inside. Because that was precisely what Roland wanted from her.

"Worse," Reyna finally struggled out. "We can do worse to you."

"Worse than killing me?" he asked with a laugh.

That was when she saw her opening and pressed into his ego and his sense of self-preservation. "We can cure you. Make you nothing more than a worthless human. Force you to live out your days just like me."

Roland reared back in shock. "He would never."

"Oh, but I would." Reyna took a deep breath. "This is my promise to you, Roland Batiste, if you do not leave here this minute, you will be hunted and cured. Forced to live your life as a human."

Reyna felt the tension in his grip on her. Practically heard the indecision working through his mind. He hadn't considered that option. Hadn't ever considered being anything but a vampire. He was too proud to allow it to happen.

Roland bodily threw Reyna onto the ground, took one last look at her, and said, "Until next time, ma cherie."

Then he bolted out of a side door. Reyna flopped on the ground, attempting to get up to follow him, but Katarina was already on her way. She fled through the same door and out of sight.

Reyna rolled onto her back and groaned. She pressed her hand to the wound, glad that the vamp venom was healing the wound so it wouldn't continue to gush out her precious blood. She felt weak and weary. Completely and utterly spent.

That was the moment that Beckham barreled in, taking up the entire doorway with his massive body and surveying the glass room. His chest was heaving. His shirt ripped in innumerable places. Blood coated his body. She didn't know if it was his or Bronwyn's. He looked like a wild beast.

"Are you okay?" she squeaked out.

"You look like death and you ask of my well-being." Beckham approached her cautiously, but when he got a look at her neck, he swore. "Who did this?"

"Roland."

"That double-crossing bastard. I'll kill him."

Reyna reached out for him. "Don't. Kat went after him. I need… heal me."

Beckham frowned. "I can't. I can barely sense you."

Reyna's eyes fluttered closed. "Okay. I'll be okay. The blood will replenish quickly."

Beckham swore again, violently, and helped her into a sitting position. "I'll try."

"No. Conserve your energy."

She thread her fingers into his hair, bringing his lips down to hers.

"You cured me," a voice rattled out.

Beckham sprang up, ready to defend Reyna with his life. When he saw Harrington slowly moving into a sitting position, his eyes widened in horror.

"He's alive," Beckham said.

"I used the cure," Reyna said.

"But it was gone…"

"Genevieve had one more. She gave it to me before we left."

"Why wouldn't you tell me that?"

Reyna frowned. "I thought he deserved to pay for his crimes. That killing him would be too easy. That was why I had Jodie broadcasting everything he said to me. So he can't come back and say he didn't intend to do everything he said."

Harrington was staring at his hands as if he'd never seen them before. "How could you do this?"

"I outsmarted you, old man," Reyna said with a smug smile. "And now you're a sickly human again."

"Reyna, we cannot keep him alive," Beckham said. "Do you know what people will do if they find out? You leave a deposed king alive, and you are risking him rallying support around him to put himself back on the throne."

"He's right," Harrington said with a smile at Beckham.

"Stop it. He deserves this. He deserves to have to live out his days as the thing he abhors. Killing him would only make him a martyr in some absurd vampire cause." Reyna pointed at Harrington with conviction. "*This* is justice, Becks."

"Maybe he deserves it," Beckham agreed, "but no one will accept this."

"Reyna," Harrington said. "Come here, my dear."

"Don't you dare," Beckham said.

"What do you have to say? This is the end of the line for you."

Harrington smiled. It split his severe features. Almost made him look…human. Fuck, he *was* human again. It was hard to wrap her mind around that fact.

"I'm glad it was you," Harrington said. "Glad that you were the queen I always knew you could be. That I was defeated by a competent opponent. I'm proud of you."

Reyna's eyes widened at his words. He was proud of her? This monster?

"Both of you." Harrington looked between Beckham and Reyna. "But this is a fate worse than death."

Then he pulled a knife from his jacket pocket and stabbed himself in the heart.

Chapter Thirty-Seven

"No!" Reyna screamed.

She launched herself toward him. Her hand moved to the knife sticking out of his chest as if she could stop this somehow. Blood gushed from the wound, coating his crisp white button-up. Then sticking to her hands as she attempted to stop it.

She needed him. She needed him alive.

She had chosen justice. She had chosen good. Had used the cure when anyone else would have ended his worthless life for the horrors he'd inflicted on her. And he had done this anyway.

He was supposed to pay for his crimes. This was all supposed to happen a different way.

Her hands were red with blood as she put pressure on the wound. But it was no use.

"Why?" she gasped.

Harrington gurgled incoherently and then the light went out of those intelligent eyes. They went blank and empty. Gone was the visionary man. The ruthless monster. The sick lonely broken boy. A nightmare and a genius.

"Reyna, he's gone," Beckham said gently. He lifted her off of the ground and pulled her tight against his chest. "He's gone."

"I know," she said, leaning her head into Beckham's shoulder. "But I wanted more."

"We all play the hand we're dealt."

She sighed against him and nodded. This wasn't over. Harrington was the first step in a long game. His death wasn't a tragedy. It was a mercy. One he didn't deserve. But they would end this without him all the same.

"Let's go save the world."

• • •

"William Harrington is dead," Beckham bellowed to the remaining fighters, from the front of the observation deck. "Roland Batiste has fled the building. And Bronwyn…" He gestured to his sister, tied up and unconscious. "She no longer leads your army."

All fighting stilled at the news. At the commanding presence Beckham issued.

"I am the new leader of Visage, and I command you to stop. Or I will hunt you all down and rip out your bloody throats myself," he roared. "Get down on your knees and surrender."

A few snarled their disapproval, but the look on Beckham's face silenced them. Along with much of his inner circle walking down the stairs to stop any further protests. They might have been Harrington's army, but they knew power when they saw it.

Beckham gestured for Reyna to come forward. She squeezed Jodie's hand before stepping toward him. He clasped her hand and she was surprised to find that his was shaking. He was still so weak from what they'd gone through together, but no one else knew that. They saw what he projected, not what was underneath.

"I am Beckham Anderson and this is Reyna Carpenter. Together we have brought you into a new age where vampires and humans are equal," Beckham announced gallantly.

Then he lifted their hands into the air. A cheer rose up from the remaining members of Elle, who had fought for this cause. Who had done everything that they could to make this a reality. Something like relief flooded her system for the first time in so long.

Katarina rushed in at that moment. Her eyes found Beckham's and she shook her head. "He got away."

Beckham sighed. "Let's finish this up and then we'll go after him again. We can't let Roland remain loose."

"I can't believe he got away," Reyna said.

"He would have killed you otherwise. It's a trade."

Katarina joined the rest of Beckham's circle, the friends they'd called in for a favor, and the anti-vamps who were now rounding up the remaining vampires and cordoning them off into separate rooms. The rest of Elle was releasing any of the people who were still locked up. Vampires and humans working together to walk forward into a new world.

Reyna's friends were standing around a body at the base of the stairs and she glanced at Jodie, who followed her down.

What they saw there turned her stomach. Reyna had seen so much death and destruction, but…Tye. He'd been so good. He'd deserved better than what had happened to him. To any of the fallen.

Meghan leaned into Gabe's arms, tears freely flowing down her face. Drew was pale and hugged Reyna when she came near.

"It's over," he whispered. "It's really over."

"This is just the beginning," she said quietly. "Now we have to rebuild."

"We need a memorial," Meghan whispered.

Reyna released her brother to look across the room full of the fallen. "A memorial for everyone who sacrificed themselves to get here. For Tye, Sydney, Washington, Xavier, Tony, Everett, and so many more."

"So much death," Meghan said.

"We'll never forget them," Reyna said.

Gabe turned to her then. "Well, General, what do we do now?"

Everyone's eyes shifted to her, and she took in each and every one of her friends. She thought about all the others still working to fix this mess. About Brian and Laura back in Beckham's safe house. All the anti-vamp people who had risked their lives and worked with the vampires they claimed to hate. About every person who had ever fought for this cause.

"We live."

It was the best she could offer them. And at the same time, it was everything.

Beckham touched her arm. She smiled at her friends and left them to grieve.

"We need to get you medical attention," Beckham said.

"I'm okay," she lied.

"You're going to run yourself into the ground."

"Look who's talking."

Beckham brushed her hair off of her face and smiled at her. "You did an incredible job today. I'm lucky to stand at your side."

"Forever and always, right?"

He nodded decisively. Forever and always.

Reyna stared up into his dark eyes, so full of longing. It was amazing that she had ever believed him expressionless. She opened her senses to him and enveloped his heart, body, and soul with all the love in her heart. He pushed right back, colliding, capturing, encasing her. They were both weak from blood loss and using their powers, but they were strong in all the ways that mattered.

She stood on her tiptoes and wrapped her arms around his

shoulders. His hands moved up into her hair, tilting her head and melding their lips together.

They had won.

The world was still turning.

There was much work left to do—a world to save.

But here, now, there were just two blood matches who had found the cure to their souls.

EPILOGUE

Reyna wrapped her arms around Beckham's torso and hugged him tight. The motorcycle hummed noisily between her thighs. Wind whipped her hair in her face as they zipped out of the city and into the countryside. They traveled through clear blue skies with the sun shining and birds singing. Travel into the city had improved markedly. Only six months post-Harrington and already the world was looking up.

Beckham had taken control of Visage in what he called a temporary capacity. She'd been by his side every step of the way. And while every single step was harder than the next, she never wanted to be anywhere else.

Not when they released the remaining prisoners of Visage and discovered that Everett's brother, Edmond, had been killed quickly after Everett had stopped giving them information. Or when Beckham offered actual free housing to those in need. Using those rooms for good instead of the horrors that had been committed down there. Or when Meghan and Gabe had spearheaded a conversion of the yard into a memorial for the fallen soldiers. Their names chiseled into stone and wrapped into a semicircle as a reminder and a remembrance.

Miraculously Zoya had pieced together Washington's research on the cure from a backup server, and a genius task force of scientists had replicated it. Now it was being offered free of charge at any Visage hospital. A surprising number of vampires had come forward for it.

Within those notes had also been the research on Jodie's blood, which Jodie had decided to destroy rather than give to the scientists. The experiments had done enough damage. They had enough information on the antidote from within Visage. They didn't need the information on Jodie. When Reyna and Jodie had gone to Visage to liberate the people who had been experimented on, they'd discovered that June had gone into Visage to find Jodie and it had been her blood that had been the ultimate reason the antidote was made. But once Visage was overthrown, all the vampires had killed the human subjects on their way out.

Reyna and Jodie had spent a long time crying over the deaths of their fellow imprisoned humans. They'd insisted on holding a funeral service for them, and while putting June to rest had been difficult, having Reyna and Katarina at her side the entire time had made it bearable.

Thanks to a rather large cash infusion into the economy, courtesy of William Harrington, it finally looked as if the country was coming out of the recession that had held it in its clutches for so long.

Which meant that Brian and Laura could buy a real house in the suburbs to raise their baby boy. Drew had decided to stay in the city and had a new boyfriend—Philippé—much to everyone's chagrin. But Reyna liked to see her family happy. Even if Visage saw it as another triumph for vampire and human equality.

Reyna felt at ease for the first time in years.

There was always more to do. But not today.

Today, their cares were more singular. And she could finally breathe in the crisp summer air and actually enjoy it.

They were nearly to their destination, when Beckham suddenly pulled off of the road.

"What are we doing?" Reyna called over the sound of the motor.

Beckham didn't reply. His silences were just as weighted as they had always been. She could have reached into his emotions, but she could read him without it. And sometimes it was fun to guess.

He came to a stop and stepped off of his motorcycle. "Your turn."

Reyna's eyes widened in horror. "What?"

"I've been teaching you to drive for months, Little One. You can handle her."

"Um, your motorcycle? You think I can handle your precious beautiful motorcycle? I nearly crashed the car. I thought Gerard was going to kill me."

Beckham's lips lifted at the corners at the memory. "Are you suggesting that you don't want to drive my motorcycle?"

"Are you out of your mind? Of course I want to. Give me anything that goes fast and I'm in."

"Oh, I know," he said with a feral look in his eyes.

Reyna blushed. "That too."

Beckham immediately launched into an everything-you-need-to-know-about-a-motorcycle speech. It was probably the most he'd ever said at once. And by the time he was done, her eyes were a little glazed over. She'd always wanted to learn to drive, but she had needed a car to do that. Now that the worst was over, she was finally getting that opportunity, and she really wasn't that bad. Hopefully the motorcycle would be okay too.

It took her a few tries to get the basics down. She only landed in the gravel once and she was pretty proud of that. Beckham had actually rolled his eyes at her. Priceless.

"Aren't you worried we're going to miss our appointment?" Reyna asked.

"It was moved back. I thought it a prudent opportunity."

She laughed. Of course he had.

"You're ready," Beckham finally said an infinite amount of time later.

"Yeah?" she gasped.

He nodded and then kicked his leg over the back of the bike. His thighs pressed against hers, his hands sliding up her waist and over her arms.

"Easy does it."

She started the motorcycle as he'd instructed and then eased it back onto the open highway. Beckham was close enough to take control if he had to but gave her enough room to breathe. It was a perfect example of their relationship. The only time she didn't argue with him taking control was in the bedroom. And even then…

His lips pressed into her neck. "You're doing great."

Reyna tilted her head back and laughed into the summer air. This was bliss. Beckham pressing into her back, the open road before her, and no cares in the world.

When they reached their destination, Beckham helped her bring the bike to a stop. She jumped off, feeling alive and wild from the adrenaline. She handed her helmet to Beckham and offered him a kiss. He obliged.

"Are you ready?" he asked.

"Are you?" she countered, suddenly sobering.

This was the hardest part of their week. Every week.

It didn't matter what else they had to face at work, with Visage, with the cure. Worse even than the fact that they never found Roland despite their best efforts. Nothing was as troublesome as standing outside of the mental facility that Bronwyn had been placed into almost six months earlier.

Beckham nodded and took her hand. They walked into the cozy home that was the best place in the state. It didn't look like a hospital, which Reyna appreciated after all her time in Visage's sterile rooms. There was wicker furniture on the porch. The interior was soft and feminine, painted in calming colors.

The same woman, Martha, who was always there, checked them in. "Beckham, Reyna, we're so glad to see you today."

"How's she doing?" Reyna asked.

"It's not a good day. But hopefully your presence will calm her down."

Reyna clutched Beckham's hand. The bad days were the hardest on him. He took full responsibility for what he had done to Bronwyn. And it ate at him that there was nothing he could do to fix what he had broken. Except be there as often as he could and get her the help she'd always needed.

"You want me to show you the way?" Martha asked kindly.

"We can go on our own," Reyna said. "Thank you."

Reyna took his hand and guided him through the facility. Bronwyn's room was at the end of a hallway. There was no lock on her door, a big upgrade from where she'd been before, but all of the exterior doors had them, just in case.

They glanced through the small window and peered in on Bronwyn sitting on a couch. She had a cross-stitch in her lap and was making gorgeous flowers come to life out of needlepoint.

"She used to do that as a kid," Beckham said.

Reyna nodded. She knew.

After they'd given Bronwyn the cure, she'd reverted to an almost childlike state. No longer a military leader or a powerful vampire, she retreated into herself and became the thing she had been before her mind had been shattered.

"Are you ready?"

"Can I talk to you first?"

She arched an eyebrow but nodded. "Why do you look upset?"

"I'm not sure how you'll react."

"Should I be worried?"

He shook his head. "I want to take the cure."

"You do?" she asked, wide-eyed with surprise. "You want to be a human again?"

"Yes."

"Why? I thought you wanted to be a vampire."

He considered. "I wanted it at one time. But I'm no longer the man who wanted it."

"Are you sure?"

"Reyna, I want to spend this lifetime with you. I want to you and me, married with children and growing old together."

Reyna's heart melted. "Really?"

"There is nothing I want more than to be with you."

"What about the company?"

He shrugged. "We'll figure it out. I can run it as a human as much as a vampire. You have been doing just as good of a job."

"Okay," Reyna said in shock. "I can't believe this is happening."

"Say you want this lifetime with me," he whispered against her lips.

"I want everything with you."

Beckham kissed her once more and then opened the door to his sister's room.

The cure was an opportunity.

A new adventure.

Not just for the vampires who had been turned against their will, but the ones who had walked into the darkness willingly. She would be there when he stepped back into the light. And every day after that.

They would weather this as they had done everything else…

Together.

THE END

Acknowledgments

The Blood Type series came about because I read an article about very very rare blood types. So, I would first like to thank the science publication *Mosaic* for publishing photographer Greg White's pictures of a blood bank as well as the article on these rare blood types. Also *Gizmodo* and *The Atlantic* for writing follow up articles on the subject and delivering me all sorts of inspiration. I would also like to thank the Blood Bank Guy, because even though most of your work is over my head, it helped my limited understanding of hematology.

Many people had their hands on this project, and these things don't develop in a vacuum. Thank you to my agent, Kimberly Brower, who never stopped believing in this series. To the incomparable team at Red Tower—Liz, Rae, Hannah, Meredith, Victoria, Lindsey, Melanie, Heather, Curtis, Bree, LJ, and everyone who touched this book along the way—thank you for all that you did to make this the beautiful book that it is. Getting it into stores, the incredible packaging with the prettiest covers around and the best sprayed edges, and all the editorial help, publicity, and pep talks. Thank you, thank you, thank you!

To my wonderful alpha readers—Rebecca Kimmerling and Anjee Sapp. #youmaycallmegraves And the incredible beta reader team—Katie Miller, Lori Francis, and Sharon Goodman. Also, the incomparable Staci Hart. I love you for calling me from the Netherlands to talk me through edits, reading over my changes, and generally making these books as strong as possible. As always my wonderful and unbelievably talented friend, Diana Peterfreund. For plotting retreats and Disney World trips and crazy cocktails and watching old movies online together and always being there for me. And Danielle Sanchez, who pioneered this series from the start!

Thank you Ava Harrison, Corinne Michaels, and Rebecca Yarros, who read book one so long ago and never stopped demanding me to write more. To all my incredible author friends, you are my people—A.L. Jackson, Carrie Ann Ryan, Rachel van Dyken, C.D. Reiss, Kandi Steiner, Emma Hart, Erin Noelle, Jessica Prince, Kayti McGee, Kendall Ryan, Kristin Cast, K. Bromberg, Laurelin Paige, Mari Mancusi, Meghan March, Rachel Brookes, S.C. Stephens, Sierra Simone, Susan Stoker, and Wendy Higgins.

To the readers who have promoted this series and pushed new readers to try my work. The ones who have screamed from the rooftops about Beckham and his broody ways. The ones who couldn't stop begging me for the next book after that massive cliffhanger. I hear you. I love you. I am so very thankful for you and your beautiful reviews. You made this series possible. You made it the success it is. Your love made Beckham and Reyna a reality. Thank you for every kind word, email, message, post, shout-out, and scream into the void when you read my cliffs. You are truly the best readers I could ever ask for!

Finally, my husband Joel, who I forced to watch *Buffy the Vampire Slayer* and *Supernatural* with me until they became his shows too so that he could understand my deep love for vampires. You make my world a better place. You are my blood match, my soul mate, my once-in-a-lifetime.

SHE BROKE THE MONSTER TREATY…
AND HE'LL MAKE HER PAY.

Some things aren't supposed to exist outside of our imagination.

Thirteen years ago, monsters emerged from the shadows and plunged Kierse's world into a cataclysmic war of near-total destruction. The New York City she knew so well collapsed practically overnight.

In the wake of that carnage, the Monster Treaty was created. A truce… of sorts.

But tonight, Kierse—a gifted and fearless thief—will break that treaty. She'll enter the Holly Library…not knowing it's the home of a monster.

He's charming. Quietly alluring. Terrifying. But he knows talent when he sees it; it's just a matter of finding her price.

Now she's locked into a dangerous bargain with a creature unlike any other. She'll sacrifice her freedom. She'll offer her skills. Together, they'll put their own futures at risk.

But he's been playing a game across centuries—and once she joins in, there will be no escape…